OH DANNY BOY

JOSIE RIVIERA

INTRODUCTION

To keep up on newly released ebooks, paperbacks, Large Print Paperbacks, audiobooks, as well as exclusive sales, sign up for Josie's Newsletter today.

As a thank you, I'll send you a Free PDF ... The Beauty Of ...

Josie's Newsletter

Did you know that according to a Yale University study, people who read books live longer?

5 STAR READER REVIEWS

Amazon Review by Reader Forever:"

Oh Danny Boy is a book full of emotion and very well written. J. Riviera takes us to Ireland and creates quite a believable setting with her descriptions and voice. I visited Ireland two years ago and enjoyed this armchair trip again. I could hear the Irish locals in their own towns. The story is sweet and touching, with Clara trying to save her brother and keep a family life. Danny is a great hero, strong and tender, who will sweep you off your feet. A recommended read."

Amazon Review by Sara5:

"Love, forgiveness, fear, happiness, just a few words to describe what a few of the characters are going through and feeling. This book is overcoming your past and dealing with the present. It is a must read book for your TBR list!"

Amazon Review by Rebecca M:"

Danny and Clara meet early in the book, when she is trying to save her brother Seamus from jumping off a bridge, while drunk and depressed.Danny happens along in time to help her. He has an immediate attraction to her, but dismisses it. He's here to further his Coffee shops, not find a girlfriend. Yet, it develops further than he thought it could.It's a lovely story, even with some strife, and well worth reading. I highly recommend it. Josie Riviera does a wonderful job developing the characters, as well as the story."

This book is dedicated to all my wonderful readers who have supported me every inch of the way.

THANK YOU!

PRAISE AND AWARDS

USA TODAY bestselling author
Oh Danny Boy is an Amazon Bestseller

"Seamus, don't jump!" Clara Donovan heard her own cries, the shouts resounding through the misty night air. She raced across the sidewalk toward Farthing Bridge, her gaze riveted on a horror she didn't want to believe. Her older brother Seamus sat on the edge of a tall bridge with his head slumped in his hands, a bottle of whiskey beside him. The arched stone bridge spanned the River Farthing, connecting the town to a once-popular marketplace.

No. It couldn't be. Her breath burned in her chest as she took in gulps of dampness and drizzle. *Don't stop. Run faster.*

When she reached the bridge, she elbowed through a group of late-night revelers. Several pointed up at Seamus. "He's off the rails!" someone shouted.

Her brother seemed unaware of the gathering crowd. He swung his legs back and forth like an underwound metronome and stared into the ice-cold river below.

She shook off the image of him on her living room floor several days earlier. He'd been passed out drunk. Should she have phoned a treatment center? No. She could fix her brother's problems. He simply needed encouragement, surrounded by his loving, supportive family.

Seamus. Gentle Seamus. Kind and fiery-haired, quick to temper, quicker to make amends. Her heart squeezed at the scruffy, dejected man he'd become since his wife had died.

Clara put her hands on her knees and took in calm, even breaths. Quickly, she assessed the corroded pedestrian catwalk leading to the top of the bridge, the skull and cross-bones sign that warned *Danger*.

She stared upward at her sweet brother. "Dear saints in heaven, Seamus," she whispered. "You promised me that you'd never drink again."

She stuffed her wool gloves into her jacket pockets and bent to lace her weatherproof boots tighter. There was no time to dash around the river to the street that crossed the bridge, and she certainly wouldn't ask anyone in the crowd to lend a hand.

She yanked off the "Danger" sign and threw it to the ground. That pressing feeling in her chest, like she was running out of air, slowed her movements. Dragging in another breath, she grasped the slippery wet handrails and stepped onto the bottom rung of the catwalk.

"Missus, are you trained for this?" a man from the crowd inquired.

She glanced around. The man stood a hairsbreadth away. He was tall with piercing blue eyes and carried a guitar case. His dark brown hair had a reddish tinge and his navy wool jacket strained against his athletic form.

"Thanks. I can manage on my own."

Despite her refusal, she hesitated. Was she trained to climb to the top of a rusted bridge when she was crippled with fear and could hardly breathe? Umm, no. But she was desperate, and desperation made people do things they thought they could never do.

"I insist." The man set his guitar case on the grass and stepped forward. "Who's sitting on the top of the bridge?"

"My brother!"

"I'll follow behind you. No worries."

No worries. Dear saints in heaven, her brother was about to jump off a bridge.

She gripped the slick railings with both hands and began climbing, acutely aware of the guitar player's encouraging whispers behind her. She counted each step until she reached the top, scrambled to her feet, and raced to her brother. Seamus's chin was hunkered in his hands, the empty whiskey bottle beside him.

She stopped a foot away from him. "Seamus, come with me."

His legs stopped swinging. He turned to her, his metallic-grey eyes glazed with drink. "What're you doing here?"

"I'm looking out for you, same as always." She attempted to keep her tone light. "The weather's a wee bit fierce up here. The wind and rain are driving my hair sideways."

Inwardly, she shuddered. He was a sight wearing tattered clothes, his flaming red hair caught in a ponytail.

"And who's that dodgy bloke behind you?"

"Someone who's offered to help." She struggled to control her trembling. Her brother's big-boned body was precariously close to the edge.

Seamus's mouth twisted. "It's better if I end my life. I'm on me tod, I'm all alone."

She extended a hand. "You're not alone. I'm here for you."

Despite the chilly night air, Seamus was sweating. "I long for my wife. My beautiful woman ..."

"We all miss Fiona very much."

Seamus's fingers found the empty whiskey bottle and flung it into the river. "I'm warning you. Leave me alone or I'll jump." Slowly, he stretched out his hands.

"Seamus!" Clara hunched over, sick to her stomach, listening to the hoots and jeers of the spectators.

"Shut your gob!" Seamus hollered to the crowd. "Are ya' thick?"

Clara caught her breath. Stay calm. Level-headed and composed.

She straightened. "Those people won't help you, but I will."

What was she supposed to do now? Move slower, speak gentler? On watery knees, she started forward.

"You're managing perfectly," came the whisper behind her.

The guitarist. She'd almost forgotten. His breath was warm and reassuring against her hair.

She extended her hand again. "Please, Seamus, please. Come with me."

Seamus openly sobbed. "I'm no use to anyone."

"Think of Anna and me. We're your sisters and we love you." Clara tried to smile. "What would I do with myself if you weren't sleeping on my couch every night? You know I don't like to be alone."

Seamus squinted at her. Using his worn shirtsleeve, he wiped at the tear-stained bags under his eyes. "I lost all my money on the horse races. Five hundred euros that I'd borrowed from a friend, and one hundred euros of Anna's money, too. The bookies were certain Green Dragon would win the second race, but the ponies double-crossed me."

Clara dug her nails into her palms. "We'll pay the bookies all the money you lost." How, she had no idea. Her income as a factory worker and part-time dance teacher was scarcely enough to pay their current living expenses.

In the distance, insistent sirens blared, angry red lights flashed.

"Keep talking," the guitar player told her.

What to say? The wrong words might send her impulsive brother over the edge. She chanced a peek at the guitarist and lost her footing. Gasping, she held in a scream.

His arms went around her. "I've got you," he said softly.

She steadied herself and shook off his hold. Without making a sound, she ventured another two steps until she stood behind her brother. "We'll return to my flat and I'll light a fire in the hearth. Won't that be grand?" She heard her voice shake, the rale insistent.

"And make me a cuppa tea?" Seamus's copper-red beard showed days of neglect and grew in dirty spikes below his chin.

She placed her hands firmly on his shoulders and gave a reassuring squeeze. "I'll brew the entire pot and fry a proper Irish breakfast in the morning."

Several beats passed. Seamus seemed to be trying desperately to concentrate. He looked up at her. "You don't cook."

"I can manage fried eggs and bacon rashers."

He relaxed beneath her hands.

She licked her lips, her mouth so dry. "Please come home. Please. We're a family. We'll work this out together like we always do."

Seamus rubbed at his eyes, sniffled, and started to stand.

The guitarist stepped around Clara. Carefully, he assisted the wobbling Seamus to his feet.

The crowd applauded. They'd observed every detail of her family's private business. Clara pressed her lips tightly together, willing herself to think of her brother and nothing else.

Her sobbing brother slumped into her arms. She hugged him for a long time, then roughly shook his shoulders and stared into his bleary eyes. "I understand you're in a lot of pain. You'll be independent again, you'll see. It took me a long time, remember? And now I'm fine."

"Yeh." Seamus's lopsided grin showed missing teeth. He nodded so quickly that he stumbled, so unexpected they both cried out. She clung to his beefy hand, his body still so close to the edge of the bridge, as she stared into the frigid waters of the River Farthing far below.

"You'll both be safer away from the bridge." The guitarist's voice came loud and urgent. He guided Clara and Seamus to the side of the road, removed his jacket and placed it on the damp grass.

"Who are you, bloke?" Seamus asked.

"Danny Brady." He wheeled, clear in his intent to walk away.

"What about your jacket?" Clara called out.

Danny half turned and looked upward. The clouds had parted, the sky bathed in moonlight and stars. "No rain and no worries. Keep the jacket."

An emergency vehicle swerved onto the bridge, and Clara squinted into the blinding headlights. Several paramedics sprinted toward her and Seamus. A Channel Four television news van streaked past, reversed, and screeched to a stop. A woman reporter and cameraman leapt from the van and scurried to the guitarist.

Clara recognized the reporter, Maeve Flanagan, an anchorwoman for the local television station. Maeve clutched the microphone, speaking urgently, then held the microphone out for Danny. He spoke lengthily, the bright camera light illuminating his china-blue eyes.

"Where are you from, Brady?" her brother shouted from across the road.

Danny's handsome face showed signs of fatigue. "Dublin." He focused on Clara. "Do you have a name, missus?"

"Clara Donovan." She nodded at her brother. "And this very foolish man is my brother Seamus."

From across the road, the reporter shouted, "May I quote you, Ms. Donovan?"

Clara stretched out a tired arm. "Absolutely not! And please take your slanderous reporting elsewhere!"

Maeve muffled the mouthpiece with her palm. In a loud voice, she asked, "Do I have permission to make a plea to the community on your behalf, Ms. Donovan? There are resources available for poor—"

Clara cut Maeve off with a wave. Heat flushed through her body. "My family fends for themselves, Miss Flanagan! If you want to do something for us, then stay away!"

CHAPTER 2

*D*anny watched as Clara Donovan poured boiling water into a bone-white teapot with shamrocks painted on the sides, moving easily in her tiny kitchen.

He'd rung the Gardaí, the police, as soon as he'd spotted the desperate, drunken man on the bridge. They'd arrived, along with the paramedics, a few minutes afterward, though fortunately they hadn't been needed.

Danny had gone for a short walk along the river's edge to clear his mind from the numerous business decisions plaguing him. His coffee shop's grand opening had brought him to the town of Farthing for a fortnight. He hadn't known the town existed until his planning board had scouted the area and discovered a fresh, natural spring located nearby, ideal because the water was clear and pure for brewing coffee.

When he'd volunteered to help her, Clara Donovan's dark, shining eyes had reflected panic and fear, despite her protests. So, he'd climbed the catwalk behind her, intending to leave as soon as he was certain that she and her brother were safe. Then he'd reversed, reconsidering, rationalizing that he shouldn't leave a helpless woman with a drunken brother at the top of a bridge until help had arrived. He'd pushed off the insistent reminder that he'd vowed never to get involved in other people's problems. He'd only been mindful of the desperate scene playing out before him.

After the Gardaí had filed a report and the paramedics had left, Danny offered to drive Clara and Seamus home. At first she refused, telling him she lived only a few blocks away.

He offered a second time. Surely, Clara and her brother were in no condition to walk any distance, he said. In a gesture of friendliness, or perhaps to thank him, she agreed by inviting him to her flat for tea and scones.

Despite the late hour and tomorrow's long work day, he accepted. After he'd assisted her brother into the backseat of his Mercedes, Clara slid onto the front passenger seat.

She raised a brow. "Quite a posh car. You fancy the metallic silver?"

He wrapped a hand around the steering wheel and started the engine. "I've worked hard for this car," was all he said.

When they arrived at her flat, he supported a tottering Seamus through the downstairs foyer and up the stairs, then persuaded Seamus to drink a glass of water and down some Ibuprofen. After that, he assisted Seamus to the bathroom and then helped Clara guide her brother to the living room couch, where Seamus immediately fell into a deep yet fitful sleep. Apparently, that cuppa tea for Seamus would have to wait until morning, Danny thought with a grin.

Danny had set his guitar in her foyer and removed his damp, grass-stained jacket, insisting he build a fire in the hearth while Clara changed out of her wet clothes.

"Would you put the kettle on when you're done lighting the fire?" she called from the bedroom. "We can keep an eye on my brother from the kitchen."

"Aye." Danny shoveled coal into the fireplace, added a fire lighter and kindling in the middle of the grate, then turf. He waited for the smoky fire to clear, then strode to the bathroom and worked the soap in his hands up to his wrists, rinsing until the black sooty dust was gone.

As he made his way into Clara's kitchen, a lemony scent wafted through the air, a mixture of sweet and tart, and he sniffed appreciatively. Her faux marble countertops and stainless-steel sink and appliances sparkled, the forest-green vinyl swept clean as the finest hotel. The kitchen walls had been painted a luminous green hue, her cabinets a cozy charcoal. Several lush potted ferns added freshness and lightness, giving the intimate space a snug, appealing appearance.

He filled the kettle with water, placed it on the stove to boil, and strode to the window. Why, he wondered, was the window dead bolted shut? The neighborhood seemed a bit run-down, although safe enough, illuminated by a lamppost on the street corner and with a stone wall beyond.

Clara padded into the kitchen wearing thick socks, black leggings, and a clingy long-sleeved T-shirt that accentuated her slender, graceful figure. Danny shifted from the window to watch her. She was a fetching contrast between vulnerability and self-determination.

"Your flat is charming," he said. "Did you decorate it yourself?"

"Yeh, and thanks. I enjoy decorating and painting on a budget. One of my favorite colors is green."

"Duly noted." He grinned. "The color of our emerald isle."

"Green is relaxing and reminds me of nature." She went to her cupboard and brought out cups and saucers. "Thank you. You've done so much for me and my brother tonight."

"No bother." He basked in the respect lighting her chocolate-brown eyes. She'd banded her thick hair back, emphasizing her high cheekbones. Despite her olive complexion, she was still pale, still looked shaken.

"Can I assist?" he asked.

"With setting the table? No bother. I'm extremely self-sufficient." She gestured to a pair of stools. "Brewing tea is my specialty, as it is for most anyone who's lived in Ireland long enough."

"Aye." He perched on one of the stools. "However, coffee is my specialty."

She pulled some napkins from a cupboard drawer. "So you're from Dublin?"

"Aye."

"A Dubliner who drives a fancy car. You're posher by the minute."

He didn't reply.

Now she carried the white teapot to the kitchen table, setting it among gleaming porcelain cups, a sugar and creamer, and the napkins. She set the scones near the butter and raspberry jam, the teapot on a trivet.

"Coffee's too bitter for my taste," she continued.

Not my coffee. My coffee is the best in all Ireland, soon to be the most successful coffee chain in the world.

He answered her smile with one of his own and zeroed in on the scones. "I thought you didn't cook?"

"I bake." She pointed to a garden stool in the corner, piled neatly with bakery cookbooks. She plated a scone and handed it to him. "They're better with butter and jam."

"Plain is best. Then I can taste all the ingredients." He sampled a bite, the biscuit soft and chewy. He detected a citrus zest, which explained the lemon scent wafting from her kitchen, the same subtle fragrance he'd sniffed on her hair when he climbed behind her on the catwalk.

"Your scone is delicious. Do you use a special recipe from one of your recipe books?" he asked between bites.

He could sell lemon scones in his coffee shop for three euros and make a small profit on each. A quality product sold at a fair price was one of the reasons his coffee shops were so successful.

"No special ingredients—only what's on hand in the kitchen." Her dark-lashed gaze was clear and warm, her cheeks slowly regaining a flush of color.

He set the scone on his plate, his gaze staying on hers. "You're a very brave woman, Clara Donovan."

"For baking scones?"

He smiled. "For climbing to the top of a precariously high bridge to rescue your brother."

She was silent for a moment. "I've become an expert at dealing with disastrous situations."

"You were rushing up the most dangerous flight of stairs I've ever seen."

"Seamus rambled on and on about jumping off that same bridge several weeks ago, and I'd calmed him down. He'd seemed to listen to reason and promised me he'd never think those scary thoughts again. I was frantic when I saw him tonight." She gave a regretful shake of her head. "I should've arrived home earlier. I work on the edge of town, and one of the trains broke down."

"Don't blame yourself for what happened tonight."

"My brother is my responsibility." Her composure seemed to slip a notch. "When I didn't see him in my flat when I got home, I phoned all our friends. Then I prayed that my worst fears … He'd promised to stay away from those awful gambling places." She wiped quickly at her eyes and focused on a snoring and twitching Seamus. "My dear brother has always loved his whiskey."

"You can't keep a grown man under surveillance twenty-four hours a day," Danny countered. "Though his promises will sound sincere, don't believe him. Assume every word coming out of his mouth is a lie."

Danny had garnered that wisdom from hard-earned experience. No one this side of Scotland had made more excuses and promises to quit the drink than his parents had before they'd committed suicide.

"Harsh advice, Mr. Brady." She added quickly, "My brother is a good man."

"Danny," he corrected. "And don't offer excuses because you'll hurt his chances to get better. A suicide attempt is a serious cry for help, and he should be admitted to a licensed rehab center."

"I'll not commit him to an institution where he'll be alone, doctors evaluating him and filling his veins with drugs so his brain's in a fog. You don't know what Seamus has done for me."

Danny held up a hand. "You're doing him no favors. You only enable when you coddle him."

"Once he's sober, I'll have a serious chat with him again." She sighed, and a slight wheeze sounded. She clasped her hands around the teapot. Danny studied her lovely, expressive face, her valiant attempt to keep her features composed.

"Are you all right?"

Her chin lifted. "Yeh, of course." She tucked an errant strand of hair behind her ear, the blonde ends falling to her shoulders. She poured the tea through a strainer into his teacup. "How do you take your tea?"

"With cream." He poured cream into his cup and stirred. "I'll be in town for a fortnight. I'll give you my business card before I leave. If you need anything—"

"I won't. Thanks."

He sat back, admiring her heart-shaped face. "I've always had a thing for beautiful Irish damsels in distress."

Her grin was dubious. "I'm not Irish. And if I'm ever in distress, I can fend for myself."

She'd needed help tonight, although he didn't think it wise to remind her.

"With a name like Clara Donovan and your Irish brogue, I assumed—"

"I was adopted by my Irish parents. I was born in Italy and lived there with my birth parents, then in an orphanage after they died." She chewed her bottom lip, suddenly quiet, and flicked imaginary crumbs from the table onto her empty plate. She seemed to be silently chastising herself for telling him too much.

He stared into his cup. He wouldn't pry. He'd built a home in Howth, far enough removed from Dublin's city centre to get away from family addictions and heartbreaking memories. He didn't want any additional secrets to carry around, not regarding adoptions, nor alcoholics, nor compulsive gamblers.

Suicide pacts and a dead sister were enough burdens for one lifetime.

He just paid the bills for the evergreen, shrubs, and red and white begonias placed at their graves every morning.

He sipped his tea, grimaced because it was still too hot. He emptied a good deal more cream into his cup and gazed out the kitchen window. A cloudburst had forced the moon and starlight aside, covering the sidewalks in murky, sodden sheets of rain.

Clara's Irish lace window curtains were pristine clean. His filthy, chaotic childhood home had been fraught with ongoing hardships and poverty.

Not anymore, he amended, because wealth kept filth and chaos at arms-length. And coffee had become his pot of gold.

He caught her staring at him and pushed his reflections

aside. Grinning, he gestured to the window. "Isn't it lovely weather we're having?"

She poured herself tea, the steam wafting from the pot, casting her face in a rosy veil of heat. "You're not afraid of a few spots of rain, are ya?"

He stretched out his long legs and crossed his arms, enjoying her infectious smile. "At least the rain gets warmer in the summer."

"Yeh." Her smile was stunning, her teeth gleaming white. She tipped her chin toward his guitar case in the hallway. "You play guitar?"

"Aye. Music is my first love."

"Are you an expert musician?"

"I've played guitar for most of my adult life. I was returning from a gig tonight when I spotted your brother."

"Whereabouts do you play?"

His restive fingers strummed a beat on the table. "A new coffee shop on the other side of Farthing Bridge. Perhaps you've heard about The Ground Café?"

She nodded over the rim of her teacup. "That coffee shop is a very successful chain. I read in the papers that the company's headquarters are in Dublin and the owner is only thirty-five years old. He's opened a shop in Farthing then. My little town must be coming up in the world. That's good, because so many families have moved out, looking for work elsewhere."

"The grand opening is this weekend. The company remodeled the marketplace off Farthing Bridge and added a bookstore and children's playground."

Seamus gave a loud snuffle from the living room. Clara opened her mouth as if she were about to say something, then coughed several times. Her rasp bumped into the tidiness of the kitchen.

Danny reached across the table and took her hand. He

studied her face, reddened from coughing. "There's a bad dose of flu going around. Are you sure you're all right?"

She shook off his hand. "I'm grand, thanks."

"Have you been coughing a while?"

She nodded, caught her breath, and took a long sip of tea.

"Do you suffer from asthma?"

She set her cup down and busied her hands with rearranging the sugar and creamer, dabbing a spill of cream off the table with a napkin. "No, and don't be troubling yourself with my ailments. It's late and I'll feel better in the morning."

This was his not-so-subtle cue to leave. "Aye. I'll head on then." He pushed back his stool.

She walked in front of him to the door, both of them silent as they passed her snoring brother.

Danny reached into his pocket and handed her a business card. "I'm at the coffee shop all weekend. I promise good craic, fun, and coffee if you visit."

She arched a slender eyebrow. "Musicians sing in a coffee shop twenty-four hours a day?"

"Usually my gig starts later in the evenings."

"Will you sing to me if I try the coffee?"

"Absolutely. Do you have a song request so I can practice in advance?" he asked. "How about an Italian song from your heritage?"

"I've lived in Ireland all my life, so any Irish song is dead-on."

"Do you know 'Oh Danny Boy'?"

"Of course." She rubbed at her eyes, smudged with dark circles.

Aye, he was being unfair because she was clearly worn out. Nonetheless, he enjoyed her company. She was unassuming and fearless and down-to-earth.

She began singing softly in a perfectly in-tune soprano voice.

He added his baritone voice. A bit off-key, he acknowledged, blaming it on the late hour.

She regarded the crackling fire burning in the hearth, then gazed at her brother. Tears glittered in her eyes, and she stopped singing.

"There're more verses," Danny prompted.

Her sigh sounded so sad, so poignant. "I don't know what the lyrics mean. However, I'm always moved to tears when I hear 'Oh Danny Boy.'"

"No one knows the true meaning of the words. They seem to signify a loss."

"The loss of a loved one," she finished.

"Aye." And he'd endured enough losses for one lifetime.

He shrugged on his wet jacket, the expensive wool scratching against his neck. With a final "Cheers," he strode out Clara's flat door.

CHAPTER 3

The following morning dawned with a powder-blue sky, scarcely interrupted by low-hanging clouds. Clara quietly closed her flat door behind her so as not to awaken Seamus. She breathed in, filling her lungs with hope and optimism she couldn't explain. A sunlit breeze carried the promise of spring, and the eighteen-hour winter nights were finally lessening.

Anna, Clara's older sister, pulled up her battered car to Clara's flat.

An hour later, the women deposited their groceries in the boot of Anna's car. They'd both dressed for a shopping day in town. For Clara, that meant dressing in comfortable clothing —a ruffled turquoise blouse with a matching belt, slim ankle jeans, and saddle-brown loafers. Anna preferred to shop in black platform booties, a faded denim blouse, and ripped salmon-colored skinny pants.

Anna zippered her black faux-leather biker jacket and ducked into the driver's seat while Clara slipped into the passenger side. Both women fastened their seat belts.

"Thanks for driving your car today," Clara said. "It's odd that the brakes went on my car with no warning."

"At least you discovered the problem while you were in your driveway and not on the highway." Anna screeched out of the parking lot and made a sharp left, nearly clipping a parked taxi. Clara gripped her seat while the taxi driver sat long and loud on his horn.

"Bunk off!" Anna shouted, then looked at Clara. "I didn't hit him, did I?" Her coal-black penciled eyebrows always seemed lifted in a question, as if she didn't quite believe that a woman as dark-skinned and gorgeous as herself could've landed in Ireland's rainy climate. She was an exotic beauty with flashing amber eyes who had been born in sunny and hot Portugal.

"The taxi driver was waving his hands and swearing, so I'd venture you came close," Clara said. "Since you were forced to enroll in driver education classes after your last accident, you should know there's blind spots you can only see when you turn around."

Anna ran her fingers through her straight black hair, frosted with royal-purple highlights. "I can't because my hair would get mussed."

Clara grinned. "You could've bought an extra can of hair spray if you hadn't spent all your money on Irish cheddar cheese and cream crackers."

"That's all the groceries I can afford. I'd made arrangements to enroll in university this semester before Seamus mooched the little money I'd saved and gambled it away. Another hundred euros that he'll never repay."

"You've been putting off university for years."

Anna pulled into traffic and shrugged. "I'm not smart enough."

"You earned the highest grades in secondary school."

When she was done fixing Seamus, Clara decided, she'd work on Anna's low self-esteem.

Anna sighed. "Seamus's mental condition is more serious than my education. He belongs in The Flyaway Treatment Center."

Sternly, Clara shook her head. "The center relies on donations and we don't have any money. Besides, I know what's best for Seamus."

"Who's with him today while you're out?"

"Liam Lynch."

Anna pumped the gas pedal and merged into the passing lane. "Liam's a bloody bad influence. He used to sit around on his computer all day long. Besides, he steals anything that isn't bolted down."

"Liam's changed. He's working full-time and quit the drink."

"Sometimes you're a bit too optimistic, Clara."

"Life is so full of sadness. I choose to see the good." Clara ran her fingers along the sleeve of her grey jacquard-weave coat. "Liam's living in Donegal now, and he told me he only returns to Farthing from time to time."

"He's full of …" Anna slapped on the brakes as the traffic light switched to red.

"Didn't you date him for a while?"

"Yeh. He's a good-looking chap, though good looks won't make the kettle boil. Does he still bleach his hair?"

"Bleached and spiked."

Anna adjusted tortoise-framed sunglasses, showing off her perfectly manicured vivid violet fingernails. "I wouldn't be surprised if Liam is off the rails again. Seamus's friends are a bucket of snots who drink and gamble and don't work."

"I was skeptical too, until Liam showed me his pay stubs to prove he's working. Besides, it's essential to Seamus's well-being that he spends time with his friends because it occupies his mind."

"You're not a social worker."

"I'm his sister and I love him and that's enough." Clara drew in a lungful of air and wheezed, earning her a frown from Anna.

"And then there's Jack Connor," Anna said, "the love of your life, for reasons I could never fathom."

"Jack Connor," Clara repeated, struck by how the mention of his name sent a tremor to her very bones. She resisted the compulsion to glance behind them, forever believing he followed her. He was far away, locked behind bars, she reminded herself. She tried to keep the memories of him at bay, although oftentimes she'd replay the worst memories.

Within a few months of their dating, he'd moved into her flat. Slowly and systematically, he'd rearranged her life, forbidding her from seeing family and friends. She'd quit her shopkeeper's job because Jack had been so jealous of her working outside the home. The isolation had left her depressed and anxious.

Silently, she shook her head. She'd never seen it, the lies, the deception, the control. She'd been spineless and gullible and oh-so-trusting. And irresponsibly dependent.

He'd been an expert at fraud, and she'd been ten times a fool for believing him. Even as she'd endured his physical and mental abuse, he'd also been cheating on her with other women.

She pressed a hand to her throat, recalling Jack's terrible blows. The external bruises had disappeared; the unsettling memories persisted. His final beating had landed her in the hospital and her lungs had never been the same. Fortunately, her condition improved when the weather became warmer.

"Our brother must have professional intervention," Anna was saying, snapping Clara back to the present.

"I know what's best for him," Clara said, and ignored Anna's blatant scowl.

As they passed the River Farthing, Clara scanned the stairs leading to Farthing Bridge. Her heart raced at the chilling recollection of Seamus, his feverish, over-bright eyes staring down into the unforgiving water. Determinedly, she jerked her gaze to the road. "My ex came out from rehab meaner than when he went in."

"Seamus and I warned you a thousand times to leave Jack. He was useless, only fit to find mice at a crossroads. What were you thinking?"

"I was a complete fool." Before she'd finally come to her senses and decided to leave Jack for good, she'd been reduced to going through the motions of life completely numb.

"I hope Jack rots behind those prison bars," Anna said. "Those pale eyes of his and his hulking body always sent me shivering into a near coma. And that awful spider tattoo covering one side of his neck was enough to freeze me in one spot for days."

"He won't be released from prison for several years. And when he is, my restraining order states that he won't be able to come anywhere near me, so I have nothing to fear."

Despite her brave declaration, Clara shivered. While the order guaranteed her safety, she couldn't shake off her uneasy feelings of late, because she swore she'd seen Jack in Farthing only a fortnight ago. She hadn't told anyone, didn't want to set her siblings in a panic. Silly imaginings, she'd told herself, merely old fears conjuring Jack's heavily built image under a flash of moonlight.

"Enough about Jack," Anna said. "Our dear brother is our concern."

"I might be able to get Seamus a job in the factory if RJ Dougal Restaurant Supplies starts hiring," Clara said.

Anna flashed a sardonic grin. "And how will you get him to and from the factory? Drag him when he's hung over and too wrecked to stand? Even if he finds a job, you'll struggle to make ends meet."

"I'm hoping the dance studio will offer me a full-time dance position. I'd like to teach more preschool classes."

"There's not much demand for full-time dance teachers in a depressed town with no jobs."

Perhaps she should try to find a dance teaching job elsewhere, Clara thought. Perhaps Dublin. Mentally, she added the travel time, knowing the public transportation expenses would far outweigh any extra income.

She blew out a sigh. She'd prefer to open her own dancing school. However, she was twenty-nine, with bills and responsibilities, and owning her own business was far beyond her reach. For now, she'd focus on what she did best —getting by on what she earned and taking care of her brother.

Anna flicked on the car's right blinker. "Wanna try the new coffee shop that everyone's talking about? We have a couple hours to spare before Seamus expects you."

Anna didn't wait for a reply. She zipped across the bridge and straight into The Ground Café's busy parking lot. She circled the lot twice, finishing up a string of curses at the lack of spaces before parking on the grass.

Clara adjusted the standup collar of her grey coat as the women exited the car. "Seamus was still buzzed when he woke at five this morning before dozing off again."

Anna considered that information. "Any thoughts on how he'll survive without you the next few hours?"

Clara managed a smile, although she didn't respond.

They headed for the coffee shop, and Clara felt the hum of

excitement before she saw the revitalized marketplace. Three vans with Channel Four News emblazoned on the doors, satellite dishes perched on their roofs, were parked across the street from the coffee shop. While the women took their place at the end of a long queue, Clara admired the spectacular renovations. The old buildings in the shopping plaza had been restored, the round cobblestoned sidewalk fitting together like a giant puzzle. Fresh golden-yellow and orchid flowers adorned the window boxes along a row of upscale boutiques. An art gallery exhibited locally painted Irish landmarks. Nearby, a children's playground painted in bright primary colors featured a wooden fort, pirate ship, and swings. Children played noisily while their parents sat on adjacent park benches and sipped coffee.

The Ground Café's well-known logo of a pot of gold, along with the statement "This coffee house runs on love, life, and laughter," was prominently displayed above the main entrance. The door was partially opened while the unseasonably pleasant weather cooperated. Aromas of freshly brewed coffee, thick cream brownies, and Irish salad wraps enticed customers. Every few seconds, a sharp burst of relaxed hilarity sounded from inside the shop.

As they waited in the queue, Clara opened her purse and withdrew Danny's simple white business card, outlined in gold trim. Embossed in black letters:

Danny Brady

The Ground Café

Beneath was a 1-800 phone number.

Why so fancy? And why wouldn't Danny's personal cell phone number be printed on the card, unless the company moved him from shop to shop? Was he not ambitious enough to become successful on his own, and was dependent on a coffee chain to earn a living? Except that he drove a Mercedes, she considered.

"I met the guitarist who sings here. He said he'd be working this evening," Clara said.

"The guy who helped you with Seamus?"

"Yeh. He suggested I come by tonight." Clara checked her watch and grinned. "We're early."

Anna rooted in her purse for her lipstick and then applied it, a flaming-red shade. "What's his name? Is he good-looking?"

"Danny Brady. He's tall and his hair is dark brown." With a reddish tinge, Clara added to herself as a faint smile touched her mouth. How could she begin to describe his boyish features, the light sprinkle of freckles across the bridge of his nose? Or the way he'd spoken in a quiet, reas-suring brogue, reacting promptly and decisively?

Anna fished out her compact and applied coral-colored blush. "Is he single?"

"How would I know?"

"You were with him for several hours. What did you two talk about?"

"We discussed Seamus, and the rain, and ... coffee." *And we sang together.* Clara smiled, remembering Danny's off-key harmony. She shook her head. So much for his musicianship. No wonder he couldn't book his own gig. "He said he'd only be in town a few days."

Anna studied The Ground Café's coffee logo. "Danny Brady. That name sounds familiar, like I've read it somewhere."

Clara shrugged. "It's a common Irish name."

The name Danny was so masculine, like a strong-shoul-dered Irish chap who'd grace the cover of any glossy men's fashion magazine. He'd been dressed in a casual black shirt, ripped at the forearms, and wore snug-fitting worn jeans. Laughter had pulled at the corners of his full lips as he'd teased her about the incessant Irish rain. She'd felt her face flush when he'd smiled at her approvingly.

Do you have a song request? His clear blue eyes had reflected both warmth and devilment as he'd asked that.

"Will he recognize you?" Anna was asking.

"He should." Hopefully she wasn't that forgettable. Clara feigned absorption in searching through her purse for lip gloss and didn't meet Anna's gaze.

Clara wouldn't dispute that Danny was good-looking, although there was no room in her life for romance, certainly not with a musician who traveled from town to town. Her abusive ex had cured her of falling for shiftless men who couldn't hold a stable job.

Anna, one hand perched on a curvaceous hip, had decided to flirt with a man ahead of them in the queue. He sported a topknot of wooly grey hair and looked twice Anna's age.

"We'll be inside by noon," the wooly-haired man assured Anna. He went on to talk about the gossip he'd heard about the owner of the chain. "It says in the tabloids that the owner has a lavish estate in every city in Ireland." The man pointed at a candy-blue and yellow motorcycle. "And that's his body-guard's motorcycle. A real burly fellow, I've heard. And they say the owner's got wealthy women dangling all around him, but he never keeps any one on for long. He gets tired of them fast."

Clara hung back and concealed a yawn behind her hand. Any woman, wealthy or otherwise, who was foolish enough to dangle over a man who was obviously a cold-hearted seducer deserved her deepest sympathy.

As the women neared the entrance, Clara opened her own compact and cast a critical gaze on her reflection. The late-night trauma on the bridge combined with the early-morning tending to Seamus had left shadows beneath her eyes. She adjusted her turquoise headband, securing her hair, dark roots to blonde tips, away from her face, and pinched her cheeks.

"Where does the guitarist live?" Anna transferred her attention from the wooly-haired man to Clara.

"Dublin."

"Does he have a home there?"

Clara bubbled a laugh. "How should I know?"

"You never ask the right questions when you're with men. You could've offered to show him our local pubs while he's here."

"I don't go out much anymore."

"Where's that fun-loving sister I used to know, the woman who fancied a good time? Don't let your ex ruin your future relationships. Remember, he's safely locked behind bars."

CHAPTER 4

The tang of fine gourmet coffee permeated every inch of space as the two women stepped through the brick entrance of the coffee shop. Lighting had been softened to a rosy tint, and piped-in Irish folk music, featuring tin whistle and drum, enhanced the welcoming setting.

The Ground Café, crammed with customers, was cleverly named, since the coffee shop was situated on the second floor of an old factory building. The first floor was comfortably furnished with couches, books and magazines, and free Wi-Fi. The women passed reclaimed wooden tables, each featuring a single, fresh pink rose in a glass vase. They rode the escalator, passing large wall murals depicting Ireland's famed castles, craggy coastlines and windswept cliffs.

Anna cocked her head. "Gorgeous, isn't it?"

"I would've liked to see more local artists' paintings featured along these walls," Clara said.

"You always had an eye for decorating." Anna stepped off the escalator and arrowed straight for the coffee and dessert counter.

A stunning young woman, whose name tag, pinned to her

starched cotton blouse, identified her as Kathleen greeted Clara and Anna once they stepped up to the counter. Kathleen's strawberry blonde hair was brushed into a classic top knot, her smoky-black eyes accented by shimmering gold eyeshadow. She wore a pair of black cotton slacks that hugged her rounded hips and long legs.

Behind Kathleen, a long list of beverages, from different-bean coffees, to Americano and cappuccino and lattes, hot or iced, were listed on a cork board. The glass shelves in the display case offered rows of bread and butter puddings and Irish coffee cakes. The cashier at the register poured free samples of the coffee of the day, an Irish latte described as buttery smooth.

"I'd like a tall iced mocha latte and a slice of orange Guinness coffee cake, thanks," Anna said.

Clara scanned the list of teas. "A tall green mint tea, please."

"Hot or iced?" Kathleen asked.

"Iced. And a bowl of fresh fruit."

"You're the thinnest woman in Farthing," Anna teased Clara. "Aren't you ready to relinquish that title and order something fattening like I did?" Anna swept a hand to her hips.

Whereas Anna's midsection remained flat, her hips, to her constant dismay, were full and rounded.

Clara chuckled. "If I ever stopped teaching ballet classes, I'd gain weight as quick as you can say—" She gaped at the tall, attractive man striding directly toward them. "Danny Brady," she finished.

His slightly tanned skin contrasted with his crisp white shirt and slim-fitting denim jeans. His piercing blue gaze targeted hers.

"Clara Donovan, you're looking brilliant today. If I'd known what time you were coming, I'd have reserved a table for you. Did you wait long?" He grabbed both her hands. His fingers were long, the tips callused.

Her nerves fluttered. Unsettled, she retreated a step. "The queue moved fast."

Slowly, she became aware that customers in the coffee shop were staring, and conversations had been reduced to a whispered hum. Bewildered, she attempted to wrest her hands from his grasp.

He smiled and subtly tightened his hold. "Thank you for accepting my invitation."

That slow and engaging smile. He'd used it the previous evening when he'd mentioned he had a "thing" for Irish damsels in distress.

Anna crossed her arms. "Well, aren't you two the cat's pajamas? Apparently you know each other?"

"Danny is the man on the bridge I was telling you about. He helped me with Seamus."

Clara carefully ignored the gawking, the waitresses who had stopped bussing tables to gape.

"I merely offered my support." His gaze lingered on Clara's face before moving to Anna. "And this lovely woman who looks nothing like you is …?"

"Anna is my older sister who was adopted from Portugal," Clara replied. "Our parents adopted two girls from entirely different countries when Seamus was seven."

"They must've realized that one Seamus was enough for any family." Anna laughed. "He was mad as a ditch even then."

"Mr. Brady." Kathleen focused her beaming smile on him. "Does the counter meet with your approval?"

"Aye, the shop looks grand." Apparently to ensure that Clara's hands were still tucked in his, Danny glanced down.

Somewhere, a spoon clattered to the floor.

In the momentary silence that followed, Kathleen

announced that their order was ready. Her eyes narrowed, she bestowed a frosty glance on Clara and then set the beverages, fruit, and coffee cake near the cash register. Danny instructed a waitress to bring their order, along with an assortment of sandwiches and desserts, to the third level.

Clara grinned at him. "I hope you're well-compensated, if you're some sort of manager as well as the guitarist. I've heard the owner of this company is very rich. Tell him to give you a raise."

"I'll pass that along." He seemed impervious to the commotion he was creating. "Let's go to the third floor where it will be quieter."

"We haven't paid," Clara reminded him.

"I'll take care of the bill."

Anna's eyebrows rose. "This boy's a dear. Who said there's no such thing as a free lunch?"

Danny kept hold of Clara's hand as they weaved through the customers. Anna pulled out her cell phone and followed, continually glancing down at her phone.

A woman approached, and Clara immediately recognized her as Maeve Flanagan, the reporter from Farthing Bridge. "Mr. Brady, may I request a few minutes for an interview?"

Another reporter held out a microphone, chiming, "I'm from the *Dublin Times*. Is it true you'll be offering franchises globally?" The woman peered at Clara. "And who is this woman?"

"No comment," he said.

A round of flashes went off, and Danny held up a hand, shielding Clara's face. He peered around. "Where's Ian?" he asked no one in particular.

Clara blinked and yanked her hand from his. "Who's Ian? And what's this all about?"

"Lunch hour." He shepherded Clara and Anna to a private

door. "Watch your footing. There's a tangle of wires from the cameramen."

Puzzled by the odd behavior, Danny's and the reporters', Clara asked him what time he was performing that night. "We can return then," she added.

He seemed confused. "I play guitar when the place is ready to close."

But that didn't make sense. She opened her mouth to tell him that if he was any good as a musician, he shouldn't allow himself to be slated to perform at the end of the night. He'd never be discovered if no one ever heard him.

Anna spoke first, though. A slow, incredulous smile had spread across her face as she studied her phone and then gawked at Danny. Her ebony hair swung from side to side as she shook her head and planted a fist on her hip. "The cheek of ya, Mr. Danny Brady. When were you planning to tell my sister that you owned this shop, as well as forty-nine others?"

CHAPTER 5

Clara snapped her chin up at Danny. "You lied to me! Do you think—"

"Not here." He shook his head as another round of camera flashes went off. He placed his hand on her elbow as he pushed open the private door, ushered them through, and then latched it behind them. He directed the women down a long corridor until they came to the lift.

Clara jerked free. "I'm going home."

"You and your sister are riding the lift to the third level with me. Get in."

"No!"

Danny exhaled heavily. He'd certainly made a bag of this, totally botching what he'd originally planned. He'd wanted to play guitar and sing for Clara, later in the evening when the coffee shop was quiet.

In contrast to Clara's scowl, Anna beamed good-naturedly. "I'm certain he'll offer a good reason for his deception. Won't you, Mr. Brady?"

"Please call me Danny."

"Won't you, Danny?"

He nodded, then focused on Clara. "I can explain when we get upstairs."

She drew back. "You'll likely spin more lies."

"I haven't lied. Your brother was our concern last night, not me."

"You lied by omission."

The lift door pinged open.

"Come with me." He captured her elbow again and guided her and Anna onto the lift. "We'll talk in my boardroom. I deserve a chance to explain."

Except he didn't know what he'd say.

Earlier, while unloading supplies in the storage room with several of his employees, he'd scanned the security monitors and noticed Clara walking into the coffee shop. Without a word, he'd rushed to the front of the shop to greet her. Aye, this was unlike him because he never acted impetuously. However, he had good reason because the woman was Clara, his captivating non-Irish Irish damsel.

Since his newfound prosperity, he'd learned, much to his dismay, that the prestige that went with dating wealthy men was immensely important to most women.

Not the man. Just the wealth.

Clara hadn't seemed to be one of those women. Consequently, he'd wanted to see her again, hoping the trappings of his success wouldn't color her interest. He'd wanted to tell her who exactly he was when he felt the time was right. And, he'd assumed she'd come by later in the evening, as he'd suggested.

He sighed. So much for that assumption.

Clara stood in the far corner of the lift. When the doors opened, he and Anna stepped out. Clara remained rooted inside.

"The lift doesn't go any higher. Are you waiting for something?" he asked.

She crossed her arms. "I presumed you were a guitar player."

"I am a guitar player. I told you last night how much I love music." He extended his hand, which she refused, although she stepped from the lift.

As the doors closed behind them, Danny's bodyguard, Ian, a brute of a man, barreled down the hallway toward them. His leather jacket was partially zipped, as if he'd been in the process of putting it on. Danny had met Ian in a soup kitchen in Carlow when Ian had been dirty, full of anger, and off the rails. They'd formed a friendship, and Danny had sponsored Ian's six-month stint in a rehab center. As a result, Ian was fiercely loyal, as well as brutally honest.

Danny had hired Ian as his bodyguard when he'd found that one disadvantage of being in the public eye was that customers were contacting him through email and phone, most of the time with complaints. Usually, those complaints were easily pacified, and Danny was always more than generous. He knew the value of one pleased patron was worth hundreds of euros in advertising.

Ian pushed a sturdy hand through his thinning, honey-gold hair. "Boss, you were unloading supplies, then one of the employees said you'd disappeared."

"I didn't have time to let you know that I'd gone to the front of the shop." Noting Ian's inquisitive grin as he glanced at the two women, Danny continued, "I'd like you to meet Clara Donovan and her sister Anna. They live in this charming town of Farthing. Ladies, Ian is my ... bodyguard." He grimaced, knowing another explanation was in order, yet preferring to skip the subject altogether for fear of sounding arrogant.

Clara nodded a greeting, looking thoroughly unimpressed.

"Hi, fella. What's the craic?" Anna cocked her head and

laid a hand on Ian's shirtsleeve. "Your boss was looking for you because walking through that crowded coffee shop with all those photo flashes going off was murder."

"I'm here now," Ian said with a laugh. His eyes sparkled, a brilliant hazel, the center a warm, reflective brown.

"And I'm relieved," Anna rejoined, fanning herself. "Clara turned scarlet because everyone stared at us. She loathes that sort of thing after that awful newspaper article written about her."

Danny rubbed his chin. "What newspaper article?"

"Nothing of interest," Clara said, glaring at her sister. Anna didn't seem to notice. Instead, she lingered by the lift and chatted animatedly with Ian.

"They're hitting it off well," Danny said.

Clara fastened the buttons on her coat. "And I'm going home."

"Please stay," Danny said, gesturing down the hall to his boardroom. "I want the privilege of treating you and your sister to lunch."

"The privilege?" Clara came to a standstill. "Don't use my sister as an excuse, you good-for-nothing bowsie."

He lifted a brow. "If I ever grow overconfident, I'll know who to turn to for a set-down. Will you accept dinner as my apology for the deception?"

She tossed her luxuriant hair over her shoulders. "I won't be coming back here."

"I'll deliver it straight to your door because I know where you live." He winked. "In fact, I can walk to your flat from the coffee shop."

She plunked her hands on her lean hips. "Don't threaten me."

"With dinner?" He pressed a forefinger lightly to her lips, silencing her protest. "My offer isn't a threat, it's an olive branch."

Her gaze seemed to warm, although she jerked her head away from his touch. She toyed with the strap of her purse, then resumed her pace, keeping one step ahead of him. "I accept your olive branch. Nevertheless, you're still a bowsie," she called over her shoulder.

He began singing "When Irish Eyes Are Smiling," and she rewarded him with an exasperated head shake. "You're singing so off-key, it sounds like the tune the old cow died of."

"I'm more in tune when I'm strumming my guitar as accompaniment. Or when I play my Celtic harp," he told her.

"Should I be impressed?"

"Absolutely not. I don't play either instrument very well."

She stopped at the closed door, and he took a moment to admire her shapely calves and graceful bearing. Aye, she was appealing, quick to temper, quick to forgive. As he took out his keys, he glanced back to see where Ian and Anna were. Anna had stopped in front of a collection of Waterford crystal vases and was talking about them with Ian.

Danny opened the deadbolt lock on the door, and, with a smile, led Clara into his boardroom. A tall fern stood by the entrance. The room was sparse and masculine, exactly the way he liked his decor, the walls lined in richly carved mahogany. An espresso-colored leather sofa and coffee table were placed beneath a large picture window. The window offered an unobstructed view of the southern bank of the River Farthing, as well as the entrance to the coffee shop. In the distance, the ruins of an old Norman castle stood atop a steep cliff.

"Very high-end," she said. "And your view is picture-perfect. You might consider rearranging your furniture so that the view is the focal point rather than the sofa."

"Thanks for the excellent decorating tip." He accepted her coat as she slid it off, signaling, he assumed, that she'd be staying for lunch. He hung it on a coat rack by the doorway and then seated her at the boardroom table in the middle of the room. After pouring two glasses of water from the pitcher on the table, he perched carefully on the narrow arm of her chair.

"Would you care for some ice water?" He leaned over to nudge the glass in front of her. Her fragrance reminded him of lemon and wholesomeness, sensual and citrusy.

She tensed, her frown pronounced. "I'll wait for my iced tea and fruit, thanks."

"How is Seamus faring?" Danny asked.

"He suffered dry heaves when he woke. I offered to cook eggs and rashers, but he refused. So I gave him some water and he went back to sleep. His friend Liam came to my flat to spend a few hours. I don't feel comfortable leaving Seamus alone."

"Aye." Danny placed his arm around her chair, earning another piercing frown. "I'll send eggs and rashers along with herbal tea to your flat for them both. I'm well acquainted with hangovers, and Seamus will be hungry once he feels better." He grabbed his cell phone from his shirt pocket and dashed off a quick text to one of his staff, acknowledging with some guilt that he should be available for his employees. Lunch hours were hectic, especially on opening day, and business could suffer from his lack of attention.

"You're experienced with hangovers?" Clara asked. "I'm surprised. You seem so, I don't know, so in control."

"I haven't had a drop in fifteen years, although I still remember the really, really bad headaches the morning after a night of drinking."

And the sadness and anxiety that had followed.

Somehow, at twenty years old, he'd come out of his alcohol-induced haze long enough to realize that alcohol had destroyed those he loved most. His chest still ached at the image of Glenna, his toddler sister, and her cherubic laughing face. He'd nicknamed her his little leprechaun.

The world hadn't stopped spinning when both his parents had committed suicide soon after Glenna's death. The short-term relief they'd sought in alcohol had ultimately killed them.

Danny gripped his glass and sipped his water. As a young lad, he'd trusted his parents to take care of him and his siblings. Instead, they'd scorned him, then abandoned him.

"Thanks for arranging to send lunch to Seamus and his friend," Clara was saying.

Danny set down his water glass and shook his thoughts back to the present.

She was staring at him. "You looked like you were a million miles away."

"I was thinking about the past when I should be enjoying the present and your lovely company," he said.

She continued to study him. Whatever she was searching for, she wouldn't find. He'd learned to keep his expression carefully neutral.

"Seamus and Liam will enjoy the sandwiches," she added.

"No bother. Let me know if I can do anything else." He didn't mention that he could recommend a good rehab for Seamus, and that Seamus's condition cried out for detoxification, which required medical supervision.

Instead, he simply enjoyed the fact that Clara had allowed him to sit so near, even if she was treating his closeness with chilly formality.

Kathleen swung into the boardroom ferrying a tray of chicken salad sandwiches, chocolate orange Guinness coffee cakes, a bowl of fresh fruit, and iced beverages laced with sprigs of fresh mint. She set the tray on the table beside a ceramic vase filled with pink roses, then arranged their place settings with gold-plated utensils, and snowy-white linen napkins.

"The waitresses are all busy downstairs, so I told them I would help. You know I'm here to be sure that everything runs smoothly and that the new employees all know what they're doing," she said.

"Thank you, Kathleen. You're an excellent manager." He indicated she could leave.

She briefly pouted. "Aye, Mr. Brady."

"Kathleen's been working with me since my shop's inception," he explained to Clara.

In fact, Kathleen had insisted on traveling with him from Dublin to open the new Farthing store. She was a dedicated employee, and, in turn, had accompanied him to several company functions. Up until now, he'd enjoyed her lush beauty, as well as her dedication to his business, although today she lacked something. Perhaps it was because her eyes weren't a deep, soft brown and her grin wasn't infectious.

He scanned the beverages on the table. "No coffee?" he wryly asked Clara.

She granted him a mischievous smile. "Coffee's too bitter, remember? My favorite is green mint tea."

"The coffee of the day is mild. And I have it on good authority that every cup of The Ground Café's coffee is brilliant because the owner uses fresh coffee beans and local spring water."

"Yeh, and the Irish latte is buttery smooth, based on the description," Clara said.

"Will you try a cup of my Irish latte? We add non-alcoholic whiskey."

She grinned. "After that fancy description, how can I resist?"

He glanced at Kathleen, who was still standing in the doorway. "Please bring Clara a cup of Irish latte."

"Whatever you say, sir." Kathleen's smile was blatantly sensual. Wheeling on her heels, she sashayed out.

Clara sniffed the flowers on the table. "Roses are my favorite. Why pink and not red? Did you run out of money because red is more expensive?"

He laughed. "All the roses I purchase are the same price. However, a deep pink rose expresses gratitude. Every customer is important, and it's my way of saying thank you."

"I'm impressed by your attention to detail." She retied the belt of her ruffled blouse around her slender waist, and he felt his insides warm. She was so pretty, as pretty as a wild Irish rose. "I'm impressed by your courage, Clara Donovan."

She nodded sagely. "It's not courage. I've simply learned to rely on myself."

"As have I," he said quietly.

At that moment, Ian and Anna entered. Anna shrugged off her biker jacket and handed it to Ian. He hung it with Clara's on the coat rack near the door.

"There's plenty of room at the table for all of us to enjoy lunch." Danny gestured for the pair to seat themselves around the nine-foot table. He kept his arm securely around Clara's chair.

"Then perhaps you should take your own seat," she said.

He waited several beats. This was his coffee shop, his boardroom, his chair.

She glared at him, the flecks of gold in her brown eyes sparking dangerously.

He complied and stood quickly.

CHAPTER 6

*D*anny hadn't intended to break for lunch. He hadn't intended to be sitting in his boardroom when a thousand decisions clamored for his attention. Instead, his mind was filled with Clara, and he couldn't look away from her exquisite profile. What was it about this spirited woman? She'd saved her brother, disregarding the danger to herself. She was proud and brave, yet humble.

He glanced at his cell phone, relieved to see that no employee had texted him. He'd allow himself fifteen minutes before focusing again on his business.

"You're obviously a guy who goes straight after what he wants in life," Anna said. "I admire you." She looked around, indicating a wall mounted security camera. "And you're cautious."

Clara didn't seem to ooze with the same admiration for him.

The food sat uneaten as silence settled over the room. Ian lumbered to the mounted television and grabbed the remote. "Wonder if the football match is being televised?" Idly, he flipped the channels, groaned at the latest scores, and settled on the local news. He lowered the volume, glanced at his watch, then at Danny. "I'll show Anna your famous painting in the hallway while we're waiting for Clara's latte, boss. Our lunch can wait a few minutes." He glanced meaningfully at Clara's pressed lips.

"Aye, brilliant idea." Danny silently thanked his friend for allowing him more time alone with Clara.

"Do you appreciate fine art?" Danny asked Anna as Ian helped her from her chair.

"Does fine art include graffiti, Danny? If so, I'm interested." She looped her hand around Ian's arm and fairly danced to the door with him. "Lead the way, you fine thing."

After Anna's platform booties had clattered down the hallway alongside Ian's heavy-booted shoes, Danny dragged his chair a hairsbreadth closer to Clara.

She kept her gaze on her glass. "Tell me, do you lie to every woman you bring into your boardroom?"

"Truly, I'm sorry for any deception regarding my identity." He reached for his water and gave his brightest smile. "Aren't you curious about my famous painting?"

"I'm certain your painting cost more than my wages for an entire year."

"You're probably right. And, I admit, one part of me is ashamed. However, the other part is proud that I'm able to afford a widely recognized painting that I consider an investment."

She was silent, nursing her iced tea.

"The painting accompanies me whenever I open a new store."

"So your fancy, expensive painting is an investment?" Her tone held more politeness than interest. "Or is it a good luck charm?"

"Both. This particular painting is one of Francis Bacon's most praiseworthy. His boldness inspired me." Danny caught

43

her inquiring expression. "Bacon's life was as chaotic as mine was."

Her eyes widened. "I assumed you were born into wealth and lived a charmed life."

"Me?" He laughed, the idea so absurd.

She glanced down. "I shouldn't have judged you."

"Is that an apology?"

"I don't manage apologies well."

He accepted her explanation with a brief nod. "My aunt brought me to the Hugh Lane Gallery in Dublin every Saturday afternoon. I should backtrack. After my parents' deaths, my elderly aunt and uncle took me and my two siblings, Erin and Eamon, to live with them. We were chiselers." Clara looked up. Danny avoided her scrutiny, preferring to study the mahogany paneling on the opposite wall.

"I am very sorry." Her gaze strayed to her glass, her voice heavy with sympathy. "Were your parents' deaths unexpected?"

Absently, he plucked a pink rose petal from the vase and rubbed the smoothness between his fingers. "Long story," was all he could manage.

Suicidal depression and alcoholism were signs of a serious mental illness. Nonetheless, his parents' deaths had hit him like an unexpected punch to the stomach. He should've heeded the warning signs after Glenna's death—his parents' withdrawal from family and well-meaning friends, their loss of jobs, their loss of interest.

Danny dropped the petal onto the table and focused on his response. "My younger sister died a few months before my parents."

"Care to talk about it?"

He stared down at his hands and shook his head. He still couldn't say Glenna's name aloud. The weight on his chest and limbs would press too heavily and crush him with guilt.

He should've been home the afternoon Glenna died, to attend to her, instead of sneaking off to get drunk with his teenage friends.

"Do Erin and Eamon live near you?" Clara asked.

He noted the softness in her voice. "Both of my siblings live in Dublin." Danny had learned, though, that proximity had nothing to do with how close you lived to one another. Eamon, his brother, was too busy establishing a successful medical practice in Dublin to care about anything or anyone except himself. And Erin, his sister, well, she drifted from one bad relationship to another.

Danny reached for the water pitcher and topped off his glass. "And that's enough questions about my family."

"Indulge me."

He usually resisted answering questions regarding his personal life, but Clara's interest seemed genuine. He held up an index finger and relented. "One more question."

"How was a poor kid like you able to gain entry to fancy art galleries?"

"The galleries were free. My aunt and I had to take a bus to the city centre because we lived too far away to walk."

"I'm not familiar with Dublin. I only visited there once when I was a child."

He inclined his head slightly away from her. "We lived on the north side."

The run-down, seedy section where people living in four-room tenement buildings were buried in dirty grave plots in Glasnevin Cemetery.

Not anymore, he amended. His parents now rested in peace inside an Italian marble tomb, quiet and serene beneath a mature oak tree. And Glenna's little cemetery plot sat beside theirs. He'd added a pot of gold and a rainbow to the top of her headstone.

He leaned closer to Clara. "I'd like to know more about your adoption if you're comfortable talking about it."

She returned her gaze to her iced tea. "There's little to tell. After Seamus was born, my adoptive mother and father said they'd wanted the sound of girls' laughter to brighten their home, so they adopted two girls from abroad. And Anna and I were those two little girls. We provided the laughter my parents sought, and topped it off with female drama." Pensively, Clara swirled the ice in her glass. "In his teens, Seamus was often on a drunken tear. So, my parents got more than they bargained for raising the three of us."

Danny chuckled. "Have you revisited your Italian orphanage?"

"No, and I won't be able to afford the trip anytime soon. I might have an older brother who was also born in Italy. I'll probably never meet him. He's long-lost to me now."

"I'll take you to Italy, luv. The country is magnificent." He stopped himself from saying more, surprised that he'd offered her a trip without thinking it through first.

She was a complete stranger. Nevertheless, he felt like he'd known her a long time. He reminded himself that they'd shared a traumatic experience rescuing her brother, and that people in those types of situations often felt a closeness to one another afterward.

"I'll pay my own way if I ever have the opportunity to go," Clara responded matter-of-factly, as if accepting charity from anyone was unthinkable. "And while a trip to Italy sounds exciting, it's also terrifying."

"Are you afraid of flying?"

"I've only flown once in my life, and I was young when I traveled from Italy to Ireland. I hardly remember the flight, although we landed in Dublin." She straightened and set her glass down, perfectly aligning it with his.

"Aren't you curious about your Italian roots?"

"Of course. It's the memories ... my poor judgment ..."
Tears brightened her eyes and she made no attempt to hide
them. "Forgive me. I didn't sleep well and last night's events
—" She accepted his offer of a linen napkin and dabbed at
her eyes. "Only the present counts, right? That's what
everyone says. Keep looking ahead."

"Your past mistakes will haunt you if you don't confront
them."

Who was he to give advice? his conscience admonished.

She smiled wryly and placed the napkin on the table.
"Have you ever thought about writing your sage words down
in a song?"

"I've written several songs. Perhaps you'll inspire me to
write another."

"First, a title is essential."

Clara. The title came instantly to his mind. Her name
meant bright and clear. A perfect title for a woman who
brightened any room.

"Write a song about coffee beans." She offered an auda-
cious grin. "You can begin with 'How warm and robust is the
scent of coffee.'"

He laughed. *Forget the coffee. I'd rather sing a song about you.*

She continued to the tune of "Irish Rover," and he
hummed along. He knew the melody well.

She exaggerated the high note of the chorus and raised an
elegant brow. "No word rhymes with coffee."

"Toffee?"

She took a breath and continued singing.

Her deep set eyes were ringed by thick black lashes and
sparkled with amusement. Once, he'd been looking for a
woman like her—a woman who was beautiful, kind and
brave.

Once. Not anymore. Kyla, his ex-wife, had cured him of
pursuing relationships with women. Women were better

kept at arm's length. He enjoyed their company, but in the end they'd only betray him, betray his trust. He'd grown immune to their charms.

He rubbed his forehead. He'd tried to make his marriage work. And he'd failed. All his relationships with the people he cared about—his parents, his siblings, even his ex-wife—had proven disastrous.

However, not his business. His businesses flourished and never disappointed him.

So what was it about Clara Donovan that started a thaw in his frozen heart?

He folded his arms and admired her entrancing face as she sang several more bars. "'Convincing me to like Irish lattes is your intent.'" She hesitated and looked at him. "What rhymes with *intent?*"

"Relent. 'If you try my latte, you'll relent.'"

She chuckled. "Or *you'll* lament ... the loss of a sale."

"Money doesn't mean everything to me," he said.

The room grew quiet, the silence interrupted by the murmur of the television.

"I think it means a great deal," she said softly.

His thumbs longed to stroke the blush of enjoyment highlighting her smooth, unblemished features. She was a compelling woman, a surprising treasure he'd never expected to find when he came to the unsophisticated town of Farthing. Firmly, he reminded himself that he'd only be in town a short while; and treasures proved fleeting and were seldom worth the effort because whatever shimmered on the surface was rarely found inside.

"I can't think of any word to rhyme with 'lament,'" she said.

"Neither can I." Perhaps it was because he couldn't tear his gaze away from her moist lips. "Am I forgiven for all my missteps today, luv?"

"Some of them." She smiled, that same vivid smile when he'd teased her about the rain the previous evening.

He relinquished his plan to return to the coffee shop in fifteen minutes.

As if on cue, his cell phone buzzed, intrusive and insistent.

"Are you needed downstairs?" Clara attempted to tuck an errant strand of hair behind her ear, though it wouldn't cooperate.

"In a wee bit." He wanted to spend time with her, not his unrelenting business. "What do you do for a living, Clara Donovan?"

She seemed to make a valiant attempt to keep her features impassive. "I try to keep my brother out of harm's way, which is a full-time job. I also work in a factory, RJ Dougal Restaurant Supplies, plus I teach dance classes at the dance studio in town."

"That's a lot of work for one person."

"I like my factory job, but I adore teaching dance because I love children. You should see how enthusiastic the kids act when they practice their ballet steps, their little faces all puckered with concentration."

Danny noted the gentleness that had crept into her voice when she spoke about children, her cheeks stained with a spark that also lit her eyes.

"So, you're a dancer," he said. "Last night on the bridge, I noticed how graceful you were."

She settled back in her chair and gave a self-deprecating chuckle. "You must've been looking at someone else. I slipped more than once."

He lightly pushed that wayward strand of hair from her face. "And I was there to save you."

"Thank you." Her expression softened.

"No bother." He shifted. Perhaps if she sat on his lap, she could thank him with a kiss.

A clicking and clattering of heels echoed from the corridor.

"Quite an impressive business here, Danny!" Anna announced, strolling into the boardroom with a moon-struck Ian behind her. "And all these pink roses." She nodded to the vase on the table. "Nice touch."

"And I just learned roses are your sister's favorite flower," Danny said.

"Yeh, she's always loved roses," Anna said. "I got restless staring at that one Francis Bacon painting so Ian showed me the kitchen. I didn't realize there was an art to making coffee or that there was so much equipment required—coffee grinders, espresso machines, refrigerators, dishwashers. And you sell your CDs in the lobby."

At Clara's inquiring gaze, Danny explained, "They're mostly instrumental CDs."

"And more money in your pocket," Clara murmured.

He chuckled.

"Your employees are extremely helpful and knowledge-able," Anna continued.

"My staff is very dedicated," Danny said.

Ian's thick blond brows furrowed. "What the boss isn't telling you is that he works sixty hours a week alongside his employees, and that's why they're so dedicated."

"I'll submit an application to help you out, Danny," Anna dove in. "Both my sister and I need jobs. I've always wanted to try waitressing."

"I could certainly use good waitresses," Danny said. "And I offer complementary food and beverages to all my employees before and after their shifts."

"As you know, I already work two jobs, although thanks for the offer," Clara demurred.

"I don't work any jobs and I love free food." Sitting down, Anna grabbed her chicken salad sandwich, coffee cake, and latte. She peered at Clara over her cup. "Wouldn't it be brilliant to make ends meet for a change? The government doesn't pay me nearly enough money for the pain and suffering caused by my terrible accident."

"That was a year ago, and you've conceded you're much better. And you can't work in the coffee shop until you're off disability allowance," Clara reminded her sister.

"The allowance ends very soon," Anna said.

"Let me know when you're available, Anna," Danny put in. "The offer's open."

"Perhaps you'll consider hiring Seamus instead of me," Clara said to him.

"You should know up front, Danny," Anna said, "before you do a security check, that Seamus spent some time in Farthing prison. It was nothing serious."

Clara glared at Anna. "After Seamus finished secondary school, he enrolled in computer classes online. He's very smart when he applies himself."

Danny hesitated. His business didn't call for office help because he employed professional accountants. And Seamus could cause serious problems if he reported for work drunk. However, if Ian befriended Seamus, then Ian could recommend a good rehab. Knowing her brother was safe and employed would lighten Clara's emotional, as well as financial, load.

Danny extracted a business card from his wallet, dashed off his phone number and handed the card to Clara. "Assuming Seamus can stay on the rails, he's hired once I interview him. I don't require a computer person, but more kitchen help is always appreciated. Here's my cell phone number."

Ian grinned and snatched up his sandwich. "The boss

fancies you, miss. He never gives his private number to women. They'd badger him relentlessly."

She leveled a stare at Ian and then Danny. "Please tell your boss that he never need fear badgering from me." She examined Danny's script, then stashed his business card in her purse. "Assuming Seamus is agreeable, I'll send him around tomorrow. I promise I'll keep him straight."

"And I'll want a job as soon as my disability allowance ends," Anna said. "Someday I'll tell you all about my accident and how I wasn't at fault." She lifted a forkful of Guinness cake. "And that the paltry sum the government awarded me wasn't nearly—" She broke off as she ate a bite of cake. "Wow, this cake is deadly. Do you give out your recipes?"

Danny shook his head. "Sorry, my company doesn't share any recipes."

"Top secret?" Anna barked a laugh. "Crack on, because I don't bake."

"My specialty is lemon scones," Clara said, "and I'm not giving away any of my secrets, either."

Danny smiled. "I'm intrigued."

"Nothing else to say," she averred. "That's why they're secrets."

"I'd consider buying your recipe." Very quietly, very slowly, he whispered, "If I'm around you much longer, you'll be privy to all my secrets."

She quickly looked away and toyed with her bowl of fruit.

Between alternating bites of sandwich and cake, Anna pointed to the television screen. "Hey, Danny, you're on TV."

Ian grabbed the remote and turned up the volume.

The television came alive. A familiar face, the reporter from the bridge, came into focus.

"I'm on the scene of a suicide attempt," she said into the microphone. "The incident happened around midnight on Farthing Bridge, and Channel Four News arrived first at the scene. Fortunately, this story has a happy ending, thanks to Mr. Danny Brady, owner of The Ground Café." The camera panned out to the bridge, showing a dejected Seamus and furious Clara, shouting and shaking her hand at the camera.

Clara stared at the television screen, and her face whitened. She shoved back her chair and stood. Danny came to his feet as well, reluctantly watching the TV screen.

"Mr. Brady is considered one of the wealthiest men in Ireland," the reporter was saying. "He's in Farthing to open his fiftieth coffee shop." She extended the microphone to Danny. "Can you tell us what happened on the bridge?"

The camera focused on Danny's face. "I was nearby and immediately phoned the Gardaí."

"AND YOU BRAVELY CAME TO a desperate man's rescue," the reporter chimed in.

"I did what I could to help."

The camera swung to the reporter. "Whether he's in the kitchen brewing his famous coffee or saving a despondent man, Danny Brady is Ireland's national hero. This is Maeve Flanagan reporting from Farthing Bridge."

Ian grinned as he strode over to Danny and clapped a hand on his boss's shoulder. "Fair play! That's a load of brilliant publicity. The customers will surely rush the place."

True. Except that Clara's nostrils were flaring and fury blazed from her eyes, which wasn't quite so brilliant.

"You and I know that's not what happened," Danny said to her. "The media sensationalizes everything."

Her hands were braced on the table. Her look was hurt and reproachful. "How dare you use my brother's desperation to promote your wretched coffee chain? Is that the reason why you were so insistent on helping me?"

"Of course not. I'd never circuit a terrible situation into one for my advantage."

Clara threw her purse over her arm and marched to the doorway. "Let's go," she directed Anna.

"I haven't finished my absolutely divine dessert." Anna was attacking her orange Guinness coffee cake like she'd never eaten before. "Besides, Mr. Brady promised us all jobs."

Clara spun. "You'd actually work for this swine?"

Anna put down her fork. "If I hope to attend university, then, yeh, I'd gladly work for him. Ian said Danny pays excellent wages."

"You'd go against your own family?"

"Have you noticed there's no jobs in this town?" Anna's gaze raked furiously over Clara's stung expression. "I don't see any dancing schools beating down your door. Now sit down and wait for your Irish latte."

"I've waited long enough." Clara's gaze fired up as she whirled on Danny. "You'll lose customers in droves if your barista spends an hour preparing one latte." She grabbed her coat. "Money isn't as important as families sticking together."

"And our family needs to eat," Anna said. "Anyway, how are you getting home? I drove."

"I'll ring a taxi."

"I'll take you home after you've finished your lunch," Danny said, walking over to Clara. "Please don't leave." He placed a hand on her shoulder, assuming she'd shrug it off.

He was right.

"I won't accept charity from a good-for-nothing bowsie." She quit the boardroom, almost knocking over a stone-colored wastebasket set near the tall fern by the doorway.

"Don't go after her," Anna advised as Danny started for the hallway. "Give her time to cool off. You're better off waiting until tomorrow."

Ian sank into his chair and pulled a roll of antacids from

his pocket. He popped one into his mouth. "And send a bouquet of roses to Clara's house in the meantime." He clutched a linen napkin and mopped the perspiration settling on his forehead. "I didn't intend to offend her, although it's brilliant you're the town hero, right, boss?"

Danny sighed, crossed his arms, and slumped against the doorway. "Aye, just brilliant."

CHAPTER 7

*H*e was riding the city bus, Clara was sure of it. She'd been walking to the dance studio to teach her evening ballet class when she'd spotted him.

Jack Connor's thick features had been pressed against the bus's grubby window. He'd waved, and she'd almost lifted her hand to wave back, a reflexive reaction. Then she'd shivered, drawing her jacket close around her shoulders.

Those cold, leering eyes, that lecherous grin. She'd recognize Jack anywhere. But he was locked away in a prison near Cork, miles from Farthing. Wasn't he?

She rubbed at her eyes. Seamus hadn't slept well the previous night, alternating between shaking uncontrollably and cursing her for being a "rugger bugger" and separating him from his whiskey. Which, in retrospect, meant she hadn't slept well because she'd lectured and cajoled him, insisting he required lots of rest so that he'd be clear-eyed for his interview at The Ground Café.

Yes, she'd relented, because Anna had been right. Their brother needed a job.

Seamus had phoned the coffee shop to schedule an interview, and Clara rang a taxi for him, although her flat was only a short distance from the shop. A threat of rain was in the forecast, and she'd wanted him to look his best. Her car's brakes were still being repaired, and, cell phone in hand, she'd decided to take a chance on the rain and walk. Her quilted jacket sported a hood to keep her dry.

She'd treaded across a handful of puddles left over from a recent rainstorm while her cell phone buzzed three times, the caller ID flashing *Danny Brady*. He wasn't phoning from the coffee shop. He was ringing from his private cell phone number.

When she reached the dance studio, she changed into her leotard and tights and retrieved the three missed calls. Danny's first message sounded professional, confirming that he looked forward to meeting Seamus at the interview.

Expectation and optimism had brightened Seamus's eyes when she'd assured him that he'd probably be hired, and would keep the job as long as he never reported to work ossified, drunk.

The second voice mail from Danny assured her that Seamus had interviewed well and had gotten the job.

"Your brother is very intelligent and witty, exactly like his sisters," Danny said. "I'm starting him off as a dishwasher, though he can easily work his way to a more lucrative position—depending on his interests—whether they be in the office or interacting with customers." Then, in an apparent side note, Danny added, "I trust you enjoyed the dinner I sent last night and didn't throw it out your flat window. I'm hopeful you'll come by the coffee shop after you're finished teaching your ballet class, because I've thought of some new lyrics for our song. I'm tied up with business appointments for a few hours and I'll ring you when I'm finished. Seamus told me about your ballet class, in case you were wondering how I knew. He said you finished around seven o'clock."

She frowned, bristling like an out-of-sorts porcupine. Why was her brother so long-winded and loose-tongued? She valued her privacy, and Danny Brady didn't need to know where she was every minute of the day.

The third message from Danny was brief. "I apologize for the article in the newspaper. There's a photo of us when we walked through the coffee shop, although I had shielded your face. And I've refused to give your name to the reporter who wrote the article."

There was a newspaper article with a picture of her and Danny? Clara groaned aloud.

Assuming Danny wouldn't answer his phone because of his meetings, she punched in his number and left a brief message. "Hi. It's Clara. Pink roses were sitting on my doorstep last night when I returned home. Thank you, they're cheery and … extravagant, and dinner was lovely. Oh, and I'm certain your song will be the next top hit and receive loads of radio play. Sorry, tonight isn't good for me."

She was meeting her brother outside The Ground Café so they could walk home together. Danny would be preoccupied and never know that she'd come and gone. She'd learned that trick from her orphanage days, slipping in and out of places quickly and unseen.

* * *

CLARA WIPED the sweat from her hairline, exhilarated and exhausted from teaching her ballet class. The five-year-old girls in matching pink tights and black leotards, the boys in black leotards and tights, had been squirmier than usual. She'd abandoned her lesson plan, instead engaging the children in imaginary play and movement games, twirling about with them on the hardwood floor. Afterward, several parents had detained Clara with endless questions regarding the upcoming dance recital. Her phone had buzzed and she hadn't dared answer the call.

Madame Sophie, the director of the dance studio, had stood at the rear of Clara's class and taken copious notes, presumably assessing Clara's teaching. Madame Sophie held absolute control, partly because of her longevity, and partly because her late grandfather had founded the studio three decades earlier.

Once the parents and students had departed, Clara stepped to the side of the ballet barre and retrieved her voice mail message:

"Your class was done at six forty-five. Where are you? You always pick up your phone and it's only a short walk from the town centre to the coffee shop," Seamus said.

I'm leaving now, she texted quickly. That is, as soon as she'd spoken with Madame Sophie. The woman now stood at the far end of the ballet barre, her platinum-white hair pulled into a tight bun, which only emphasized, rather than enhanced, her scowling features. Her top-heavy body was hidden beneath a hip-length tunic. Her long blue-grey jacket and matching pants disguised her stout midriff.

I got the job, Seamus texted back. *The boss is grand.*

Clara choked on her salty retort. Why did everyone raise Danny Brady to such an exalted position? So he'd deigned to step down from his lofty boardroom to offer Seamus a job as a dishwasher. It was insulting, degrading. Nonetheless, it was a stable job in a depressed town offering little employment.

She managed to text back, *Congrats, Seamus!*

As soon as Clara closed her phone, Madame Sophie trooped over. She adjusted her blazing-blue reading glasses while blasting a barrage of complaints, concluding that "Ms. Donovan's" recital choreography wasn't on par with the studio's standards. Another half hour went by, and Clara had rearranged the choreography six times before Miss Sophie finally nodded her approval.

In the employees' locker room afterward, Clara changed into street clothes. She was ready to leave when Colum O'Brien, a fellow dance teacher, entered. Colum had been a principal dancer for the Dublin Ballet. Nearing fifty, he'd returned to Farthing to care for his troubled nephew, a nineteen-year-old boy who'd launched a graphic design business.

Clara could always count on Colum to come to her defense, and oftentimes she believed that he was the only reason she still held her teaching position.

Now he regarded her with his kind, green-eyed gaze. "My dear girl, have you had a rough day? You look as weak as a kitten."

With a sigh, Clara leaned against her locker. "Nothing I do seems to satisfy Madame Sophie."

"She's tough on you because she sees your talent."

"Either that, or she'll only be satisfied when she drives me out for good. I'm certain she'll keep me on probation forever."

"Two years have passed since you were arrested."

"Yeh, and my one night in jail was wretched." Clara rubbed a hand through her hair. She'd been so frightened, her fear of being locked in a small, airless space. "Do you recall when Madame Sophie told me that she kept me employed part-time as a favor, because 'convicts shouldn't be around small children'?"

"Since that incident, you've taught so many dance classes at no charge that I've lost count," Colum said. "You've more than made up for your mistake and I don't believe that Madame Sophie feels that way about you anymore."

"I want the children to embrace dance and movement, to be comfortable in their bodies." Clara scanned her surroundings, taking in the studio she'd come to feel such affection for. The worn pink ballet shoes and cotton balls strewn on the floor, all those years dancing with bloodied toes and aching muscles, because she'd valued the discipline and art of dance.

"You're an excellent teacher who clearly adores children." Colum threaded a hand through his salt and pepper hair, revealing trim, muscled arms, the result of lifting ballerinas in the air for twenty-five years.

She smiled. "How do you always know the right thing to say?"

"Age and experience oftentimes brings a wee bit of knowledge."

"Thanks for being one of the nicest men I've ever met." Clara buttoned her jacket. "I'm meeting my brother at the new coffee shop in town. He got a job."

Colum bent to retrieve a pair of light pink ballet slippers and fiddled with the elastic drawstrings. "I hope he sticks with it."

"He will."

"You're his sister, so you should know him better than most." Colum set the ballet slippers near the changing cubicle and grabbed his camouflage-colored parka. "I'll walk you out and grab a smoke before my next class."

"You realize that a dance teacher who smokes in front of a dancing school sticks out. Kinda like selling candy outside of a health club."

Colum tossed a contrite smile. "I'm quitting next week." He pulled out a pack of cigarettes as they left the locker room. With a quick farewell, Clara headed in the direction of the coffee shop.

Her wristwatch showed seven thirty, and she followed a short cut through one of the alleyways to make up time. The neighborhood was safe, and the Keegan sisters, who were Clara's former school chums, had lived on the street for years. The night sky was somber and overcast, the streets silent. Wild, overgrown brush haphazardly lined the broken sidewalks, a litter of mismatched, cracked cobblestones.

Clara peered at the Keegans' second-story flat windows. All the rooms were dark. She'd heard that their grandmother had been hospitalized recently, and made a mental note to ring them.

That was why, she later rationalized, she hadn't heard heavy footsteps pounding through a puddle she'd just crossed. She'd been pondering Grandmother Keegan's ill health.

"Howya, Clara. Are ya on your way to meet that fancy guy from Dublin?" Behind her, the man's voice rang frighteningly familiar.

Jack Connor.

She felt the gut-wrenching slice of fear, a chunk carved from her belly, before she whirled around.

Too stunned to move, she stared into his pale eyes. The lurid tattoo of a spider seated on a web ran along Jack's neck, a manifestation of the man himself. His hulking body sported a stained leather coat, the collar frayed. She had bought him the coat three years earlier from a thrift shop, that first Christmas when he'd exuded charm and chivalry.

She blinked, shuddered. She'd been a dense fool. She should've realized all that trumpery was for show. But somewhere deep inside, in a place she didn't want to admit, she'd been secretly pleased that a guy had showered her with gifts and undivided attention.

"You're a cute one, ain't ya?" Jack's furry brows knit in a glower, a predictor of the utterly callous fury sure to follow. "Surprised to see me? Or upset that you're on the front page of the newspaper again?"

"I haven't seen the papers." It was a miracle she spoke so

calmly when her insides were churning like mad. Surely he could hear her shallow breathing.

He stepped closer, smelling of old sweat and cheap leather. "I'll steal you a paper. Then we'll go for a cold pint and laugh at the want ads, just like old times."

She retreated a step. Her terror came with her.

"I don't drink anymore. I don't steal, either." She attempted to scoff and wheezed instead. And the wheeze, she noted distractedly, sounded far away. "Why are you here?"

He kept his hands beneath his coat. "The weather's nicer in Farthing than in County Cork."

"And what about your prison sentence? You're supposed to be behind bars."

"My brother knows the judge. We appealed, and I was released for good behavior." Jack's menacing sneer sent a string of goose bumps along her arms.

Silently, she chided herself. She hadn't kept track of Jack's prison sentence. Instead, she'd trusted a judge and legal system to keep him locked away.

"The court ordered me to rehab," Jack said.

"Did you go?" she asked.

They were a scant three feet apart. Her gaze flew to the main road, and she counted off the number of seconds it would take to reach the intersection.

"I don't need more rehab and I don't take orders from no judge. You and me, we make our own rules, remember?" Jack's chilling monotone pinned her to the sidewalk. "Now I'm homeless, Clara. You were an orphan and you know what it's like. Will you take me in? I still love ya."

"Leave me alone. Our relationship was over a long time ago."

Why had she once confided to him that she had been a waif, wandering the streets of Italy, then stealing after she was placed in a neglectful orphanage? And why had he conveniently forgotten that she'd subsequently been raised by a loving family?

She lifted her chin. If he saw her fear, he'd use it against her. "You're a grown man, and I haven't been homeless for a long time."

"We're alike, you and me." He slurred each word. "Our past is who we are."

Time stopped. She scanned the overcast sky and gathering clouds. Somewhere in the distance, thunder rumbled. She assessed the alleyway, the clumps of open dirt behind random shrubs. The intersection was closer, a few yards in the opposite direction. She could outrun him.

Before she could take a step, his fingers clamped down roughly on her arm. "You can try, but I'm faster."

She flung off his hand. "Stay away or I'll call the Gardaí.

"I CAN HANDLE THEM, as long as your yoke of a brother doesn't come near me. He's touched in the head, you know."

"I'm leaving."

"Without this?" He reached into his coat and brandished her purse. "Didn't even know I'd lifted it, did ya?"

Her purse had been hanging from her shoulder, and she hadn't even realized he'd taken it. He'd always been able to whittle her down with threats, quick actions she didn't expect, so that she felt like a complete idiot.

Despite her fluttering nerves, she managed to speak dismissingly. "You're a disgrace."

"I've been called worse." There went his high-pitched laugh before he narrowed his glassy stare. "You were good at stealing, remember?"

Remember this. Remember that. She'd pushed it all away to a locked compartment in her mind, and now he was forcing every horrific occurrence to the surface.

She stiffened her spine. No. She'd promised herself that she'd never be controlled by a man again.

"I'm not proud of what I did," she said.

Jack sighed dramatically. "I'm locked away for a couple donkey's years and now you've grown soft. Guess I can't fault ya because you're surrounded by such good friends." He inflated his words by scanning the dark flat windows. "Although the Keegans moved out a while ago, so maybe you need new friends."

Her cell phone rang incessantly from inside her purse.

She stretched out her hand. She was shaking. "Give me my purse."

"Is that your new fella ringing, that Brady millionaire?" Tauntingly, Jack swung her purse in front of her. "He'd better not fancy my fine oul doll or he'll be digging himself an early grave."

"It's Seamus," she said.

And Danny was most likely a billionaire, not a millionaire.

"I saw you on TV," Jack went on as if she hadn't spoken. "They're making that Brady fella out to be a Holy Joe for saving your crazy brother. Seamus was about to jump off that bridge."

"Go back to Cork." This was the brave new Clara, fortified by a strong will, protected by a restraining order. "You'll be thrown in jail if you stay in Farthing."

"I'll be here a while. There're some scores needing settling."

A garda drove past the main roadway and idled at the traffic light.

Jack's eyes widened. He wavered. Clara grabbed her chance and screamed as she dashed for the garda. "Please help! This man is—"

With one vicious jerk, Jack ripped the sleeve of her jacket and hauled her into the bushes.

The traffic light changed, the garda kept going, the distance between them widening.

But there was another car, and she heard the engine before Jack did. A metallic-silver Mercedes sped directly down the alleyway. And the garda had reversed to the other end of the alleyway. Clara and Jack were blocked from both sides.

The Mercedes bulleted in their direction, its headlights blinding them.

"My darling Clara," Jack growled, "you'll be lookin' at heaven's gates for this."

"Stay away from me!" she shouted.

A deluge of rain soaked through her jacket as the skies parted.

Jack raised his fist, and she winced, an old reflexive reaction, preparing for his hard blow. Instead, he shoved her. As she fell to the ground, he threw her purse into the bushes and sprang into the shadows.

CHAPTER 8

*D*anny screeched his Mercedes to a stop. He vaulted from the car, his breath freezing in his chest. In the pouring rain, Clara was lying on the ground face-down.

He knelt beside her. "Clara!" He lifted her, shook her shoulders. "Clara, are you all right?"

She wiped at her face, smearing mud across her temples. "I ... I'm grand."

She didn't look grand. She looked dazed, her complexion ashen.

With an anxiety that made his hands shake, he searched her face for signs of bleeding and ran his hands along her torn jacket sleeve. Big droplets of rain ran down her face, her hair. There were no cuts and no bones seemed broken. He jerked off his wool coat and tucked it around her, wiped the mud from her temples with his shirtsleeve. "Does anything hurt?"

"I ... I don't think so." Sobbing, she mumbled and ferreted through the bushes. "Where's my purse? I can't find my purse."

"I'll get your purse." He retrieved it and guided her to her feet.

"I'm cold," she whispered.

"Aye, it's damp." His legs were unsteady as he brought her to his car. Pure, blind fury had surged through him when he saw the hulking man shove her.

Danny eased her onto the passenger seat and bit back his fury beneath a reassuring smile. He set her purse on the floor mat. "You'll be warmer in a wee bit when you get out of this night air."

She wrapped her arms around herself and rocked. Water dripped from her clothes. "Thank you for—for finding my purse."

He leaned into the car. "It's more important that I found you." He closed the door, catching his breath, gripping the handle until his knuckles whitened.

The garda was walking from his car at the end of the alleyway toward him. "It's necessary that we file a report, sir," he called out.

Disregarding the rain, Danny stalked to him. "This woman was attacked and all you're concerned about is filing a report? Find the man who attacked her!"

"We need names." A thick fringe of bangs hung beneath the garda's peaked hat. He peered at the Mercedes. "I recognize the woman. Clara Donovan, correct?"

"How would you know her?"

"She's been at the prison before."

Most likely Clara had visited her brother when Seamus had been in prison.

"What's your name?" Danny asked.

"Doherty. Jimmy Doherty, sir."

In a sharp, authoritative tone, Danny said, "The only report you'll be filing is when that man is thrown in prison, Garda Doherty!"

"Aye, sir." The garda got back into his car and gunned down the roadway.

Danny's fury was interrupted by a heavier rain bucketing down as he strode to his car. He pushed his wet hair from his forehead, settled into the driver's seat and set the heat blasting. The windshield fogged, and he switched on the defroster.

He focused on Clara. "Better?"

"A little." She was trembling, shaking her head as if in denial. He wanted to hold her tightly in his arms, although she looked so fragile, he feared she might break if he squeezed too hard.

Instead, he gazed at her wet, tear-stained face and took her hands in his. "We'll sit in my car a while."

"All right." Her soaked hair curled in ringlets around her heart-shaped face. Her dark eyes were overly bright. She licked her lips. "How did you find me?"

"My appointment finished early, and I noticed your brother waiting outside the coffee shop. He kept checking the time and mentioned you were meeting him and that you were late. The weather looked like rain, so I volunteered to pick you up at the studio. One of the instructors, Colum, I believe, was standing outside on the stoop, smoking, and said you'd left. We chatted a bit. He seemed like a nice chap."

"Yeh, I consider him a trusted friend. We've worked together at the dance studio for a while, and he always looks out for me."

"He pointed toward this alleyway," Danny continued.

She leaned against the seat. "And you alerted a garda."

"Aye, a precaution. You didn't answer your phone, and Seamus and I were concerned." Danny shook his head. That was an understatement. His pulse was still racing.

She stared straight ahead at the windshield wipers swishing away the rain.

Danny took a deep breath. "Clara, who was that man?"

She pulled from his hold and rubbed her hands along her muddy leggings. "Jack Connor, my ex-boyfriend."

Danny nodded slowly. "I assumed so."

"How would you know about Jack?"

"After Seamus finished his interview, we chatted. He told me more about you, including your relationship with Jack."

"My brother has a tongue that would clip a hedge. Sometimes, he never stops talking."

"Fortunately, I'm a good listener." Especially, Danny was coming to realize, if the subject involved Clara.

She chewed her lower lip. "I could've headed Jack off if he hadn't caught me unawares and lifted my purse."

"Aye. You're fearless." Danny offered a supportive smile. "However, for my peace of mind, will you promise to ring me if you see him again? He's a dangerous, unpredictable man. You have my number and can put me on speed dial."

A pair of mutinous eyes stared back at him and she didn't reciprocate his smile.

"Give me your word."

No answer.

"Give me your word," he demanded sharply.

Time ticked in charged silence before she finally swung her gaze to the windshield wipers and muttered, "Yeh."

She was a stubborn, foolish woman if she believed she could outwit a man as ruthless as Jack Connor. From what Seamus had revealed, Jack was prone to fits of unpredictable rage.

Danny stared at Clara's delicate profile, the dogged set of her chin. She was a spirited, splendid woman who needed him, whether she admitted that fact or not. Despite her rebellious gaze, she was as tense as when she'd raced up the rusty stairs to the top of Farthing Bridge.

She tucked her hands beneath the warmth of his wool

coat. "So you offered my brother a job today and then the subject swung around to me."

"Something like that." Danny stroked the damp hair from her forehead. "I'm grateful to Seamus, because I couldn't have helped you if I didn't know about your situation with Jack. Now that I do, I can assure you that you should never be afraid again. I'll protect you."

She waved a dismissive hand, although her soulful brown eyes seemed to seek reassurance. "And how will you manage to protect me?"

His wealth. His resources. He'd garnered respect and influential friends because of his prosperous business. Aye, some enemies in the guise of disgruntled customers too. That was the reason he'd hired Ian.

Danny paused. He could enlist Ian's help to ensure Clara's safety. He hadn't used Ian as a bodyguard for months. Besides, Danny thought, he was a coffee shop owner, not a head of state. He didn't need a bodyguard.

"I'll protect you the way I manage everything in my life," he answered. "Every detail is arranged so that nothing will go wrong."

A fresh stream of tears slid down her cheeks. "Jack will make certain he can't be found, and no one will talk. I know how living in the streets works."

So do I, Danny wanted to say. And people living in the streets answered questions if the right amount of money was offered.

He placed his arm around her and she bent her head to his chest, soaking his shirt with her sobs. He let her cry, all the while whispering soothing assurances, hugging her closer. When her tears subsided, she wiped at her eyes. "The judge assured me Jack would be locked in prison and never bother me again."

Danny lifted her chin. Solemnly, he said, "I assure you

that Jack Connor will be found, then locked away for a very, very long time."

* * *

CLARA DREW A LONG, inward sigh. Danny was offering assurances because he felt sorry for her. She'd known well-meaning people when she'd lived in the Italian orphanage. In the end, she'd fended for herself.

No doubt Danny pitied her because she'd cried so hard. Her chin trembled. She was pathetic.

She didn't know what was worse—false assurances or pity. However, Danny's conviction that he'd find Jack Connor and send him back to prison was the only promise she had, and whether it was true or not, she clung to it as a lifeline.

Despite Danny's calm assertions, his expression had changed from frantic worry when he'd first spotted her, to composed decisiveness. Beneath his quiet exterior, she could sense his anger was simmering, albeit carefully restrained.

He adjusted the heater on the dashboard. "Comfortable?"

"Yeh, I'm about dried off."

"Care to tell me exactly what happened tonight?" he asked quietly.

She watched him from beneath her lashes and briefly nodded when it became apparent he was waiting for a response.

"Did Jack say anything to you?" he pressed.

She waffled, played with the strap of her purse. "What do you mean?"

"Did he threaten you?" Danny grabbed her hands and waited until she met his gaze. "Did he say where he was going, or anything that might assist me and the garda in finding him?"

"I can't recall specific details. It all happened so fast."

Except when Jack had said, *You'll be lookin' at heaven's gates for this.*

She feared Danny's reaction if she told him. He'd most likely find an excuse to drop her off immediately at her flat and then attempt to find Jack himself.

No, she told herself firmly. She had placed Danny in too much danger already. He owned coffee shops for a living. He wasn't a private investigator. He'd grown up in Dublin and visited art museums with his elderly aunt on weekends.

Resolutely, she squared her shoulders.

Danny leveled her with a bold stare. "Should I believe you?"

"Of course," she lied.

"You'd have no reason to protect Jack, would you?"

She bridled. "When we were together, he beat me so often that I lost count and he ruined my life for a long spell. Of course I wouldn't protect him."

But she *did* want to protect Danny.

She tucked her purse neatly on the floor. She should tell Danny everything. She should. She would. Just not tonight. Her emotions were poised to career out of control at the slightest prompting.

"Anything else?" he asked.

"I told you. No." She responded louder than she'd intended, torn between her decision to protect him and the pressing, unexplainable fear that her decision, either way, would result in disaster.

"You're a magnificent, although imprudent woman if you think I believe for one second that you're telling me every-thing. Don't forget, I'm available anywhere, anytime, when-ever you want to talk."

She gazed at his face, so recklessly good-looking, nodded

briefly, and resumed her absorption of the rhythmic swishing of the windshield wipers.

With a sigh, Danny pulled his cell phone from his shirt pocket. "Your brother is probably pacing every inch of the coffee shop. He's waiting there in case you arrived there before I found you. Do you want me to call him?"

"Seamus," she groaned. "How could I have forgotten about my dear brother?" Mentally chastising herself, she elected to spend extra time with him over the next few days to make up for her absence.

Danny punched in Seamus's number, waited for the phone to ring through, then spoke quickly. "Aye, lad, Clara's with me and she's safe. Get yourself into the shop, enjoy some dinner, and we'll be there in a wee bit. We'll explain more when we arrive. Aye. Aye." Danny clicked off. "Be prepared to answer a thousand questions. Should we call your sister next?"

Clara hesitated, trying to recall Anna's whereabouts. Her hesitation was punctuated by a wheeze, which Danny politely ignored.

"Anna is visiting a university in Wicklow and she's seeing Ian afterward. I'll phone her tomorrow morning." Clara attempted a half smile. "Thank you for everything, Danny."

"Please, don't thank me. I'm excelling in the course, Rescuing Lovely Farthing Damsels in Distress 101 ever since I met you. Besides, I had an ulterior motive tonight. We can all dine together at the coffee shop. The owner said it's all right."

His joking did exactly what he'd most likely intended and roused her into a full-fledged smile. "I can't eat. My stomach's in a knot, and the desserts at your shop are too heavy."

His brows rose. "They are?"

"Yeh, beginning with the Guinness coffee cake my sister devoured yesterday."

He chuckled. "Will you join me for a cuppa tea then?" The kindness in his tone, his earnest blue-eyed gaze, made her feel ungrateful and impolite for refusing his dinner offer.

She nodded. "A cuppa tea sounds brilliant." The strain of the evening had brought a catch to her voice. "And despite what happened yesterday in your boardroom, I appreciate all you've done for Seamus."

"It's no bother. And I admire you because you've gone way beyond the definition of a devoted sibling."

"You don't know what Seamus has sacrificed for me."

"Care to elaborate or should I speculate?"

She shifted. "Seamus was devastated after his wife, Fiona, died. And although I knew he was depressed, I didn't offer him any support. Instead, I was self-absorbed with my own problems because of Jack."

"Very understandable," Danny said.

Silence settled. He seemed to be waiting for her to say more.

She continued to stare straight ahead. The wipers were relentless, the Irish rain incessant. "I'd assumed our relationship was over. Then one night, Jack crept through the kitchen window and broke into my flat. I screamed, tried to ring for help … he grabbed the phone from me."

"Is he the reason your windows are bolted?"

"Yeh." She tightened her hands into small fists. "At the time, I hadn't seen Jack around Farthing for weeks and I'd started to feel safe again. If Seamus hadn't arrived when he did …" She squeezed her eyes shut to block the memories.

"Go on."

She stole a peek at Danny's concerned expression. "I can't."

Danny laced his long fingers around hers. "I didn't mean to upset you."

She accepted his hold, admiring the quiet authority

surrounding him, evident in his deep, calm voice and bold, certain strides. He was a man, a real man, unlike any man she'd ever known.

She didn't continue her Jack story, didn't say that Seamus had rushed her to the hospital because she'd suffered a broken rib and numerous bruises from Jack's beating. Or that Seamus had hunted down Jack once she was settled in the hospital. Her brother had never revealed the details. Jack had simply disappeared from her life and been locked in a Cork prison soon afterward.

And now Jack had returned. It couldn't be possible. Not again, when she'd fought so hard to be rid of him. She shook her head in denial, pulled from Danny's grip, and clenched her clammy palms together.

"Your brother told me the same story," Danny said quietly.

"Then why did you ask me?"

"I'm a good listener," he reminded.

"And Seamus could talk the teeth out of a saw." She closed her eyes to stop her weeping. What had started as a conversation about her ex was quickly becoming a crying free-for-all.

Danny reached across the seat. "I carry paper napkins in the glove compartment, which I reserve for crying women I've rescued," he said with amusement.

She gave a self-conscious laugh. "You've known that many?"

The amusement vanished from his face.

She grimaced. Of course he'd known many women, all of them much prettier and more sophisticated than she.

"Actually, you're the first crying woman I've ever cared about." He feigned levity, although his expression had sobered. The sincerity in his voice, the smiling gentleness that returned to his gaze, chipped a piece of the wall away from her fiercely guarded heart.

He pulled out a paper napkin. Stamped on it were the words "The Ground Café" and the recognizable pot-of-gold logo.

She dabbed at her eyes and grinned, before tucking the napkin in her purse. "Always the businessman, yeh?"

He grinned. "I might meet a potential coffee customer passing through the alleyway."

She managed a trembling smile. "You should warn them about coffee being bitter."

Lightly, he touched her cheek. "Not my coffee." His hand traveled to her nape, a light, soothing caress. She should push his hand away, she told herself. Her breath felt thick and heavy in her throat, and she didn't move.

"Somehow, someway, I'll convince you to love my coffee." His arms shifted protectively around her. "You're an extraordinary woman, Clara."

He bent his head. His lips hovered only inches from hers. He smelled of coffee and cream, the scent reassuring. A breath away. She saw the banked fire of desire in his gaze, and deep inside her a response rose, a longing for his strength, the safety of his powerful, gentle embrace.

She leaned into him, didn't resist when he kissed her, savoring his hard mouth pressing against hers.

He lifted his lips a fraction. "I will protect you, luv." Affection burned in his eyes, deepening them to a rich indigo, the blue specks reminding her of an ocean, deep with complications.

"I'm glad I came to Farthing," he said. "I wasn't supposed to be here. At the last second, one of my managers called in sick, so I drove from Dublin to oversee the grand opening. If I hadn't, I never would've met you."

His hair gleamed the color of a rich mahogany, damp

with rain. He'd pushed a strand off his forehead, which only accentuated his sharp Irish features. His well-built arms swelled beneath the sleeves of his work shirt.

Her heart gave a lurch. He was so handsome, so fearless, and he gazed at her with such affection.

"I'm glad you came too," she said softly.

The rain had softened to a light pattering against the windshield. She snuggled closer to him, her cheek touching his chest, and she accepted his comforting embrace.

Practicality intruded. Danny Brady moved in wealthy circles she could hardly fathom. And she'd pledged to safe-guard her heart and never be any man's fool again.

Just for tonight, she'd accept his thoughtfulness, his solid arms keeping her secure. Just for tonight she'd focus on the safety he offered, assuring herself that she'd never be impru-dent enough to fall for him. She could never love anyone. She'd thought she loved Jack and he'd left her bruised, vulnerable, and ashamed.

Danny tipped up her chin. "Nor would I have had the pleasure of saving you and your family at every juncture if I'd stayed in Dublin and lived my quiet, uneventful life."

She smiled slightly. "Somehow, I'm sure that your life is the opposite of uneventful. And I could've handled the dire situations myself."

His eyebrows came together in a mild scowl, and she chided herself. She shouldn't repay his kindness with churlish responses. If Danny hadn't rescued her in the alley-way, she could've ended in the hospital. Or worse.

The image of a hulking Jack, the unnerving spider tattoo on his neck, prompted her to shiver.

Danny brushed a kiss on her temples. "You'll catch a chill if you sit in your damp clothes much longer. Let's get back to the coffee shop." With noticeable reluctance, he dropped his arm. "I wrote new song lyrics. Would you be interested in hearing them?"

"You're trying to take my mind off what happened tonight with a song?"

"Aye."

"Sing away."

A combination of affection and incredulity tapped through her. Something as average as writing a song and wanting her to hear it actually gave joy to a successful man like Danny Brady.

As he merged the car into the traffic on the main street, he sang to the tune of "Irish Rover": "My lovely Irish damsel would rather eat an English toffee, if she drinks my Irish lattes, she will relent."

She laughed out loud. "You changed the words."

"Aye, and the changing of the words was intentional." He clicked his blinker and passed a slow-moving car. "Are you working this weekend?"

Now where had that come from?

"I teach a dance class on Saturday morning. Why?"

"On Sunday I'm headed to my main office in Dublin to update several computer files. My lawyer's been researching the specific laws and regulations regarding international franchising, because each country is different. The paperwork is all signed, but I need to reword a couple paragraphs of the agreement and it shouldn't take long." He began singing again. "So will you accompany me on our first date? I'm hoping you'll *consent*."

"I've never been asked out on a date to the lyrics of a song before."

"Should I switch my Irish charm on high to persuade you?"

He'd done enough of that for one night, she thought, feeling a funny squeeze in her stomach at his inviting smile.

His damp work shirt hugged his strapping shoulders, and the spell of his heavy-lidded gaze kept her eyes riveted to his. He seemed to grow handsomer by the hour.

"I'd like to go, although I can't," she said. "Anna is counting on our weekly picture show outing, and I'm treating."

"She can go with Seamus. I'll treat them both, and that way Seamus won't be alone. Any other excuses?"

"Housework?"

"Your flat is immaculate." A roguish gleam came to his eyes, and he sang in his baritone voice. "I've invited her to Dublin and hope she will *consent*." He emphasized the last word with an infuriating grin.

She gave in. "All right, yeh, I'll go with you to Dublin. Teresa's Irish Dancers is a prestigious dance academy in the city centre. Perhaps they're hiring instructors. I've always dreamed of owning my own dancing school and naming the school after myself. Does that sound vain?"

"On the contrary, I'm very impressed. If anyone can succeed, you can."

"Unfortunately, funding is required to set up and design a studio." She sighed. "Followed by advertising costs, insurances, permits, leases. Perhaps once Seamus's gambling debt is repaid, I can apply for start-up financing."

"I can lend you the money."

She shook her head. "Thanks. However, if I ever open my own business, I'll do it on my own." She gazed at him for a moment to make sure he understood, and then glanced at her watch. "Doesn't your gig begin at ten o'clock?"

"There'll be no guitar playing at The Ground Café this evening." He leaned over and brushed a kiss on her hair. "The guitarist had a much more important engagement tonight rescuing a damsel in distress."

* * *

Later on at her flat, after Seamus was settled on her couch, Clara went to her bedroom and dressed for bed. She tried to sleep. Instead, she stayed awake for hours listening to the rain drumming against her bedroom window. Despite her best efforts, the frightening image of her ex haunted her. Jack was supposed to be behind bars. He wasn't. And because he wasn't, her life had veered madly off course.

The hours passed and her thoughts swirled. Why was Jack in Farthing?

There're some scores needing settling.

That same gut-wrenching slice of fear she'd felt earlier fairly hissed through the air.

She sat upright and slapped a hand on her forehead. Revenge. Of course. Jack wanted revenge, the man who had once-upon-a-time professed undying love. Now she knew better. He'd been professing a controlling, selfish love. Looking back, she realized that his declarations were an elaborate scheme to exert a tight hold over her.

Clara furiously plumped her pillow before abandoning sleep altogether. This situation with Jack was all her fault. How could she have been so thoroughly blind and gullible when the signs of his brutal and controlling nature were evident early on? She longed to retrogress and give that Clara from two years ago a hard shake. Why hadn't she seen what was so evident to everyone else?

The moon was high overhead when Clara came to an irrevocable decision. She'd created her own twisted, difficult mess, despite her family's warnings, and she'd be the one to rid herself of Jack for good. She'd ask about his whereabouts on the streets until someone led her to him. She knew his old hangouts. She'd start there.

And then, once she found him ... then, what?

She took in a long breath, blew it out slowly. And then she'd order him to leave town. Surely he'd listen to reason when she reminded him about the restraining order. Violating that alone could send him back to prison for a long time.

Danny, on the other hand, relied on the Gardaí.

Although she appreciated his offer to help, he lived in a different, high-class Dublin world, far removed from the everyday life of common Irish folk. He didn't understand the cold, calculated life of the streets. And if he'd once been there, he'd banished that existence a long time ago.

She swung her feet to the floor and padded to the window. The rain had stopped. She drew aside her lace curtains and peered at the empty, quiet streets.

Except the streets weren't empty nor quiet because a hulking man, illuminated by a full moon, stood by the stone wall across from her flat.

Her breath hitched. The space in her bedroom filled her ears with a dull roar.

The figure moved, and she blinked for a second, disbelieving.

She rubbed her eyes and drew the lace curtains together. Her blood thrummed in her ears. She flew to her bedroom door and flung it open, fully intending to shout for Seamus.

His thunderous snores resounded from the living room couch, stopping her short.

She withdrew to her bedroom. Without making a sound, she closed the door. She wouldn't wake him. Her dear brother had endured too many hardships already.

She went to the window and slowly drew back the curtains again, scanning the street for signs of movement. The sidewalk was bathed in the light of a clear moon. There was no man, not even his shadow.

She ran her hands through her hair and shook the tension

from her neck. Clearly, she was becoming a raving lunatic. She was supposed to be moving forward in her life.

She sat on the edge of her bed and regarded her pale, thin face in her full-length mirror. Should she ring Danny and let him know?

And let him know what, exactly? That she'd imagined the hulking shadow of a man lurking in the dark streets near the stone wall across from her flat?

Adamantly, she shook her head. No, absolutely not.

You promised, a nagging voice reminded. Danny was there for you tonight when you needed him.

I didn't see anyone for certain, she sternly prompted herself. Why get Danny all nettled up for nothing? Her mother had lectured her once on the wisdom of silence, quoting a traditional Irish proverb: Melodious is the closed mouth.

There was no disputing the fact that Danny Brady had extended himself for her and her family. He'd established a flourishing business and managed a stunning number of coffee shops and staff. Nevertheless, without a blink of hesitation, for the past three days, he put her catastrophes above his endless responsibilities.

More important, he was caring. And intelligent. He'd said little about his family, off-handedly mentioning a brother and sister who lived in Dublin, as well as his parents and young sister, unexpectedly deceased. He'd kept his features carefully neutral while he'd spoken of them.

And then there was Danny, the musician. He'd framed clever, funny lyrics to his song, all geared to asking her out on a date to Dublin while diverting her attention from the upsetting events of the evening. Considering his jam-packed schedule, he hardly had enough time to devote to his coffee shops, let alone his music. However, *despite* his busyness, he'd treated her as if she were the most important person in the world.

She climbed into bed, mulled her thoughts around. There was definitely more to the man than she'd realized when she'd first met him at the bottom of Farthing Bridge.

So she'd go with him to Dublin. Someday, she'd look back on her date with one of the most eligible, famous bachelors in all Ireland and shake her head in disbelief. He wouldn't be in Farthing long, so she might as well enjoy his consideration and attention.

She stared stiffly at the ceiling as unexpected tears welled. Why did the thought of him leaving create such an unexpected emptiness in her heart?

She yanked her night shirt to her ankles and brushed away her tears. She could scarcely understand herself anymore, let alone a successful, fetching Irishman with sharp cheekbones set off by eyes the color of a cloudless spring day.

She reminded herself that he was hardly a saint. He'd begun their relationship by choosing to keep his identity a secret from her. Sure, she'd been furious when the truth had been revealed. However, he was also the same man who made her laugh out loud at his teasing banter. And she hadn't laughed, truly laughed, in a long time. And it felt so good.

Will you accompany me? I'm hoping you'll consent. His eyes had sparked with devilish gleam as he sang that, before lingering on her lips.

There was no use in waffling. He wanted to be with her and, in truth, she enjoyed spending time with him. He'd chosen his life's course as she'd chosen hers. So what if they were different? In the short time she'd known him, she'd come to believe in his honesty and integrity.

I will protect you, luv.

His lips had moved tenderly on hers.

Aye, he desired her, though if the tabloids were accurate, he desired many women. And she'd be the biggest fool this side of Sunday if she believed he cared. She was simply a diversion while he established his thriving coffee business in her economically depressed town. Still, no one could fault his generosity, earnest spirit, or easy smile.

She moved her musings ahead to Sunday. Perhaps he'd end their day together in Dublin with another kiss. Perhaps he'd write a love song for her.

She sank against the pillows and smiled. There was absolutely no substitute for a road trip to Dublin with a heartbreakingly handsome musician.

CHAPTER 9

*A*ll week, artfully-arranged bouquets of light-pink roses had been waiting at the doorstep of Clara's flat when she came home from work. One dozen roses. Every evening. She'd asked Danny why he'd chosen the lighter shade, and he'd responded that a light pink rose meant admiration.

"Do you like them?" he'd asked.

"I love them. The fragrance is exquisite." She didn't want to hurt his feelings, nor sound unappreciative by adding that one bouquet of a dozen roses would have been more than enough. Seven dozen was a bit extreme.

Her flat was beginning to smell like a florist shop, until Anna volunteered to help Clara disperse the flowers to a hospital in town.

The cards attached to the bouquets were always written in Danny's confident scroll:

"So glad I'm in Farthing, luv," one had read. "Ring me as soon as you read this so I know you've arrived home safely from work. Your favorite barista, DB."

Their week together had been delightful, save for one

ongoing disagreement. Danny had mentioned, much too casually at dinner that first evening, after he'd rescued her from Jack, that Ian would be escorting her to and from work each day. Ian was pleasant and loyal, Danny said, an asset to Danny's company, but he needed more to do and—

She'd checked Danny's suggestion in midsentence and flatly refused his offer. She could handle her affairs perfectly fine by herself, and, she'd added in a blandly polite tone, "A bodyguard isn't necessary for a small-town woman like me. Thanks, anyway."

After several heated disputes, Danny had reluctantly agreed.

Since Danny's shop had opened, her shifts at work had doubled. The factory supplied local restaurants, and The Ground Café was placing large orders. She had gladly accepted the overtime hours, hoping to use the money to help pay off Seamus's gambling debt. Anna had volunteered to stay with Seamus when he wasn't working so he wouldn't be alone.

Adding to her hectic week, Clara had filed another restraining order against Jack, although he'd disappeared. She'd checked some of his old hangouts and no one had seen him. She held on to the guarded hope that perhaps he'd forgotten about her and taken himself back to Cork.

At the end of the workweek, Clara was walking the two short blocks from her flat to the coffee shop. The air was unseasonably warm, the rain a light misty sheet. Her car's brakes still weren't fixed, and the mechanic had explained it was a bigger job than he'd first estimated. Her car would be in the shop at least another week.

She pulled the hood of her quickly mended quilted jacket over her head and checked her wristwatch. Nearly eight o'clock. Seamus would be finished with his shift. Tonight, Danny had invited them to stay on at the coffee shop, enjoying dinner and desserts, while he sang Clara the song he'd recently composed.

"I'd appreciate honest opinions," he had joked, adding, "Keep in mind that musicians are fragile, so don't say anything too honest unless it's complimentary."

Five minutes later, she'd arrived at the shop. As always, the exterior was well-lit, the pot of gold mounted on Kelly-green signage and illuminated by a strong spotlight.

Seamus stood smoking near the entryway. He adjusted a brimmed plaid tweed hat to sit lower on his forehead.

"Nice hat," she acknowledged.

"Thanks. It's from Donegal."

How and when had Seamus been able to travel to Donegal? she wondered. The town was several hours north of Farthing.

"What's the craic?" She pecked a kiss on his cheek, surprised when he recoiled.

"No craic or fun to be had working in a hot kitchen all day." He threw the cigarette down and ground the butt into the grass.

She gestured to the cigarette. "Your boss won't approve. Danny enforces a strict no smoking policy in his coffee shops."

"We're outside," Seamus said. "The nicotine calms my nerves after being around those chirpy employees all day." He fidgeted with the buttons of his jacket. He'd seemed edgy the past few days.

"The employees are cheerful because they're working for a good, fair boss."

"Mr. Brady has favorite employees and I'm not one of them. He works me too hard."

She arched a brow. "I'll tell him to ease off. He knows what you've been through."

"Won't do any good." Seamus lit another cigarette, hoisted

his pants over too-skinny hips and tightened the worn belt around his waist. He'd lost weight. She'd encouraged him to eat more, although from what Danny had mentioned, Seamus enjoyed two good meals at the coffee shop every day that he worked.

"Ian is probably Danny's favorite employee. I know they're good friends," she told him.

"I haven't seen much of Ian. However, Kathleen, the gorgeous barista, is never far from Mr. Brady's elbow. Is she his personal assistant?"

Clara struggled to keep a bland expression in place. "I don't know. I only met her once."

Dazzling, sultry Kathleen and her devastatingly handsome employer. Kathleen knew everything about his business. She had started with him on the ground floor when he'd begun establishing his coffee empire. They shared a past, a history together.

Feeling an unexpected jolt of jealousy, Clara dragged her gaze from her brother's smug smile.

"Sometimes," Seamus went on, "Mr. Brady and Kathleen disappear for hours and go upstairs."

"Danny's boardroom, offices, and computer are all on the third floor."

"He keeps a small flat on the third floor. I thought you ought to know, sis, before you became too involved with him. I don't want to see you made a laughingstock again, like when Jack was seeing other women while he was controlling you like a marionette."

"Danny Brady and I are just friends. He can do whatever he pleases."

"He certainly has the money for it." Seamus flicked the cigarette ashes on the ground. "Any word on Jack Connor?"

"Nothing." She rubbed her arms to stave off the sudden

chill in the air. "Danny nearly ran Jack over with his Mercedes the other night. Jack may have been scared off."

Seamus's fists tightened. "The Donovan family doesn't need no fancy Mercedes to scare off Jack Connor."

"Please, Seamus. Control your temper or you'll make a complete mess of a good thing. Your life is finally changing for the better." She peered at her brother's rough face, the dark circles under his eyes, the tufts of burnt-orange hair poking from his chin. "Are you sleeping okay?"

He rubbed his neck. "Why?"

"The last few nights I heard you pacing the living room. And I thought the front door opened and closed around two in the morning."

His brows pulled together. He drew a last drag, threw his cigarette on the grass and grabbed a fresh one. "You're mistaken, sis. I always—"

"I assumed you'd gone outside for a smoke," she interrupted.

Like Danny, she enforced a strict no-smoking policy in her flat, and Seamus had agreed to smoke outdoors. However, that was the only request Seamus respected. She usually came home after work to a pile of dirty pots and pans in the sink, as well as his soiled wash strewn in the bathroom.

It was okay, she reminded herself. Small stuff. Everyone went through hard times. Seamus required all his strength to recover from his sadness over Fiona's death, plus recover from his addictions.

He dragged more nicotine in his lungs. "I sleep like a newborn babe at your place."

"You'll always have a home with me, because we're family."

Despite his punched-tight body language, a smile lit the

creases on his freckled face. "You're a fine, pretty thing, you know?"

"You're mistaking me for Anna." She linked her fingers together and regarded her navy-blue jacket and khaki slacks. Her plain wardrobe lacked color and style, and she couldn't recall the last time she'd purchased anything new for herself. Perhaps, using some of her overtime money, she'd purchase a fashionable outfit for her upcoming date to Dublin. Something light and bright. The weather forecast for the weekend called for sunshine.

Regretfully, she shook her head. Perhaps in Danny's world a woman could shop on a whim, but certainly not in hers. She couldn't afford a new outfit of any sorts. Seamus still owed the bookies over five hundred euros, a near fortune on their combined salaries.

He had become unnaturally quiet and covered a yawn. "Mind if I head to your flat? The boss spent the last half hour looking out the shop window waiting for ya, and he saw enough of me for one day."

She hesitated. "We agreed someone will stay with you at all times."

Seamus shifted from one leg to the other. "Aww, Clara, trust your big brother. What will I be tempted by? One of your lemon scones? There's no liquor in your flat."

Several customers exited the coffee shop talking and laughing, but then sneaking uneasy glances at Clara and Seamus. Danny followed the last customer through the entry, and stood on the threshold to his shop, his arms crossed.

He regarded Seamus and Clara before he spoke. "Am I interrupting something?"

"My younger sister is being overprotective, telling a grown man he can't be left alone for a couple hours. I can't talk to her without getting lock-hard, unsolicited advice. She's making me feel like a child." Seamus threw his cigarette on the grass. "That's not the way to help a man, is it? She's stealing away my self-confidence."

Danny frowned at the smoldering cigarette. "Did you tell your sister you received your first paycheck today, Seamus?"

"I was just getting around to that." Seamus did a change about. "Sis, I made—"

"Congratulations, Seamus! Your first paycheck in over a year," Clara broke in.

Despite his unmistakably unwelcome body language, she hugged him.

Seamus stood stiffly and stuffed his hands into his jacket pockets. "I figured on walking to the city centre and buying you a gift with some of the money I earned. You've ruined my birthday surprise for ya by all your harping."

She dropped her hands. "Seamus, I'm sorry."

Danny looked at Clara. "You're celebrating a birthday?"

"Not for a while. My adoptive parents decided to celebrate my birthday on Saint Joseph's Day, which is two days after Saint Patrick's Day. The Italian orphanage didn't have a record of my actual birth date. My parents wanted to honor my Italian heritage in an Irish country so they chose Saint Joseph, the Italian saint. Too much information, right?"

"So your birthday is March nineteenth," Danny summarized.

"Yeh."

"Welcome to the thirties. I'm thirty-five."

"How did you know I was going to be thirty?"

"Your brother told me."

"Of course." She laughed and shook her head. Sometimes she believed the only reason Danny had hired Seamus was to glean information about her. Which was ridiculous, of course, because her ordinary life wasn't of interest to a billionaire. And any dirt on her had been spread across the front page of a two-year-old newspaper. She was old Farthing news.

She suppressed the inclination to pick up Seamus's discarded cigarette and throw it in the garbage. Instead, she stared into Danny's laser-beamed gaze. He was so fine-look-ing, his strong build reminding her more of a leading man in a Hollywood picture than a coffee shop entrepreneur. His gaze was thoughtful, his full mouth turned up into a grin.

Mesmerized, she felt a piece of her heart melt. Perhaps he was more interested in her than she realized.

She released a ragged sigh. Umm, no. Everyone knew that rich people weren't the least bit interested in poor people. Still, the thought that he might be a wee bit taken with her made her pulse unexpectedly quicken.

Seamus widened his stance and focused on Danny. "Clara and I enjoyed a lovely chat last night over a pot of tea. When-ever I'm thinking of going astray, she sets me straight."

"I'm very proud of you, Seamus," Clara said. "Please, go ahead and—" She stopped in midsentence. "Are you going to my flat first, or the city centre?"

Seamus pulled at the collar of his ill-fitting cargo jacket. "I'll walk to the city centre first and browse the shops before they close. I might meet Liam."

Danny's expression became watchful. "Seamus, you're welcome to spend the evening with us and visit the shops in the morning. Ian and Anna are stopping by, and I can drive you and Clara home later."

Seamus threw Danny a look of mock disgust. "Don't take offense, boss. I've been running the dishwasher ten hours today in your hot, steaming kitchen and I'm knackered. Besides, you two couples will want to spend time together without a big brother in the way." He pivoted back to Clara. "So, I'll meet you at your flat later."

There was no mistaking the urgency in Seamus's voice.

He was curt, defensive. Had he always acted like that? No, not always. The shift had been gradual.

"I thought you were walking to the city centre," she said.

"Clara, you're always analyzing every word I say. I meant *after* I shop for your gift."

Danny stepped forward. His gaze was sharp, carving a warning. "Don't talk to your sister in that derogatory tone."

Clara started at the bite of anger emanating from Danny's six-foot frame.

"My brother is only teasing," she said, attempting to diffuse the situation. "He often speaks to me that way."

Seamus seemed to shrink a hair. "Only joking, boss. I'm just a big brother winding my baby sister up. If you had a baby sister, you'd understand."

Danny hesitated. He stiffened. "I did," he said after a long pause. "She's dead."

Clara flinched. "Danny, Seamus didn't know about your sister's death."

She was making excuses, she realized. She was always making excuses for her brother.

As if reading her mind, Danny ran a hand through his hair, then pulled a business card from his wallet and gave it to Seamus. "Ring my office any time."

"Yeh, thanks." Seamus lit another cigarette, swung around, and strode briskly in the direction of the town centre.

Later, when Clara reflected on their conversation, she wondered why Seamus had rushed past her like a man who'd been given a reprieve from the guillotine. And why she hadn't realized that all the shops in town closed at six o'clock.

CHAPTER 10

The atmosphere in the after-hours coffee shop was so different from during the day, Clara mused. Quiet and calm, the customers gone, only a few employees organizing the shelves and polishing display cases. An Irish ballad about a fair maiden who'd lost her true love in Galway played softly in the background.

The scent of chocolate and butter cream, and, yes, the aroma of rich coffee beans caused Clara to halt in the middle of the lobby and sniff approvingly. Sea salt caramel candies were set in covered glass jars behind the counter. The sleek coffee shop boasted large, comfortable couches, Wi-Fi, computers set at various tables, and muted television sets. Half of the lobby was shelved with current books and magazines.

Danny stood at the cash register ringing receipts while she wandered to a display of CDs. She scanned the titles, noting his name on several covers. She picked one featuring an Irish fiddle and bagpipe and skimmed the list of songs.

"Who's Glenna?" she asked.

Danny glanced up, his hand hovering above the cash register pad. "Why?"

"Because the name of this instrumental piece is 'Ode to Glenna.' Was she a former girlfriend?"

"My ex-wife's name was Kyla," was all he offered. When Clara raised her brows, he finished, "My marriage was disastrous and short-lived. Unfortunately, we couldn't come to terms on our initial agreement, which resulted in a heavily publicized and ugly divorce."

So he'd been married. And Glenna was someone else.

"Can I take the CD home? I enjoy traditional Irish music, and I'll pay you, of course."

"Didn't I tell you that everything in my shop is free for you?" he said with a teasing smile.

She grinned. "No, but thanks. Are you singing on the CD?"

"Just one selection."

"I look forward to listening." She perused the song list until Anna rapped loudly on the front glass plate window.

"Anybody home?" Anna shouted above the Galway ballad.

Danny strode to the door and unlocked it. Ian stood at the entry beside Anna, fumbling with a set of keys. Both Anna and Ian removed their motorcycle helmets as rain pelted the windows.

"I couldn't find the keyring to the shop and upstairs office, boss." Ian hurried Anna inside. "Do you have an extra set for the boardroom?"

"I should." Danny shook his head as he walked back to the cash register. "Last month you couldn't find your motorcycle in the shopper's mart parking lot. Took you an hour to find it parked at the end of the plaza. You're becoming more and more forgetful."

"Now I park my motorcycle near the entrance, and haven't lost it since."

"How can you lose a motorcycle?" Anna reached around the counter for a caramel candy and chewed appreciatively. "A keyring maybe, but a candy-blue and canary-yellow motorcycle with shiny metal fenders?"

"Lots of people are absent-minded," Danny said. He looked at Ian. "Perhaps you're working too hard."

Anna stopped chewing. "Then this is the perfect occasion to offer him a holiday, somewhere sunshiny and warm with his girlfriend. I've always wanted to revisit Portugal, my birthplace. I may have birth siblings there."

All gazes turned to Anna. "Thanks for the broad hint. Glad you joined us," Danny said.

"A free meal, coffee, and dessert at the newest hot spot in town? Who could resist? This entire plaza was a kip, a dump, and your transformation is amazing." Anna smiled broadly. "Be warned that you've taken on an expensive venture offering free food to our family. We love to eat."

Clara grinned. "Don't tell him that. He'll worry we'll cut into his profit margin."

"Enjoying time with you and your family is my pleasure." Danny closed the cash register and placed the receipts in a drawer. "That's why I'm working. To keep you all well-fed, employed, and happy." He strode back to Clara and whispered, "And to keep you safe and protected."

Before she could take a breath and remind him that she didn't need protecting, Anna laughed and said, "We're singing with joy ever since you came to town, Danny."

"Don't tell him that, either." Clara rolled her eyes. "He's likely to burst into song at the slightest provocation."

"You have one of the boss's CDs, Clara?" Ian eyeballed the CD she held in her hand.

"Yeh. He's feeling generous and said I could take it home. No charge."

"Did he tell you that all the proceeds from the sales of his CDs are donated to a children's charity in Dublin?"

"No, he didn't." Hurt and annoyed that Danny hadn't mentioned anything about the proceeds going to charity, Clara tucked the CD in her purse and glared at him.

"I'm sorry, Clara." Danny complemented his apology with an easy smile. "Am I forgiven?"

Ian shot Clara a look of wounded dignity on Danny's behalf. "You'll soon learn, Miss Clara, that the boss says little about his good deeds. Nevertheless, he's known throughout the world for his philanthropy."

The absurdity of Clara's annoyance prompted her to shake her head. She shouldn't be infuriated at Danny because he was generous and didn't flaunt his good deeds.

"You're forgiven," she hastened to assure him.

Still smiling, Danny poured two steaming cups of herbal tea from a dispenser behind the counter, secured the lids, and handed one to Clara. "Even *I* think it's too late for coffee."

"Tea is brilliant, thanks."

He took her hand and led her to the door marked *private*, calling to Ian and Anna that he was writing a song he wanted Clara to hear. "Help yourselves to whatever, sandwiches, desserts, beverages, in the kitchen, and we'll join you later."

"Just in case your song takes longer to sing than you anticipated," Anna said with a knowing grin, "are there any slices of your divine Guinness cake left in the kitchen?"

"Aye. And tomorrow there will be an even better offering." Danny exchanged a glance with Clara. "Will you share your prized lemon scone recipe?"

"Do I get a commission?"

"How does a flat fee of ten thousand euros sound?"

"Twenty thousand is fairer," she quipped.

"Agreed." Setting his tea down on the counter, he grabbed

a pad and handed her his gold pen. "Can you write the recipe down for me?"

"Sure. It's easy and I have it memorized." She set her tea beside his and jotted the ingredients and recipe on the pad. "Tell your bakers to knead the dough first," she instructed as she handed the sheet to him. "And drizzle the glaze on the scones when they come out of the oven and are still warm."

He examined the paper and placed it in his pocket. "Thank you." His gaze dipped to her mouth before he led her through the private door. The reward for her recipe was a caress of his strong fingers against her nape and an unexpected, passionate kiss that took her breath away.

* * *

DANNY CLUNG to the feeling of Clara's lips pressed against his as they rode the lift. He'd watched the conflicting reactions flicker across her beautiful face. She'd been obviously surprised by his kiss, feigning indifference at first. He'd deepened the kiss and, with a sigh, she'd wrapped her hands around his neck and kissed him. When the lift doors opened and the kiss came to an end, he drew a shaky breath. Slowly, his hand roved up her back.

"Fast lift," he remarked.

Less than a minute later, they stood facing the door to his boardroom. He rattled the locked door handle and released it.

"Where is that keyring?" he muttered to himself. He glared at the door with one hand on his hip. "All the files are on my computer, including the song I was writing for you."

"How're you going to get in the boardroom?" Clara asked.

"How do you think?" He handed her his cup and lifted the decorative doormat in front of the door.

"My boots aren't muddy, are they?" She raised one foot and then the other, checking the bottom of her boots.

He held up a keyring that had been under the mat and smiled. He inserted a gold key into the lock, swung open the door, and gestured for her to enter as he flicked on the lights.

"A billionaire hides a spare keyring to his boardroom under the doormat?" she asked.

"Soon-to-be billionaire," he corrected with a grin. "Although I plan to become a billionaire once my franchises go global."

"Why go global when you're so successful right here in Ireland?"

"Because I'm a driven man and never satisfied." He grabbed his cup of tea from her. "I can enter new overseas markets, gain additional customers, and double the coffee shop's net worth. Someday I'll tell you more, if you're interested."

"I'm interested." She quirked a delicate eyebrow and said wryly, "No one can fault your ambition, Danny." Her statement was followed by a prominent wheeze.

He shoved the keyring into his pocket and smoothed his fingers over her shoulders. "How are you feeling?"

"Couldn't be better."

"Aye, so it seems."

There could be a remedy to soothe her breathing, although she would probably resist his suggestion that he help her pursue that. Nevertheless, he would try. "My doctors in Dublin are excellent. Would you like me to make an appointment with one of them?" He kept his tone light as they walked into the boardroom, their feet sinking into the thick wool carpeting.

She studied the carpet before meeting his stare. Her huge, dark eyes showed exhaustion. "Absolutely not. My cough will subside now that spring is approaching and the weather will be getting warmer."

Her airy response despite her obvious fatigue was so typical that Danny almost acted unconcerned. "And then autumn will arrive again. And then what?"

She rubbed a brow as if to ward off the question and didn't respond.

He set both cups atop ceramic coasters on the coffee table, pushed a pile of magazines aside and gestured to the espresso-colored leather sofa. "Please sit and rest a bit."

She collapsed against the sofa and sighed. "The money part of the overtime is grand, while all those hours lifting heavy boxes is difficult. Between taking care of Seamus and juggling my jobs, I haven't slept much."

He sat beside her, wanting to take her into his arms. She shouldn't work so hard, struggle as much as she did. A woman like Clara deserved to be sheltered and pampered, spoiled with extravagant gifts and a magnificent home.

"Shouldn't you check your computer files?" she asked.

He opened her tea and handed the cup to her. "The files can wait."

She took a sip. Several beats passed.

"What are you thinking?" he asked, deciding to engage in pleasant conversation to divert her from her tiredness.

"I'm thinking about how much my family's life has changed this past week."

"Hopefully for the better?"

She set her cup precisely in the middle of the coaster and fixed her gaze out the picture window. The view captured nighttime in the little town of Farthing, all smudged by a misty rain. The Farthing streetlights gleamed, creating a shadow play on her smooth cheeks.

"You've offered endless kindnesses—the flowers, meals, employment ..."

He moved closer and draped his arm around her. "And you can repay me by accepting my protection. Please consider my offer to enlist Ian as your bodyguard until Jack Connor is safely behind bars."

She shot him a frown. "Did anyone ever tell you that persistence isn't always a good quality?"

"It's one of the best qualities for running a successful business."

"However, I'm not a business, I'm a person."

Danny had the uncomfortable feeling he'd somehow managed to say the wrong thing, despite the fact that most everyone knew that successful businesses and persistence went hand in hand. Successful personal relationships, on the other hand, required caring and … affection.

He stood and cleared his throat. "I won't be long checking my files."

She plucked an issue of *Entrepreneur* magazine off the stack and began leafing through it. "I assure you I can amuse myself."

He took a seat at his computer and scanned the files, relieved to find the coffee shop's invoices, balance sheets, spreadsheets, and banking information hadn't been tampered with. For some unsettling reason, he'd feared someone had hacked into his files, most likely because of the unnerving mystery of the missing keyring. Satisfied, he shut down his computer and settled onto the leather sofa beside her.

She didn't glance up, apparently deeply engrossed in *Entrepreneur.*

Briefly, he closed his eyes, counting how many days remained before he was scheduled to depart for London. His lovely companion didn't seem remotely interested that he was sitting so close. He propped one foot on the opposite knee and regarded her. As always when she was near, he could think of little else. Her beauty distracted him.

He shook his head. He didn't have room in his life for distractions. He needed to concentrate on one goal, offering franchises worldwide to secure his wealth. Then he would find the peace that he'd been searching for, insulated from the poverty and insecurity he'd known.

He watched Clara in the silence. Soon, he'd be required elsewhere, although he refused to dwell on that thought, the absolute finality of his departure. After spending the week with her, he didn't want to leave her picturesque town, her quirky family. Dining with her every evening, laughing together as they walked the rainy streets, writing lyrics to a song ... These simple activities had caused him to stop and reflect on everything that had been missing in his life. Snippets of the ordinary. He'd forgotten they existed, and the joy those moments brought to his hectic, demanding world.

In the reasonably short amount of time since he'd become successful, he'd known plenty of attractive, ambitious women who had eagerly accepted any invitations he'd casually extended. Yet Clara was hesitant to spend one day in Dublin with him until he'd convinced her with a song. She wasn't a woman who'd wanted to date him for his money or fame. If anything, Clara was furious when she'd learned who he really was.

The object of his thoughts studied the open magazine in her hands and murmured, "Did you know that one of the characteristics for a successful entrepreneur is to be passionate about your work?"

"Aye. And you have a passion for teaching dance," he pointed out.

She straightened. "Once Seamus is better, I'm applying for city funding to open my own dance studio. I want to teach underprivileged preschoolers. These children have nowhere to go after school except an empty house with a disinterested sitter."

He considered her remark. "Sounds good." He emphasized the good, in case she didn't believe how much he believed in her. And he did. He couldn't recall the last time anyone's face had lit up like Clara's when she'd described teaching the young boys and girls.

"My options are limited because Miss Sophie, the director, won't allow me to teach any more classes."

"Why not?"

With a small, grim smile, Clara said, "I was in trouble a while back and she won't let me forget it."

Danny caught Clara's chin and pressed her to look at him. "What kind of trouble?"

"Browse an old copy of the Farthing newspaper." Her expression turned guarded, and she didn't meet his gaze. "Just remember there's more to the story than what's printed on the page."

He waited for her to explain further. Instead, she turned back to her reading.

He picked up his tea, now lukewarm, and gazed out the window. The sleepy Farthing streets radiated in four different directions off Main Street, the backbone of a town with ten thousand people. The six pubs were undoubtedly open and ready for business. Farthing was so different from the bustling city of Dublin, which boasted an international airport, world-famous statues and landmarks, and restaurants too numerous to list.

Once, as a child, he'd loved Dublin. Now that he was an adult, the city brought regrets and remorse, tied to a sadness that wouldn't leave his gut despite the three-story mansion he'd built. His home was ridiculously large. Located in the coastal area, its view of the sea was jaw dropping. He rarely visited the place.

His gaze traveled to Clara, and he studied the fine contours of her features, her natural, flawless complexion devoid of makeup. If he'd met her sooner in his life, would she have been able to teach him tolerance for his parents' shortcomings, the tolerance she'd exhibited so freely and patiently with Seamus? Could Clara have given him a purpose grander than procuring wealth, the pursuit that shaped his entire adult life? Could she have reignited his joy so that he felt free to compose and sing whenever he wished? In the throes of building his business, he'd regrettably put his music aside.

Danny took a deep breath and slowly let the air out of his lungs. Someday, after his international franchises were secured, he'd return to his music making. At present, though, wealth brought well-being and self-respect. He'd met hunger firsthand and preferred luxury.

Despite his ambitions, he didn't know how to quell the "what if" questions racing through his mind. His gaze perused Clara's lovely figure, the silky hair gliding across her shoulders. And her soft lips, the pouty, full outline that encouraged his kisses.

He shifted. "Whenever you're done reading that riveting article, we can chat."

Clara set the magazine on the coffee table. "What do you want to talk about?"

"Tell me about yourself."

"Haven't you learned enough about me through my chatterbox brother?"

Danny sipped his tea. "When it comes to you, my curiosity is insatiable."

She changed positions on the sofa to face him, pulling her knees to her chest. A mischievous grin played on her features. "Well, for one thing, I could've broken into the boardroom for you."

He stopped in midswallow. "What did you say?"

"The deadbolt lock. I know how to break in most anywhere. I learned to pick a lock when I shoplifted in Italy." She wiggled her fingers. "It's easy. You take a credit card, slide it into where the barrel connects with the doorjamb, wiggle the door handle a wee bit, and—"

He gaped, setting his tea on the table before he dropped it. "You stole?"

"Mainly food for me and the other kids in the orphanage, sometimes warm clothes for the toddlers."

"You stole?" Danny repeated again in sheer disbelief. She was certainly a woman full of discrepancies—unafraid, impulsive ... enchanting ... and full of surprises.

"If I hadn't, some of the littler ones in the orphanage wouldn't have survived the winter. They most likely would have died from starvation."

"How old were you when you were adopted?" He touched his throat, somewhat surprised that he hadn't been rendered speechless by her admission.

"Almost six. The older boys and I snuck out of the orphanage a lot. We learned how to dodge the security cameras in the posh shops."

"Risky business for a five year old, wouldn't you say?"

She straightened. Her defensiveness filled the air. Remorse came with it. "The orphanage didn't feed us nearly enough. I had no choice."

Danny shook his head. He visualized Clara, the protector, spine erect, brown eyes flashing, ready to take on the world for her suicidal brother at the top of a precariously high bridge. And Clara, the thin, five-year-old street urchin, sporting short wispy bangs and a helmet of shaggy hair, ready to take on the rough Italian streets so that she could steal food for the orphanage children.

Her devotion to the people she loved was incredible. He

watched her stunning smile and felt a bump in his pulse. She must've been born with that smile on her alluring lips.

And then he felt it again. Another bump, followed by a curious, urgent tug on his heart.

"The older boys taught me lots of criminal tricks," she went on. "Just think of the notorious career I could've had if my parents hadn't adopted me."

Danny's shout of laughter ricocheted off the walls. He drew her near and buried his face in her luxuriously lemony-fragrant hair. "No one except me could have come to Farthing on a business trip and met Italy's greatest crook. Do I dare ask if you were ever caught?"

"Only once, when the matron in charge of the orphanage found out." Clara's demeanor changed. She clutched her arms to her stomach, her expression revealing surprising vulnerability. With a sigh, she rested her head against his shoulder.

"What happened?" he asked softly.

She chewed her bottom lip. "The matron locked me in a closet. It was so cold in there, so dark, like the walls were closing in on me. The matron said she wanted to teach me a lesson."

"Did you learn any lessons?" Danny tempered his voice. Inwardly, he envisioned wrapping his hands around that particular matron's neck and squeezing tightly.

"I learned not to get caught."

Danny smiled. It was just like Clara to grow weary of an establishment that didn't care properly for its own and take matters into her own hands.

"You're certain that stealing was the best solution?"

She looked up at him with a wounded expression. "If I didn't steal, I would've been forced to beg."

"And you're too proud to beg?"

"I felt embarrassed sitting on a corner, rattling a tin cup and asking for handouts. I relied on myself."

He settled an arm around her. "You're not desperate anymore. You're a determined, sometimes stubborn woman who insists on assuming every burden by herself. However, if you are ever in a pinch, you have me."

"I've learned to be independent because I've been let down before. I can assure you that it will never happen again."

"I'll never let you down, luv." His profession came clear and simple. He stared into the depths of her determined, chocolate-brown eyes. She was fascinating and ingenious and resilient. And more of the pieces of how she had been formed were coming together. "Sometimes I wish you were weaker so that I could be stronger for you."

She squared her shoulders and seemed to push out her words. "You don't want my problems added to your all-too-full plate. You'll be leaving soon."

"Not yet."

"Soon enough." He felt her withdrawing, despite the fact that she hadn't moved. "So now that I've told you about my life, can you tell me more about yours?"

"Perhaps."

He knew that if they spent more time together, ultimately he'd tell her all of it—his parents' suicides, his young sister's death, his strained relationship with his siblings. And the guilt. Always the guilt. Although he didn't know why he felt compelled to share his story with her. He'd never told anyone about his past, not even his ex-wife. Only his siblings knew, and they never spoke of it because too many other sentiments from the past would roll to the surface. They'd decided years ago to bury the past alongside the gravestones in Glasnevin Cemetery.

Perhaps he'd tell Clara because she'd already inspired him

much more than she'd realized—by her wry humor, her fortitude, her willingness to carry other people's problems without harboring a shred of resentment.

He tightened his arm around her, tilted her chin, bent his head.

Her eyes twinkled up at him. "You really want to kiss me after my confession?"

"Did you ever botch a job?"

"The older boys in the orphanage said I was so good I could've stolen the sugar out of their punch."

His lips were a breath from hers. "I'm delighted to know a first-class thief in case I'm desperate for coffee beans and my finances run low."

"I'm a reformed crook. I may have lost my touch."

"If I were a betting man, I'd wager some skills are never truly lost." He buried her laughing lips against his, pleased that she'd yielded so sweetly.

An hour later, they'd finished their tea, accompanied by increasingly light banter. As they were leaving the board-room, Clara glanced at her phone. "Seamus texted me. He went to visit Anna and should return to my flat shortly."

The hour was late, the streets murky, when Danny drove Clara to her flat.

"I could've walked home," she protested for the second time.

He'd insisted. He certainly wouldn't allow her to walk home alone in the dark.

He went around his car to open the door for her. "And deprive me of an excuse to escort you to your door and kiss you good night?"

They stood on her front steps, and as she looked into his eyes, he felt his chest grow tight. The lyrics from "Oh Danny Boy" flooded his mind, the song they'd sung together in her flat only a few short days ago. So much had happened since then. He tried to push away the thought that he'd be leaving Farthing soon. He would be forced to travel the world in order to promote his international franchises. He had no other choice, his climb to success outweighing all other options.

Oh Danny Boy.

Were the pipes truly calling him?

He pulled in a shaky breath.

Droplets of rain began to fall, mingling with the fog.

From under the awning over the front entrance, they took in the quaint stone buildings on her cobblestoned street and the craggy hills in the distance. She ran a hand through her damp hair.

"What do you love most about Farthing?" she asked.

He smiled. "The wet weather?"

"It's a fine night for young ducks."

He framed her face in his hands. "What I love most about Farthing … is you."

Her gaze darkened with an affection she didn't attempt to hide. He touched her lips in a soft, warm kiss.

And in the space of a heartbeat, he knew that leaving Farthing was going to be far more difficult than he'd imagined, more difficult than his decision to quit school, or his decision to leave the safe confines of his aunt's home to start his own business.

He buried his face in Clara's hair and closed his eyes.

Her fingers spread across his jaw, urging him to look at her. "When are you leaving?"

She'd read his mind, their thoughts in unity.

"I'll be required to attend business meetings in London by the middle of next week."

"I wish you could've stayed longer. I wish …" Her voice sounded broken, a shattered whisper.

He touched her lips with his fingers, quieting her. "Don't. Don't make it more difficult than it already is."

She actually flinched from his firm tone.

"Your business is more important. I know that, I just thought …" She looked away and raised her chin. "No worries. I won't mention your departure again."

CHAPTER 11

$\mathcal{C}$lara and Danny climbed the hallway stairs and stepped into her empty flat. Clara's gaze darted around the living room. "It's so quiet without Seamus here. I'd expected him to have arrived by now."

"Why did he visit Anna at this hour?"

Clara glanced at her watch. "Why not? He's a grown man. He told me to give him more space and I agreed. I can't be hovering over him every second."

"Do you want me to stay until he returns?"

Her fingers waved an airy dismissal. "I'll be fine."

"Then thank you for a delightful evening." Danny kissed her one more time, another excuse to hold her. "And I promise I won't share a word of your secret with anyone."

She cocked her head. "What secret?" she asked with sham innocence while smiling like an angel.

He grinned all the way to his car. Out of the corner of his eye, he detected a man's silhouette. Danny waited, peering into the darkness. Seeing nothing, he reached for his car keys, but then decided to retrace his steps. The foggy night brought a disorienting inky somberness to the streets. Hadn't there been a streetlight lit on the corner the last time he'd visited her? If so, the light had gone out, leaving only a slant of moonlight sifting through the clouds.

Danny pulled out his cell phone and switched on the flashlight app, searching for footprints near the stone wall. A pickup truck's headlights switched on and unexpectedly swerved, blinding him. He shielded his eyes. The truck rammed into his parked Mercedes, leaving the front fender scratched and damaged.

"Hey! What the—" Immediately spoiling for a knock-down fight, Danny was already pulling off his coat and rolling up his sleeves as he rushed toward the truck.

It quickly sped past. "You're an eejit, a bloody eejit!" the driver yelled. The man in the passenger seat wore a brimmed hat drawn low over his forehead. He sank down in the seat and quickly averted his face.

Danny shook his head in mock disgust at himself and returned to his car. He should've reacted quicker, raced faster. He'd fought his way through the Dublin streets when he'd lived with his aunt and uncle, and was considered a pro when it came to a good, solid fistfight. He hadn't tolerated his family being called drunken meads, not by the rough, secondary-school lads, not by anyone.

He thrust aside the memories.

The rain had stopped. The air felt heavy, the sky was tar-black. He shivered, kneading the tight muscles in his shoulders. He'd been working too hard, while preoccupied by a stunning Italian Irishwoman. He pulled on his coat and checked the damage to his car. Scratches and minor dents, he determined. He'd take the car to the garage when he returned to Dublin.

As he turned the car's ignition switch, he decided he would employ Ian to keep an eye on Clara whenever she commuted to and from work. And he wouldn't tell her.

He didn't want to keep his decision from her, didn't want to unduly frighten her. However, he had no choice, and her protests be damned. Jack Connor was, in Clara's own words, dangerous and unpredictable, and Danny refused to leave her vulnerable and unprotected. This latest incident could've been a coincidence. The men in the truck were plastered, very drunk, out for a good time. They seemed to be of university age.

No. He corrected. They were older. One of the men's hair was platinum blond, probably why he had first assumed the men were younger.

Danny returned to the coffee shop and rode the lift to his small flat. He stopped in midstep before he started down the hall.

He'd never sung his new song for Clara. He'd forgotten. His thoughts had been diverted by something much deeper than his beloved music. And he recognized that his carefully controlled emotions were slowly becoming unhinged by an angelic smile and a reformed thieving orphan.

CHAPTER 12

*S*unday morning had sped by. After Clara had attended church services, Danny's Town Car had arrived at exactly ten o'clock. The chauffeur, wearing a coolly crisp uniform, had opened the back door of the sedan, and she'd bade him a cheery good morning. With a broad smile and a good day, the chauffeur had driven her the short blocks to The Ground Café.

Two jazz clubs at the end of the renovated plaza displayed "Coming Soon" signs, and an ice cream shop announced an early May opening. Danny had single-handedly breathed new growth into a tired town and rundown square.

He stood outside his shop waiting for her. His navy wool pants appeared expertly tailored, contrasting with a cadet-blue button-down shirt that outlined his muscular build. A long camel-colored coat was slung over one arm; he held a leather briefcase in the other hand.

"How are ya?" Danny nodded to the chauffeur.

Ducking into the seat beside her, Danny deposited his coat and briefcase near him. Then he greeted Clara with a broad smile and light kiss, his gaze drifting over her admiringly.

"You are gorgeous." He nuzzled her neck. "I love when you wear your hair away from your face. Your eyes remind me of a dark, rich espresso."

"My eyes remind you of coffee?"

"I love coffee."

The unflinching approval in his tone did amazing things to her pulse. She felt her cheeks heat as he helped her off with her jacket and placed it beside him.

She'd shopped at the thrift store in town, thrilled to snag a new, fitted multi-colored paisley top that she wore over a bright-red tank. Charcoal-grey cotton slacks completed her outfit. She'd secured her hair from her face in a thick, wavy ponytail.

The heady effect of their anticipated afternoon in Dublin combined with Danny's male nearness, the tangy scent of his cologne, prompted her to say, "You're gorgeous, too."

A wide grin lit his face, lending him an endearingly youthful appearance. She couldn't help but smile at his response.

Clara leaned her head against the luxurious headrest. Seamus and Anna were seeing an afternoon matinee, and Ian was stopping by Anna's flat afterward. For the first time in a long while, she'd be able to enjoy a worry-free afternoon. As her entire body lightened, her eyes drifted shut.

When she opened her eyes, afternoon sunlight filtered through the windows of the sedan and trees went by in a blur. A Celtic harp solo strummed delicately on the CD player. She blinked and took a second to consider where she was. Danny's arm was firmly around her. She sighed with contentment, settled deeper into the sedan's comfortable leather seats and snuggled nearer his warm, strong body.

His fingers brushed her cheek. "Clara, we're nearing Dublin. Time to wake up, luv."

She offered a weak grin. "I slept the entire trip?"

"All two hours of it." His chuckle was muffled against her hair. "You fell asleep so quickly, I didn't want to wake you. This week has been exhausting for you." He pulled his arm from around her and sighed. "I have some work I should review."

In the serene haze that comes after sleeping so soundly, she studied him while he leafed through a stack of documents he'd extracted from his briefcase. His spiky dark lashes offset the brilliant crystal-blue of his eyes. His face was all strong angles and chiseled features.

His entire demeanor changed as he reviewed his paperwork. Even his voice, when he said he had some work to review, had taken on a more professional tone. No longer was he the relaxed guitar player who'd sung "Oh Danny Boy" in her Farthing flat. He'd transformed into a man firmly in control, his mouth set, his posture strong. His straight coppery-brown brows drew together as he shuffled papers scribbled with numbers. He caught her staring at him and offered a rueful grin.

She let down the window and the wind whipped her hair, the air smelling of mustard-yellow blossoms and freshness. She breathed in and slowly exhaled.

"You haven't coughed," Danny noted.

"The brilliant weather and bit of sun eases my symptoms."

"Perhaps you should move somewhere exotic and sunny?"

She shook her head. "I love Ireland and would never leave."

As they entered the city, she saw sprouts of glade-green grass lining the cobblestone sidewalks, and people walked at a brisk pace, smiling and talking to one another. Dogs barked eagerly, running after rubber balls and wagging their tails with excitement. Everyone was having a love affair with the vibrant spring day. Clara lifted her face to the sun shimmering through mere wisps of clouds, brilliant streams of light. Dublin was exactly as she'd envisioned, vibrant and energetic.

Near the city centre, they drove past the famous Molly Malone statue on the corner of Grafton and Suffolk Streets.

"Tart with a cart," Danny provided with a laugh.

"Please don't start singing 'Cockles and Mussels,'" Clara warned.

Too late. He'd already begun. Clara couldn't resist joining in.

She admired Trinity College, and even the ashen-grey smoke from dilapidated smokestacks that dappled the sky. Pearls of sunlight sparkled on the River Liffey, and silently, Clara thanked Danny for the opportunity to see Dublin.

As they neared Pearse Street, Danny knocked on the window partition between the front and backseats, and instructed the chauffeur to park in a side parking lot.

"This is my flagship store." Danny pointed to a brick cornerstone building. "All my stores are set up with the offices located on the third floor."

"And a flat for you?"

"Aye." He clicked off the harpist. "Oftentimes, I work late. Otherwise, I drive to my house in Howth."

"You own a home in Howth? I've heard lots of famous people live there, including my favorite Top 40 Irish singer."

Danny placed his paperwork in his briefcase and snapped it shut. "I haven't met my neighbors. I'm so busy traveling, I don't get home often."

As the chauffeur pulled into the parking lot, Clara gaped. The large stone building extended across an entire street corner. Burgundy-striped canvas awnings ran the entire length. An outdoor seating area featured moss-green wrought iron tables and chairs. Vintage-style lightbulbs were strung in private alcoves, and outdoor heaters stood waiting to be used.

Danny assisted her on with her coat, then captured her hand as they exited the sedan and walked to the main entrance. Barring a lone security guard stationed in the lobby who respectfully stood and touched the brim of his cap as they passed, the building was empty. Danny explained that his shops were closed on Sundays in order to give his employees the day off. The scents of strong coffee and sugary caramel lingered in the lobby's air.

"Any decorating suggestions?" Danny asked. "Since this was my first store, it probably requires updating to your trained eye."

"I'm hardly trained, though I love decorating." She crossed to the far end of the lobby and looked around. "I'd strive for a cozy, contemporary feel. Concrete floors are trendy, and salvaged-wood walls would add contrast. Mix the old with the new. Antique velvet furniture could create more inviting seating areas."

"Can I hire you as my interior designer?"

She waited for him to walk over and touched his sleeve. "At present, two jobs are all I can handle. You don't get my life."

"I get more of it than you think, and the offer is open if you ever change your mind."

They spent the next hour touring the coffee shop while he explained that dozens of fresh pink roses, one for each table, would be delivered on Monday morning.

"I sincerely appreciate all my customers." He inspected a row of enormous glass jars filled with chocolate-covered coffee beans that stood behind the counter, ensuring that they hadn't been placed in direct sunlight.

She lifted the lid of one of the jars, filling her nostrils with the rich, tangy aroma, then popped a chocolate-covered coffee bean in her mouth. The taste was surprisingly sweet and bitter, and she enjoyed the different, creamy flavors mixed together. Perhaps, she thought, she might grow to like the taste of coffee after all.

Her fingers stole into the jar for another coffee bean, and she savored the intense bitterness on her tongue. "If you remodel, place the pink roses in galvanized buckets on each table."

"Aye. Good idea." He seemed to want her to keep talking about her ideas, so she did.

As he showed her the enormous kitchen stacked with commercial coffee grinders, flavored syrups, condiments, and numerous coffee supplies, she could hear the pride swell in his voice. He selected two Irish ham and cheese sand-wiches topped with Dijon mustard from the cooler as well as bottles of water, and grinned at her approval.

As they rode the lift to the third floor, she asked him what the benefits of international franchising were.

"Do you want the short or long description?"

"Short."

"Typically, it involves a franchisor, in this case, me, granting an individual or company, the franchisee, the right to run their business using my business model, identified by my trademark. 'The Ground Café' will be used for logos, and our coffees and recipes will be provided. In return, I'll receive an initial upfront fee."

"And my lemon scone recipe?"

"I'll feature the scones daily."

"Have we negotiated what I'll receive in return?"

His chuckle was impenitent. "Aye. My undying devotion and lots of euros."

She fell in with his teasing mood. "Is that all?"

"We can negotiate the details in my office." His eyes gleamed with a sensuality that made her catch her breath.

His hand firmly on her elbow, he piloted her from the lift when they reached the third floor. She paused at a bold-stroked painting. "Francis Bacon hangs here too?"

"Aye. Besides greatly admiring his work, I'm also known for quoting his sayings."

"Should I ask?"

"Francis Bacon said, 'It is impossible to love and be wise.'"

She absorbed the saying delivered in Danny's husky voice, and navigated through her emotions by trying to ignore the heat radiating through her body. "You're a shameless flirt and a true blue dub, Danny Brady."

"I'll take that as a compliment." He led her to a large mahogany-paneled office and hung their coats by the door. At one side of the office sat a trio of potted philodendrons next to an enormous bay window. The window offered an unobstructed view of the city of Dublin. A Tuscan-bronze wastebasket sat neatly in the corner. An acoustic guitar stood on a stand nearby.

"Do you play guitar often?" As she asked, she realized she'd never heard him play.

His face fell a fraction. "Not as often as I'd like."

He gestured to a grey settee flanked by two cobalt-blue pillows. "Will this area be comfortable while I work?"

She scanned the magazines fanned out on the end table alongside the settee. "Is there a copy of *Entrepreneur* in the pile?"

"*Business Weekly.*"

"It'll do nicely." She sank against the pillows.

He pressed a kiss on her cheek, and set the sandwiches and water on the table. Then he straightened, strode to a large desk, and switched on a computer.

"One of my tech geniuses is developing a software

program to connect all my coffee shops to one program, allowing me instant access to financial information wherever I travel." Danny typed in a password and waited. His brows knit into a frown when the computer wouldn't fire up.

An article in *Business Weekly* entitled "How to Start a Small Business with Little Capital" had caught her attention. When she finished reading the article, she glanced at Danny. He was still hunched over his computer and frowning.

"Hopefully, no computer problems?" she asked.

"I've been intending to change my password. Should've done it to begin with instead of spending so much effort trying to figure out what happened." He anchored his attention on her, grinned, then went back to his computer. With a chuckle, he typed in five letters followed by numbers and special characters, swiveled to meet her gaze, and winked.

"Problem solved?"

"Aye, with a brilliant new password." He propped back in his chair with his hands behind his head as his computer files opened.

She didn't hazard a guess. There was no need to. She'd noted the purposeful gleam in his eyes. Somewhere in that jumble of numbers and characters, he'd typed her name as part of his computer password.

Clara.

Now he'd think about her countless times a day, whenever he opened his computer files. She smiled, the smile of a woman who felt truly cared for. Although he was leaving Farthing soon, she was important to him.

She gazed out the window, over asphalt and metal rooftops, and sighed heavily. The thought of never seeing him again sent a quiet sadness through her. They wouldn't be discussing his departure; he'd made that point clear.

She punched up the cobalt pillows and curled up on the

settee. He was bent over his computer, his brows furrowed as he concentrated on a screen teeming with numbers.

The afternoon sunlight flooded through the window, highlighting his hair's deep cinnamon tones. He'd rolled up his shirt sleeves. Crisp, reddish-brown hair glanced through the open collar of his shirt. Besides being devastatingly masculine, Danny Brady epitomized every inch of the wealthy Irish entrepreneur. He'd succeeded because of his drive, persistence, and aptitude for business.

She could easily fall under his persuasive spell, the glamor and enchantment of the rich and famous, although she would never allow that scenario to occur.

He swiveled his chair and slanted her a smile. "We'll eat our sandwiches in a wee bit, all right?"

"Yeh, no hurry." She pulled her phone from her purse and texted Seamus. *What's the craic?*

Home from the picture show, he texted back. *Ian's here at Anna's flat. R U in Dublin?*

Yeh.

Busy with the boss?

We're sitting in his office. Danny wasn't able to log into his computer so he changed his password. Now he's working on franchise agreements.

There was no response from Seamus for a full minute. *How do you know he changed his password?*

The way he looked at me.

Hope he's hiring more dishwashers, though he hates to part with his money.

Danny's an absolute gent. You said he was grand.

What time R U headed back to Farthing? Seamus texted.

A few hours. Stay with Anna and Ian until I return.

I'm a grown man and can take care of myself. See U later.

About to text Seamus a rejoinder, Clara saw Danny was

studying her. His hands were folded at his waist, his manner relaxed.

She placed her phone in her purse. "How's business?"

He logged off. "Brilliant and, thankfully, done." Seating himself beside her, he unwrapped their sandwiches. "I'm sorry we didn't have time for a proper meal today."

She heard the sincere regret in his tone and nodded.

"My business is pressing because of these international franchises and my imminent travel schedule. America will open vast and unlimited opportunities, and I'm a wee bit nervous. Can I admit that?"

"Of course," she said. A man like him was actually nervous. She couldn't help but smile.

"There's a new restaurant in Dublin," he continued, "the Ballyburren Smokehouse, set in a traditional thatched roof cottage. And you wanted to visit Teresa's Irish Dancers, the dance academy. I checked and they're not open on Sunday. Next time for both dinner and the dance academy, all right?"

Clara concentrated on her sandwich, knowing there wouldn't be a next time. Danny was simply making small talk to avoid an issue that neither of them wanted to broach. Soon, he'd be miles away, and he'd offered no promises of continuing their relationship. Their worlds were too far apart.

She swallowed. No matter. She'd visit the dance academy and the Ballyburren restaurant on her own.

"I'd invited my sister, Erin, to my office today because I wanted you to meet her," Danny was saying between sandwich bites. "She's the proud mother of Michael, my six-year-old nephew. However, my sister's out of town because she's visiting her latest boyfriend."

Clara detected a note of sarcasm. "You don't approve?"

Danny swigged some water, polished off his sandwich, and shoved the wrapper aside. "Erin can date whomever she chooses as long as her boyfriend takes care of her and her son properly."

"And does he?"

"I wouldn't know. She's never allowed me to meet him. She said I'm too judgmental."

"I'm certain Erin is a grown woman who can make her own decisions. I can't imagine your sister's life requires your help."

"*You* are trying to run your brother's life."

His remark made her cringe.

She arranged the *Business Weekly* magazine, fanlike, on top of the others. "That's different. Seamus needs me in order to get better."

"Or maybe you want to *think* he needs you. Maybe he needs more than you can offer."

She pushed to her feet. "He's an alcoholic who's vowed to stay away from the drink because of the long cozy chats I've had with him."

"He's suicidal."

She rubbed a hand over her face, as if she could scrub away Seamus's troubles. "He's suicidal because he drinks. If we solve that, then all Seamus's other problems will go away."

"Until he realizes that he actually has a problem and he sincerely wants to fix it, he won't relinquish the drink no matter how many 'cozy chats' you have."

"Thanks for your unasked-for opinion." She picked up the discarded sandwich wrappers and tossed them into the wastebasket.

"Do you always organize and clean when you're uneasy?"

She saw the quiet tenderness in his gaze and regretted her outburst. He was well-meaning, truly interested and trying to help. Danny had given Seamus a job, hadn't he?

Clara softened her tone. "I don't like to see anything messy. Blame it on my orphanage days when everything was chaotic in my life—meals, bedtime, caretakers. In spite of that, the woman who ran the orphanage screamed for order. So I was pulled in opposite directions at a very young age."

Danny's dark brows rose. "Consequently, you like to control your surroundings and don't appreciate any interference?"

"Yeh. So occasionally when I'm upset, I tend to straighten things. It gives me something to do." She looked down at her hands. "Once, when Jack left me home alone in our flat all day, I felt so isolated. He'd forbidden me from seeing or talking to my family or friends. So I alphabetized all the spices in the spice rack. It didn't take long. We only had salt and pepper."

"Do I upset you because I want to protect you?" Danny asked quietly, ignoring her attempt at humor.

Her vision blurred. This strapping, powerful man had a way of tapping into her emotions when she least expected. And nothing broke down her guard as effortlessly as kindness.

She braced herself for another of his sympathetic remarks.

A few seconds passed. When one didn't seem to be forthcoming, she offered, "Yeh, my spine goes up because I can take care of myself. I was duped once before into believing I should depend on someone. I wasn't strong enough. This time, however ..." She balled a discarded napkin she'd overlooked and threw it into the wastebasket.

Danny came to his feet. "Don't ever do that."

"What?"

"Compare me to your ex."

"I didn't. I wouldn't." She met his steel-blue gaze. "I just meant—"

"That guy almost broke you. If you want to insult me, you're at the top of your game."

She heard the Dublin in Danny's voice—that hard, previous life he kept firmly under wraps. Attempting to avoid a heated conversation, she started for the door. "Let's ride the lift down to the kitchen. I noticed a couple slices of Guinness cake in the cooler."

He rubbed a hand across his temples. "Forgive me, Clara, if I sounded harsh. This Jack Connor thing has me so frustrated and worried for you."

"No bother."

"You've become very important to me."

She took a half-step back. No, forward. "I'm still hungry. Are you … hungry?"

His voice deepened. "Only for dessert."

Off-balance, she contemplated how best to resist him. He'd mentioned his flat on the third floor. Did he expect her to sleep with him in exchange for a trip to Dublin and a ham sandwich?

She gave herself a firm mental shake. If he assumed she'd be another one of his conquests, a brief fling after their briefer time together, he'd be sadly mistaken. He'd offered no commitment, only the assurance that he'd be leaving.

She tossed him a guarded look.

"Do you know how beautiful you are, luv? Clara, you are so damn beautiful."

His gaze caressed her with gentleness.

That was good, right? No demands. Although she'd learned from her ex that gentle words were a façade to reeling a woman in. And gentleness didn't last. Gentleness made a woman weak and pliable and trusting.

She wrenched her gaze from his and studied the philodendrons.

"Did you hear me, Clara?"

His voice warned that he would persist until he'd gotten an answer. She turned her head slightly and watched him.

Danny's molten gaze offered another layer far more dangerous than gentleness. Desire simmered in his eyes, deepening them to a dark, rich blue with flecks of navy.

She grabbed her water bottle from the table and finished it off.

She couldn't afford to be hurt again, to rely on someone other than herself. Soon, when Danny was gone, she'd be left alone, the dreaded constant in her existence. And she'd manage, just like always.

Which was better—gentleness or desire? Neither. Both. The question with no answer lodged in her throat.

She stifled an urge to find a dust cloth and begin dusting the room.

Instead, she went over to the window and watched the lively atmosphere of the rooftop pubs, the patrons soaking up the sun. She heard Danny, his stride sure and steady as he came behind her.

"I can take away those bad memories," he said. "The ones that are frightening you." Lightly, he rubbed his hand against her cheek. "If you'll let me ..."

Her mouth went dry. She could resist him. A nonchalant comment swirled in her brain, the word *no* on her tongue, a knee-jerk reaction, protection for her heart.

She pasted on an expression devoid of emotion and swung around to face him.

CHAPTER 13

*D*anny stared into Clara's fathomless eyes. The way she was looking at him filled him with the agonizing longing to hold her tight and never let go. Grimly, he reminded himself that Jack had hurt her deeply and her earlier life had been ridden with hardships.

"No one can make me forget the awfulness of the orphanage," she said. "We were hungry and cold and always dirty. The caretakers tried, although there were too many of us and too few of them. Remembering those times … It makes me so sad."

He suppressed a shudder at the deprivation she must have suffered. No one had held her. No one had loved her. Everyone needed love and acceptance, especially when they were children, especially when they were adults.

"Can you teach me how to break into a place?" He attempted to disrupt her solemn remembrances with levity. "There's a competitor's coffee shop down the street I've intended to visit. Unfortunately, they're closed on Sunday."

She rewarded his levity with a small smile. "I've never broken into a coffee shop."

His mouth quirked. "A new career path for you, perhaps?"

"That particular career path was a small part of my long-ago past."

She shook her hair with an impatient shake, and he longed to loosen her waves from their loose ponytail and run his hands through them. Did she have to be so perfectly shaped, so slim and willowy, her mouth so curved and inviting? He stroked his hands over her shoulders. Her fitted paisley blouse made her look small, fragile, defenseless.

"Someday," he promised, "you will own your own dancing school."

"It'll take me a year to dig out from Seamus's debt and then there'll probably be other bills I didn't anticipate. Maybe I'm a fool for suppressing horrific experiences, but if I dwell on them … I should look to the future, yeh?"

He felt himself becoming lost in her glorious eyes, the dark recesses pulling him in. Lightly, his thumbs stroked her cheekbones. "You're smart and you've accomplished so much since you left Italy."

She rolled her cheek against his palm. "And yet, somehow, Jack has reappeared in my life. Once, I was dependent on him to fill a void. Not anymore." She seemed to dwell on the thought, seemed to search for the right words. "Now it's up to me to make him go away—not you, nor Ian, nor Seamus. Nor a justice system that can't be counted on."

Her response brought a deluge of his own remembrances —his uninterested parents and Glenna, his beloved spit of a sister. Was he, in his effort to move forward and succeed, putting off dealing with his heartache from long ago, just like Clara? Would the past forever be nipping at his heels? No matter what he'd accomplished, he'd always label himself a poor chiseler, a child born to suicidal parents, a weak sibling who hadn't saved his younger sister. No amount of wealth would ever change that.

He bent his head and lightly rubbed his lips over Clara's.

She kept her hands at her sides.

Rather than intensifying his efforts, he reasoned that it was necessary to meet her where she was in her life. Her feelings were raw and vulnerable.

The older boys in the orphanage said I was so good, I could've stolen the sugar out of their punch.

She'd joked to hide her mortification for stealing. She was too proud to beg, aye, and too stubborn to accept the fact that Seamus's recovery required more than her love and support.

Danny slid his arms around her, relishing her nearness, the scent of freshly squeezed lemons on a warm spring's eve.

"Have I told you how much I admire your thievery skills?" he murmured with a laugh.

"Unfortunately, being a thief isn't a talent I can list on a resume. However, *your* achievements are amazing."

The sincere compliment and admiration in her gaze was his undoing. "Thank you. I'm truly happy when I'm with you."

She smiled.

His heart exploded. Their growing relationship was brilliant, delicate. Delightful.

He touched his lips to hers again. He felt her resist, her indecision, knew the exact second when she yielded. His heart raced madly when she allowed him to lock his statement with a scintillating kiss. Blood pounded in his ears as he savored the sweetness of her mouth. For a fleeting second, he considered taking her to his flat, just down the hallway. In his reckless past, he hadn't been one to let an opportunity slide by.

He lifted his head and she took a guarded retreat. "Danny, I won't sleep with you."

He rested his chin on her hair until his breathing slowed. "I know, luv."

And he wouldn't ask, because he respected her too much.

Because Clara meant more to him than an insignificant tryst. And if he was honest with himself, he'd admit that as sure as the hills of Ireland were a lush, emerald green, he was falling in love with her.

* * *

An hour later, Clara and Danny headed to his Town Car. The chauffeur opened the door, and Clara and Danny slid into the backseat.

The sedan merged onto the highway. An early evening sun shone through the windows and cast a golden glow on Clara's features. With his legs stretched out, Danny wrapped an arm around her. She'd pulled out her ponytail, and her tumbling waves fell past her shoulders. Leisurely, he ran his fingers through her glossy hair.

As the sedan took the Dublin airport exit, traffic picked up, then it calmed again when they passed the National Botanic Gardens.

"Are we headed to Farthing?" Clara asked. "Seamus is waiting."

"Your brother will survive brilliantly without you." Danny fiddled with the CD player, deciding on silence. "I've instructed the chauffeur to stop at Glasnevin Cemetery since I haven't visited in several months. My parents are buried there, along with …" He paused, staring out the window at a curving brook running alongside the roadway.

"Along with?" Clara tipped her head to one side.

"Along with my young sister," he continued softly. "Her name is Glenna."

Clara's eyes widened. "Glenna is your sister?"

"Aye. Didn't I mention her to you?"

"Not by name." Clara gazed past him. "I assumed Glenna was one of your past wives."

"I've only been married once, to Kyla." He thought about glossing over the details before forging ahead with the truth. "I was young and married her for the wrong reasons. Her wealthy family invested a large sum of money in my fledgling coffee company, assuming they'd reap a huge profit. They did. And I repaid her parents the money they loaned me. Soon afterward, Kyla and I divorced."

"What happened?"

He tapped his foot to a silent beat. "We were never suited. I tried to make the marriage work, but in the end, I was the one who filed for divorce. Kyla was furious. Nevertheless, she was well-compensated. She called me a money-monger and informed every tabloid who'd listen to her that I'd used her family's wealth for my business venture, then cast her aside. I didn't refute her claims." He shrugged. "A month later, I discovered that she'd stolen a great deal of money from my business. I confronted her and she said I owed her the money because I'd been such a disinterested husband throughout our marriage."

"Although I don't condone Kyla for what she did, she must have loved you and was probably hurt when you filed for divorce."

He answered with a derisive snort. "She didn't love me. She loved my money."

They soon reached Glasnevin in the northern section of Dublin, and the car chauffeured quickly past the trademark high walls and round watchtowers of Glasnevin Cemetery.

Danny directed Clara's gaze to the watchtowers. "Those were erected to scare away the body snatchers in the eighteenth century."

She shivered. "Body snatchers?"

"Aye. Body snatchers stole corpses for money, usually selling the bodies to medical schools."

They passed simple stone gravestones covered in a jumble of ivy, and elaborate gravestones topped by Celtic crosses. On the street near his parents' marble tomb and Glenna's grave, Danny asked the chauffeur to park the car.

Clara leaned on the door, her gaze on the rows and rows of headstones. "Glasnevin Cemetery is massive."

"One and a half million people are buried here." Danny stepped from the sedan and strode around to open her door. He took her hand, and they walked slowly on the path leading to the tomb and Glenna's grave.

Danny breathed in the cool, damp breeze and eyed the clovers dancing along the path. As he'd directed, shrubs and evergreens, offset by red begonias and silvery dusty miller, had been carefully tended at both Glenna's grave and his parents' tomb. A field of violet and sugary-pink wildflowers bloomed nearby, the uncommonly warm winter beckoning the flowers open. So much promise blooming so close to so much sadness.

Paying no heed to the damp grass, he knelt by Glenna's grave, keeping his focus on the granite headstone. Clara knelt beside him and bent her head. When they were finished praying at Glenna's gravesite, then his parents' tomb, he brushed the grass clinging to Clara's pants as they stood.

"We'll be going back to Farthing with green knees," she said. "Though kneeling to pay our respects is more important than any grass stains."

"Infinitely more," was all he could manage. Tears he'd bottled swam precariously close to the surface.

"You live in Dublin. Why haven't you visited the gravesites more often?" she asked.

He took a deep breath. His chest ached. "Busy with work," he murmured. In truth, he'd found one excuse after another for not visiting, when the reality was he couldn't manage the grief.

A cold sadness clogged the late afternoon air. The space where they stood was fragrant with the scent of pine needles. Nearby, a liver-colored tree sparrow perched on the branch of an elm tree, greeting them with a nasally *chu-wit.*

"Glenna's gravestone is strong and erect, just like she must have been. So beautiful."

"Sorry. What did you say?" He looked at Clara. He'd gotten caught up in staring at the intricately carved Celtic cross topping Glenna's polished headstone.

"The gravestone is beautiful." Clara pointed to the brilliant rainbow etched on one side of the somber stone, the pot of gold and flaming-orange-bearded leprechaun on the other.

Danny focused blindly ahead, concentrating on the scarlet sunset tucking itself behind rolling hills. In the pressing weight of the bleak graveyard, he could almost feel Glenna's childlike presence.

"I used to call Glenna my little leprechaun. She was so mischievous and innocent."

A poignant memory rose unbidden.

"Leprechauns are real, Danny," Glenna said, crossing her thin, freckled arms. "And I'm gonna catch one and he'll lead me to a pot of gold so we won't be poor anymore.'

Danny tousled her flaming-red hair. "Aye. Well, if I find that wee man smokin' a pipe, I'll take off his buckled shoes and carry him to you myself."

And Glenna had giggled with delight.

For one heart-stopping beat, Danny thought he could hear her trusting voice calling out to him.

She had enjoyed every moment of life with the pure unworldliness of a child. If she were alive, she would've been in the middle of the wildflower field performing cartwheels and chasing butterflies, rather than gazing somberly at a frost-grey headstone.

"How did she die?" Clara asked gently.

He looked off toward the watchtowers. Dusk was creeping in, the cemetery becoming deserted, the other mourners returning to their cars. Soon it would be pitch-dark. The chauffeur got out of the sedan and motioned Danny with a slight wave. Danny nodded, delaying, the memories nudging him.

He shifted. "Glenna was always searching for a pot of gold. Sometimes we'd spend hours in the hedgerows adjoining our land, playing, making up games. She loved cow parsley. We used the stalks as pea-shooters while we chewed on the leaves."

Clara nodded, her expression encouraging him to continue.

"And then one afternoon in late September, Glenna was poisoned by the leaves of a hemlock bush she'd apparently found growing at the edge of our yard. I found her lying on the cold grass, limp, unresponsive. Did you know that cow parsley and hemlock look very similar?"

"No, I didn't." Clara hesitated. "Was she alone in the yard?"

"Aye. And if you're thinking she was too young to be out wandering alone you'd be right. My parents had been inside our house, passed out drunk on the couch. The judge ruled Glenna's death an accidental poisoning."

A kind understatement. Glenna's death was partly the result of his alcoholic parents' inadequate supervision and neglect, and partly because he hadn't been with Glenna when she had needed him most.

He kept his tone carefully controlled. "My little sister never lived long enough to find her pot of gold. I blame my parents. I blame myself."

He glanced around. Had he said the words aloud? Judging by Clara's expression, her fingers that had somehow become laced tightly with his, he assumed he had.

All his life he'd tried to save what inevitably couldn't be saved. He'd talked, he'd argued, he'd shed tears. Despite his best efforts, he couldn't seem to control other people's actions.

"Absolutely not your fault," Clara said adamantly. "You were a kid too. You were probably at school right then."

"I'd skipped school that day. I'd decided to get drunk with my friends. If I had come directly home, Glenna might still be alive." He pushed a hand through his hair, attempting to push away the inevitable self-disgust swelling like poison in his veins. "At the burial, I begged my parents to add a pot of gold to Glenna's headstone. They refused. They were hard-hearted bastards. I told them that it was their fault Glenna had died—they were neglectful drunks. They shouted that I should slither back to the streets where I belonged, because I was the drunk who would never make anything of himself. My brother Eamon was the smart one."

She shook her head. "You shouldn't speak ill of the dead. They were probably lashing out at you to cover their own grief."

He pulled his hand from hers. "You don't understand. It was their fault, and they wouldn't accept the blame."

She stiffened at the dangerous edge in his tone, but then sympathy and support flooded her beautiful eyes. "You're not justifying their negligence. You are strong and brave. Forgive so that your own healing can begin."

"I can't be disloyal to Glenna and forget what happened."

"You're not forgetting." She lifted her gaze to his. "You're finding your own happiness. Otherwise, these resentments will gnaw at you and you'll never be at peace."

He ran his fingers across the stony Celtic cross, the faded

etching of Glenna's name, the absolute finality of her death. Bottled rage at his parent's neglect simmered beneath his own fury at himself. He didn't want to deal with it. The subject was too painful. Work was the answer, the only alternative, immersing himself so that he could prove his worth.

A heaviness settled in his heart.

Prove his worth to whom? His book-smart brother, who had been their parents' favorite child? His dead parents?

And for what?

So that he could boast that he was the richest man in Ireland, thereby showing his dead parents that he hadn't been a failure? That Eamon wasn't the only one who could be successful?

"The pot of gold on The Ground Café's logo is your tribute to Glenna," Clara said softly. "Soon, that logo will be seen throughout the world."

"Wealth buys many things, fixes many things," he murmured.

"But not this."

He drew in a breath. Waited. "Not this."

Glenna's last day of her life was seared in his brain. He'd begged her to hold on, squeezed her fragile, cold hand tightly in his.

"Don't you dare leave me alone with Ma and Da, Glenna. They don't care about us. We only have each other," he'd pleaded. "Don't leave me."

It was too difficult, all those terrible recollections emerging. He knuckled away a tear, attempted to find some sense in the tragedy that shouldn't have happened.

The wind picked up, more frigid than slight, rustling the leaves on the thin and spindly tree branches.

Clara gave his fingers a gentle squeeze. "You were a devoted brother and Glenna's death wasn't your fault. You were only a teenager and despite what you believe, your parents must've been devastated. Losing a child so young ... I can't imagine."

He wanted to accept her grasp, her reassurance. "If my parents were devastated, I never saw a shred of remorse. If anything, they drank even more those months following her death. I damn well tried to stop them from drinking and I damn well failed. I thought I could fix them. I couldn't. They both committed suicide a few months later. They needed more help than I could give them."

She seemed to absorb every word, every sadness, into her own heart. "So then you went to live with your aunt and uncle and finished secondary school."

"I never finished. I left the schooling to my brilliant older brother. Eamon's an esteemed physician in Dublin now, very up-and-coming in the medical field."

"Experience is more important than any schooling." She stepped in front of him and offered a quivering smile. "Danny Brady, I believe you've achieved great things and the best is yet to come, although I'm still waiting for your apology."

Momentarily speechless, his lips parted with no sound. "For what?"

"For talking so unnecessarily harsh to me a few moments ago, in that imperious tone of yours. And here I was nice enough to accompany you to Dublin and missing the Sunday matinee picture show."

Taken aback, he brushed his knuckles against her cheek. "Will you still let me buy your recipe?"

"My price keeps increasing for every second that you don't apologize."

"You said that you don't like to apologize."

"This is about your apology, not mine."

"You drive a hard bargain."

She was the only woman he'd ever met who could take

him from sorrow to laughter to passion in under one minute. "And I sincerely apologize for my earlier rudeness."

As they walked to the sedan, Clara gripped his hand firmly. In times past, he'd wanted to be alone in his grief. Today he was grateful for her presence.

He glided his thumb against her fingers. "I've never asked anyone to accompany me to Glasnevin before."

"Thank you for sharing your past with me." And before they slid into the sedan, she gave him a kiss.

Clara, his enchanting Clara, brought balance to his unsteady, demanding world.

The chauffeur pulled the sedan into traffic. Clouds were gathering in the twilight sky, promising rain as the Dublin streetlights stretched farther away. Clara rested her head against his shoulder, and he stroked her hair.

She'd listened to his tale about his parents and young sister without judgment, urging him to forgive. In the end, it wasn't Clara's reassuring words that had moved him. It was the respect shining from her chestnut-brown eyes, her unabashed belief in him, her ability to see only the good. Her affirmations meant more than all of his extravagant estates and luxury cars combined.

He pressed her nearer. "May I take you out to dinner tomorrow evening? I've heard there's a posh restaurant in the next town over from Farthing, The Duckling and the Quail. Do you fancy duckling?"

She shook her head. "Never had it."

"Mouthwatering quail?"

Another head shake. "We're of the fish and chips mentality."

"Me too." He laughed and pressed a kiss on her cheek. "Surely there'll be some type of normal food on the menu we can eat. I'll make reservations and ring Ian and Anna to stay with Seamus."

After a lengthy, relaxed silence, Clara remarked, "You've managed to find the most expensive restaurant within thirty miles of Farthing. My dance class finishes at seven. I'll need to go home to shower and change first."

"I'll come by your flat at eight."

He held her tightly, wanting to escape the tragedy of his past in her goodness. And he wanted to make their last few days together as unforgettable for her as they would be for him.

CHAPTER 14

The following morning, Clara lingered in bed later than she'd planned. Seamus had kept her awake the night before, complaining that both Ian and Anna had lectured him about "staying on the rails … or else."

"Or else what?" Clara had inquired while she'd started the wash and tidied the kitchen. She was too tired for this conversation, she thought. She stayed, although she would have preferred to go to her room and think about her day with Danny and what she had learned about him.

"Or else they'd force me into a treatment center," Seamus had replied.

At midnight, Clara had finally pleaded exhaustion while making assenting noises in Seamus's direction before bidding him good night.

Just now, she'd been relieved when the door to her flat had opened and closed at seven, the exact time Seamus departed for his shift at the coffee shop.

She smiled. Despite his ranting the previous evening, Seamus had proven himself a responsible worker, reinforcing her belief that nothing was more important to his recovery than his family's love and encouragement.

She sank deeper under the covers and listened to the soothing sound of rhythmic rain against her bedroom window. Stretching, she sighed contentedly and closed her eyes.

She and Danny were getting on brilliantly. Although they'd known each other for only a short while, they'd formed a strong connection, a bond she couldn't deny.

And tonight she'd be seeing him again.

Mentally, she went through her closet, deciding what to wear to the posh restaurant. Months earlier, she'd purchased a ruby-red silk cocktail dress at the local thrift shop. The dress was stunning and sophisticated, its sheath design clinging subtly to her slim curves.

She'd called Anna the previous evening and asked to borrow her beaded faux-crystal headband. Danny had said he'd liked Clara's hair best when she pulled it back to show off her dark eyes.

And dinner with him at such an exclusive place. Why, hadn't the prime minister himself dined at The Duckling and the Quail?

The meal would be superb, coupled with Danny's easy laughter and impeccable manners. At the end of the evening, she envisioned him wrapping her in his arms and kissing her in that sensually confident way of his. Just thinking about his kisses heated her entire body.

On her nightstand, her cell phone chimed and her eyes fluttered open. Noting Danny's caller ID, she picked up on the first ring.

"Good morning, Clara. It's your favorite barista."

She grinned into the phone, basking in the warmth of his deep voice. "Good morning."

"You still in bed?" His tone took a husky turn.

She sat up and propped the pillows behind her. "How did you know?"

"Your brother reported for work at the coffee shop and he's a virtual chatterbox, remember?" Danny's soft laugh sounded tired. "Sorry to ring on such short notice. Unfortunately, I need to cancel our dinner tonight. My lawyers are convening in Dublin this afternoon, and I was just informed that I must be present. More papers require my signature and I need to go over some eleventh-hour details regarding my trip."

The laughter, she noted, was gone from his voice.

"When are you leaving?"

"Shortly."

She slumped against the pillows. "Is your chauffeur driving you?"

"No. My car needs some repair work done. I'll drive it to Dublin myself." Danny seemed to falter for a second. "Ian may come with me. He has … a project in Dublin to attend to."

"That's a fret. We were in Dublin yesterday."

His weary sigh was followed by a pause. "Aye."

She accepted his response. He sounded as frustrated as she felt. Noting the clock, she pushed to her feet. Cradling the phone against her shoulder, she pulled on her robe and padded to the kitchen. "How long will you be gone?"

"I'll fly directly to London from Dublin because there's no sense delaying these meetings. I promise I'll make it up to you when I return to Farthing in a couple of weeks."

"No worries." Deflated, she lowered herself onto the kitchen stool.

Two weeks without him.

She stood and started the kettle to boil. "Will you ring me?"

Immediately she regretted her question, hated the underlying neediness. Her wounded self-respect prompted her to add, "Of course I'll want to know you've landed safely."

"I'll ring you tonight when I arrive in London." He punctuated the silence by clearing his throat. "I'm going to head on then."

A woman was talking to him in the background. Clara sensed he was rushed.

She squeezed the phone. "Safe travels, Danny."

"I'll miss you." He waited for a beat. "Will you miss me?"

She brought the phone close to her ear. Perhaps he wasn't handling his unanticipated departure as dismissively as she'd thought.

"I'll miss you a great deal," she replied honestly.

"Imagine my arms around you while I'm gone, ensuring that you are safe." He lowered his voice. "Keep your thoughts on last evening, when we were in the backseat of the sedan. Remember that."

They'd kissed as if they were a couple of love-struck teenagers.

Briefly, she closed her eyes. "I will."

"I'll return as soon as I can, luv." He hung up with a quick click.

She stared at the phone. Should she be a little hurt that he hadn't offered more than a quick farewell? For a man who'd seemed so concerned about her welfare, he was leaving on extremely short notice with only the promise of a memory.

Frustrated, she showered quickly, got dressed, and ran a hairbrush through her damp hair. As she sat finishing her morning tea and lemon scone, a pounding on her entry door brought her quickly to her feet.

"Anybody home?" Anna waltzed into the kitchen with her purse slung haphazardly over her arm.

Clara put a hand to her heart. "I nearly had 40,000 canaries. You scared me half to death."

"Only me." Anna screwed up her face and shook the wetness from her hair. "It's raining stair rods out there." She bent and smiled at her reflection in the stainless-steel toaster on the counter, then fluffed candy-blue hair strands to frame her face. "How do you like my new hair color?"

Clara chose her words carefully. "It suits you better than royal purple."

"I chose this color to match Ian's motorcycle."

"A perfect match."

"He's a cupcake. Tonight, we're riding his motorcycle to a pub the next town over. I'm wearing a candy-blue sweater too."

"Even better." Clara muffled a smile, then frowned, considering. "Ian's staying in Farthing this evening?"

"Yeh, where else?"

Clara sank onto the kitchen stool, pushed her teacup aside and started to ask about Ian. Hadn't Danny said that Ian would be driving to Dublin with him?

"You should lock your flat door, by the way," Anna interrupted before Clara could speak. "Your useless toe rag of an ex is roaming somewhere around Farthing and you don't want him barging into your flat unannounced."

"Jack Connor would never be awake before noon. Besides, Seamus asked on the streets, and word is that Jack returned to Cork and is living with his brother."

"He's not back in prison then?"

"Nope."

Anna shook her head. "Sometimes I still can't believe that you were once arrested and put in prison because you stole from our friends. The Murphys, of all people. They'd owned their furniture store for years."

"Jack was so controlling. I did whatever he said to do. I was in a fog."

"Seamus and I tried to tell you that he was manipulative. You wouldn't listen."

"I wasn't myself. I was with Jack every second. He was all I heard, all I saw ..." Clara wiped at her eyes. Her cheeks felt hot. Shaking away her thoughts, she glanced at the clock and stood. "I'd wet some tea for you, except I'm already late for the bus."

Anna set her biker jacket and pink suede purse on an empty stool, plunked herself down, and forked the last bite of Clara's scone. "I'll drive you to work. You'll be soaked before you reach the bus stop."

"Thanks. I don't know when or if my car's brakes will ever be fixed. Now the mechanic's saying the cost to repair the brakes will be more than the car's worth. His advice is to give up the car. I don't really need one, anyway." Clara went to the stove and threw two teabags into the teapot. She poured Anna a cup and brought a sugar bowl and two more scones to the table.

"True." Anna added several heaping teaspoons of sugar to her tea before biting into another scone. "So, on a much more fascinating topic, I assume you had a whale of a time yesterday in Dublin with Danny? Happy out?"

Clara sat opposite Anna. "Dublin was grand."

"There are definite advantages in dating a billionaire. By the way, the reason I burst in this morning was to bring you my headband." Anna reached into her purse and brandished the sparkly headband, waving it gaily in Clara's direction. "Tonight you're actually dining at The Duckling and the Quail!"

"Not anymore." Clara attempted a swallow of tea. The warm liquid stayed trapped in her throat as a nagging realization struck her. Danny Brady would always choose his business above his personal relationships. And that realization brought a clearer insight into his priorities.

He had to have known how unpinned she would feel, how much she'd been looking forward to their evening together. Sure, she'd had plans canceled on her before. And she'd carried on, just like she would this time.

She swallowed the tea, set down her cup, and pushed it aside. She'd never mention her disappointment to him. Her pride was too fragile. Besides, she'd vowed she'd never allow a man to make her feel vulnerable again. "Danny's leaving for Dublin today because of some unexpected meetings. Then he's off to London for a couple of weeks."

Anna pushed the sparkly headband back into her purse. "You sound disappointed."

"A little." Clara went to the sink and rinsed a clean cloth, then returned to the table and wiped bits of crumbs onto her plate.

Anna finished off her scone and licked her fingers. "He'll be back."

Clara feigned absorption in the crumb-wiping. "If he returns, it's because he'll want to ensure that his fiftieth coffee shop in Ireland is a huge success before he enters the international franchise market."

"He employs at least one hundred other employees who could oversee his coffee shop in our little town," Anna said with insolent amusement. "He'll return to Farthing for one reason. You."

Clara stopped in mid-swipe. "What do you mean?"

Anna appraised a third scone before biting into it. Chewing, she dabbed at her lips. "He talks about you all the time. Ian told me, so the info is straight from the horse's mouth. And anyone can see Danny has a glad eye for you. He's in love with you."

Clara went to the stove to freshen her tea while Anna's

remarks swirled through her mind. The persistent drumming of raindrops against the window had stopped. A thin ray of sunlight wafted its way through the window and into a corner of the kitchen.

Shaking her head to emphasize her point, Clara turned to face her sister. "Danny and I have become good friends because he's seen me through a couple trying ordeals."

The truth was, they'd become more than good friends. The heat in his kisses, the kindness in his smile, the tenderness in his gaze, were all evidence that he cared. If they kept seeing each other, their relationship might develop into something more, something deeper. Something lasting.

She curved back to the sink and switched on the faucet, washing imaginary bits of food down the drain.

Will you miss me too? The caring in his voice, like a honeyed caress, had effortlessly brought down her defenses.

"So you're just good friends?" Anna asked.

Clara slanted a glance at her smugly beaming sister.

Anna washed down the scone with her tea in a poor attempt to hide her glee. "I've seen the secret smiles you two share."

Clara shut off the faucet. "Get outta that garden before your imagination wanders too far," she warned with a half smile. "Will you promise that you won't talk of my relationship with Danny Brady again?"

"Yeh, I will promise," Anna said, and both women burst into laughter. In Ireland, many times "Yeh, I will" actually meant "No, I won't." And in that instance, Clara knew Anna would never change. Anna loved romance and happy endings and good craic. Besides, they shared a sisterly bond.

The women were still chuckling as they left the flat. Clara locked the door, and the women walked arm-in-arm to Anna's parked car.

A blink later and unbeknownst to the women, Seamus and Liam entered Clara's flat through the same door.

* * *

CLARA HAD DECIDED that a fortnight without seeing Danny was long enough. She'd missed him more with each passing day.

Every evening, he'd rung from London. Besides entertaining her with hilarious accounts of pompous lawyers conducting their endless business meetings, he'd encouraged Clara to recount details of her childhood. She'd told him about her brief time in the orphanage in Italy and her happier upbringing in Ireland. The wonderful life she'd enjoyed with her loving, adoptive Irish parents had dimmed her memories of her desolate orphanage days.

He'd listened intently, interjecting affirmations, urging her to talk for hours. During their lengthy conversations, he'd listened as though she were the most important person in the world. On several occasions, she'd attempted to shorten their nightly talks, reminding herself that he was a billionaire businessman with a thousand other concerns vying for his attention. Still, his interest in her seemed insatiable and the affection she felt for him had only deepened.

Now she counted the hours until his return.

During Danny's two weeks away from Farthing, she'd thought she'd seen Ian several times as she'd walked to and from the city centre. After all, the burly guy was hard to miss. She'd asked Danny once about Ian's whereabouts. He'd denied that Ian was in Farthing, vaguely remarking that Ian was working on some project in Dublin before changing the subject.

Even stranger, Anna had also denied that Ian was in Farthing, offering an ambiguous excuse that Ian was needed in Dublin for some project. Anna had kept herself scarce, explaining that she was applying to several universities and working on applications.

Despite all that denying, Seamus, on the other hand, had never seemed happier.

On March 17, Saint Patrick's Day, Clara returned home immediately after work. The night hummed with festivity, and as she'd walked from the bus, her nostrils had been over-whelmed by the smells of pub food and thick, dark beer.

She met Seamus outside the street door to her building. He was dressed in a new pair of denims, an indigo-colored hoodie, and his brimmed tweed hat.

They faced each other with only a patch of moonbeam lighting the sidewalk between them. The streetlight had been broken weeks before and had never been fixed.

Clara fished in her pocket for her keys. "Where are you going?"

He lit a cigarette, the flare of the match showing every unshaven stub on his square chin. "I'm workin' on a deal to buy a new car. You've said that your car isn't worth fixin'."

"It isn't. However, the car dealers are all closed at this hour."

"This here's a private negotiation, Clara," Seamus drawled in an icy tone.

"We don't need a car. We can walk most places and I ride the bus to work. If you've saved any extra money, use it to pay your gambling debt."

"It's paid."

"How?"

"I'm savvy with my money, Clara, and I worked out a deal with the bookies." He smoked silently for a beat. "And now I want a car. Furthermore, I won't allow my little sister to catch a bus to work anymore."

"You don't earn enough money to afford a car." Nasty

little tendrils of suspicion began to take root in her mind. Was he gambling again? Was that how he'd gotten so much money in so little time?

"The car is an old banger, but it runs." Seamus frowned at her censorious tone. "Don't fret. I'm takin' on extra hours at the coffee shop and your man has actually given me a raise."

"He's not my man."

"Yeh, right." Seamus flicked the ashes of his cigarette in quick, juddering movements. "Besides, my friend's letting me buy the car on credit."

"Who is this mysterious friend?"

Seamus expelled an enormous ring of blue hazy smoke and squinted at Clara in the patch of moonbeam. "She's a fine, large doorfull of a woman. I'll let you meet her soon."

Clara smiled, trying to think positively. A good, sturdy woman would bring joy to Seamus's life. A good woman was exactly the person he needed.

She drew back to admire him. Her strong-willed brother, so brawny, so dapper in his new clothes and tweed hat.

"I'll be home for the evening," she said, "and Danny's ringing me at nine. You'll not be out late? Saint Patrick's Day is always mad here, and there'll be trouble brewing." She extended her arms for a hug. He narrowed his eyes and tapped his foot, visibly fidgeting.

She dropped her arms. "Good luck with your car deal."

Seamus threw the still-smoldering cigarette on the ground and crushed it with the heel of his shiny black boots. "I'm always in the field when luck is on the road. This time, however, my luck is changing. I guarantee it, Clara." His eyes darkened to slits of charcoal. His expression gave away nothing.

He spun decisively in the direction of the city centre. He had a little too much swagger in his walk, she decided later on. And his eyes had been too bloodshot.

Luck. Gambling. She wanted to call out a warning for him to be careful, although her mouth went dry. For a second time, she worried that he might be wagering on the horses. However, after all their long cozy chats and his sincere reassurances, that troublesome thought was simply unthinkable.

CHAPTER 15

*T*wo days after Saint Patrick's Day, Danny returned to Farthing.

Without fanfare, he knocked on the door to Clara's flat at six o'clock on a rainy March evening.

She opened the downstairs door and her mouth flew open. She'd resigned herself to spending her birthday by herself, half deciding to tackle the thankless job of cleaning her refrigerator and oven.

"You're looking brilliant, luv." He favored her with a look of unabashed approval.

He needed a shave, and the rain had given his hair a copper sheen. One of the buttons of his linen sport jacket had been buttoned in the wrong hole, as if he'd been in a hurry. He looked incredibly tall, devastatingly handsome, and completely desirable.

She blinked back tears of delight at the invitation in his compelling blue eyes. Without words, he was telling her how much he'd missed her.

"Danny, you're ... not in London?"

In a laughter-tinged voice, he said, "I don't think so." He

smiled, that primal, intimate grin that ignited her insides. His feet were braced apart, a bouquet of a dozen red roses clutched in his hand. "Happy Birthday."

She shoved a hand through her hair. "I expected to spend the night alone. Seamus hasn't been around much lately and Anna said she was busy studying for some university entrance exams. I even offered to assist Colum with a very active preschool class at the dance studio because he says he can't control that age group. However, he said the attendance was small and he could handle the children by himself."

She knew she was babbling and immediately quieted.

Danny smiled. "Is that all?"

"Thank you." With a prim nod, she accepted the roses from Danny's outstretched hand and inhaled the delicate aroma.

The rain finally registered, and she pulled him into the foyer.

Caught between delight and confusion, she added, "This morning when you rang, you said your meetings in London ran longer than you'd anticipated. I didn't expect to see you until tomorrow."

He grinned. "I'd planned to charter a private plane to Dublin if I missed the flight from London. And that's what I did."

"You didn't tell me *that* part."

"I wanted to see you. Judging by your smile, you wanted to see me too."

"How many hours have you been traveling?"

"I was up before dawn. Seeing you was more important than a few hours of sleep."

She bit back a teary chuckle, fearful to show too much emotion, powerless to stop the joyful sniffles because she'd missed him. He'd effectively dissolved the pity party she'd decided to have for herself because no one had wished her a happy birthday.

Danny tenderly wiped the corners of her eyes. "I thought we'd enjoy your birthday celebration in my flat at the coffee shop, nice and quiet, just the two of us. We'll have dinner there."

"I should change first." She gestured to her worn denim jeans and ripped grey sweatshirt. "And I'll place your beautiful flowers in a vase with water."

He glanced at his watch. "Will fifteen minutes allow you enough time to get ready?"

"Are you in a rush?"

He averted his gaze, looked at his watch again. "I'm only in a hurry to be with you." He added a swift, nipping kiss on her lips that made her smile. "I'll wait here in the foyer."

She whirled toward the stairs and called over her shoulder, "Give me ten minutes." She'd change into the ruby-red silk cocktail dress that she'd contemplated wearing to The Duckling and the Quail. And she'd twist her hair into a quick French braid, using her faux-pearl clips to hold it. Silver hoop earrings would complete her outfit. It was her birthday, after all, or at least the day her adoptive parents had designated to celebrate her birthday. And it was Saint Joseph's Day, a traditional day to wear red.

She didn't know the date of her actual birthday, a quiet voice in her mind prompted, because she'd come to Ireland as an unruly, untidy, and uncombed shoplifter from a dirt-poor orphanage.

She chased away her negative thoughts. The drop-dead handsome man who'd appeared at her door had remembered her birthday. He'd grinned at her, all male charisma, and her heart had taken a solid bump. She had so much to be thankful for.

She met Danny in the downstairs foyer in ten minutes

flat. He was standing exactly where she'd left him and was texting someone. He glanced up, quickly snapped his phone shut, and held out his hand.

"You look exquisite, Clara." He flashed a gleaming white smile so appealing, her knees felt watery. He reached into the inside pocket of his sport jacket and pulled out a box wrapped in luxurious gold foil.

"Happy Birthday."

"You already brought me flowers and—"

"And you would deny me the pleasure of buying you two gifts for your birthday?"

She hesitated.

"Open it," he prodded. "I hope you like it."

In her shabby foyer, Clara unwrapped the most beautiful diamond necklace she'd ever seen. Eye-catching and brilliant, several heart-shaped diamonds in an exquisite white-gold setting. She fingered the stones. "Surely these can't be real diamonds."

He seemed taken aback. "Of course they are. Eighteen carat. I insist that my girl have only the best."

My girl. Her heart squeezed.

She leaned nearer him. "I could never wear a piece of jewelry this extravagant. Suppose I lost the necklace? Suppose—"

"Suppose I put the necklace on you? It would please me greatly if you'd wear it tonight." He fastened the necklace around her throat. She glanced at her reflection in the entry-door window and smiled shyly at herself.

His mouth captured hers in a breathless kiss. When the kiss ended, she stayed in his arms. Her hands stroked the beginning of a beard on his chin.

"Do you like the necklace?" he murmured against her lips.

Her eyes welled with tears of joyfulness. "I love diamonds. They're beautiful, although I've never owned any."

"Be prepared," he teased. "This is only the beginning of what I plan to give to you."

When they reached The Ground Café, Danny helped her out of his Mercedes. Because of the rain, she'd donned a khaki raincoat to protect her silk dress. Fortunately, the earlier rain shower had settled to a light drizzle.

"The parking lot is empty," she said. "Where are all the customers?"

"I closed the coffee shop at six because of your birthday."

She lifted her brows. "You? Giving up business and losing money?"

He accepted her barb with a glint of amusement, which seemed to lighten his eyes to a cornflower blue. "Only for you, luv."

As they entered the empty shop, Danny flipped on the lights and gestured to the tea dispensers behind the counter. "Would you fancy a cup of green mint tea?"

"You remembered my favorite tea."

"I remember everything about you." He poured the tea. Then he tidied a bagged coffee display and refilled a bin of sugar. Another thirty seconds, and she imagined him grabbing a broom and sweeping the floor.

He seemed as jumpy as a schoolboy, humming the tune to "Oh Danny Boy" as they made their way through the empty shop to the lift.

She grinned over her tea and drew in the nutty, toasty aroma combined with strong, refreshing mint. This exquisite-tasting tea was one of the many reasons why his businesses had flourished; because of his attention to excellence, cleanliness, and detail. His standards were high, reflected in his first-rate products. Customers had shown their appreciation by patronizing his coffee shops in droves.

When they reached the third floor, they passed his boardroom, and Danny waved to a young guy with sparse carrot-red hair and thick glasses hunkered over a laptop. He nodded in return.

"Aiden is my top accountant," Danny explained. "I depend on him because he never gets rattled. He's also honest to a fault. He came in tonight to begin working on our yearly audit, and he's checking the numbers for the Farthing store to ensure that the spreadsheets balance out. It's imperative that I demonstrate to my potential franchisees that I run a sound business."

"So, is your business venture in my modest town successful?"

"I haven't checked the numbers in a few days, though the shop has shown a bigger profit than expected." His gaze shot to hers. "You've never seen the inside of my flat."

She didn't reply as a previous conversation with Seamus sprang to mind.

"Sometimes Mr. Brady and Kathleen disappear for hours and go upstairs."

Could the gorgeous Kathleen have shared hours with Danny in his private flat? How many nights had they spent together? Could that striking woman with the strawberry-blonde hair have experienced his sensual kisses, the delightful pleasure of his hard body pressed close to hers? She was utterly devoted to him and had been with him since, literally, the ground floor of his coffee shop endeavor.

Despite the warmth of the tea steaming from her cup, Clara's fingers felt chilled. She tried to reassure herself that Danny had chartered a private flight to see her, not Kathleen.

"I've arranged for a dinner to be sent up at nine o'clock," Danny was saying. "Nice and quiet, just the two of us."

Clara shot him a look of annoyance. Why did he keep repeating himself?

They reached a closed door. "I'll hold your tea," he said,

gesturing to the door handle. "The flat's unlocked, although I know that breaking into a place is one of your—"

"I can certainly hold a cup of tea and open a door at the same time," she snapped, his drollness irritating her. Not to mention his ear-to-ear grin.

She clicked the handle and stepped inside. The room was dark and silent, except for a muffled giggle somewhere in the room.

"What's going on?" she asked.

The lights came on and a crowd shouted, "Surprise!"

CHAPTER 16

"*H*appy thirtieth birthday!"

A cacophony of tin whistles and shakers greeted Clara. She yelped and jumped back. All around the room were people wearing iridescent-green party hats, laughing and playing a variety of musical instruments—tin whistles and hand drums and tambourines. Colum grinned and waved, along with Ian and several of Clara's friends. Anna stood next to Ian in the middle of the room. Besides holding a party-blower, Anna threw Kelly-green confetti into the air and waved a pastel-green balloon emblazoned with the number 30.

Clara blew out a suspended breath. Wasn't Anna supposed to be home studying? And Colum should've been teaching his preschool dance class. And wasn't Ian working on a project in Dublin?

Anna snaked her way to Clara and bussed a kiss. "Wow! That shocked look on your face was priceless." She blew into her party-blower, then inspected Clara's necklace. "Umm, are those real diamonds?"

Clara fingered the heart-shaped stones and nodded. "The necklace is a birthday gift from Danny. Isn't it gorgeous?"

Anna gave a triumphant giggle. "I told you there were advantages to dating a billionaire."

Clara smothered a laugh. "He really is so good to me."

"And because of him, I've avoided you like the plague this past fortnight. I was so nervous that I might spill your surprise birthday after he rang me to work out the details."

Clara grabbed her sister's arm. "Details? Who? What? How?"

"Ask him." Anna's accusation came out in a rush as she pointed to Danny. "He arranged everything. Do you know you're called the surprisee?" Anna whirled, all animation, her pale-pink floral dress swaying, her leopard stilettos accenting her shapely legs. "He instructed me to decorate his living room in green because he said green's your favorite color. Isn't his place posh? I love the sleek, modern fireplace. Imagine what you could do with a place like this with your decorating ideas."

Clara surveyed the large living room, the bright-green streamers wound around every lampshade, the table towering with platters of sandwiches, coffee, and fruit punch. On a side table, an etched silver tray held sliced red apples and fresh strawberries.

Clara caught Danny's guilty, albeit pleased, expression. Laughingly, he shrugged and held up her green mint tea. She hadn't realized he'd taken the cup out of her hands.

"You planned all this?"

"I'm the culprit." He set the tea on a cherry-wood credenza and came to stand beside her. He helped her off with her raincoat, slung his arm around her, and kissed her. "Happy birthday, beautiful," he whispered. "I'm sorry that I haven't finished writing my song for you. I really wanted to sing it to you tonight."

She heard the suppressed excitement in his voice and smiled. No wonder he'd been so jittery. He'd acted like a fresh-faced lad, bursting with his secret surprise ever since he'd knocked on her door.

"Will you have your song finished by tomorrow night?" she teased.

He hung her raincoat and his jacket by the door before returning to her side. "No. Unfortunately, I've been too tied up with meetings."

Clara recognized two of Danny's employees from the coffee shop. They were dressed like waiters and traveled through the crowd offering appetizers to the guests— smoked salmon in new potatoes and cucumber-ham rollups, as well as nonalcoholic emerald-colored cocktails and chocolate mint shakes in glittering crystal glasses.

Danny plucked two cocktails from a tray as one of the waiters passed them and handed one to Clara, then he asked everyone in the room to take a glass for a toast.

A burst of pride surged through her as Danny stood alongside her. Tall and elegant, he projected an impressive, take-charge appearance, an aura of capable command that was an integral part of his character.

He centered his gaze on her. His eyes sparkled, a beam of forget me not blue, mesmerizing and oh so attractive. Raising his glass, he said, "Several weeks ago, I came to Farthing to open a coffee shop. Clara and I hadn't known each other twenty-four hours before this charming, gorgeous woman accused me of being a bowsie, a good-for-nothing male. I'd told her that I was a musician and loved music. She advised me to stick with making coffee because I sang so off-key that I sounded like the tune the old cow died of."

The group laughed.

With a smile and shake of his head, Danny continued, "Many of you know that one of my life-long aspirations was to open a chain of successful coffee shops. This aspiration was far easier to accomplish than my second—to live up to the example this fearless woman has shown me." He lifted his glass higher. "Sometimes I don't understand her ability to forgive so freely, but to quote our great Irish poet and novelist, Oscar Wilde, 'Women are made to be loved, not understood.' Slainte!"

Clara flushed as she met Danny's tender gaze. When the surge of toasts ended, she nodded at Seamus. He'd stood in a far corner of the room, and when she caught his glance, he tipped a glass in her direction. "Happy birthday," he mouthed. Then he turned to Ian, and the two men started talking.

What was Seamus drinking? Water? The liquid in his glass looked clear. The question nagged, even though Danny was leading her to the CD player and asking if his music selection was to her liking. Seamus was soon forgotten.

The hours went by in a fairy-tale haze. Clara noted that Danny spent a good deal of time speaking with Colum. She smiled, listening to the two men before she continued mingling with the other guests.

As the evening progressed, Danny's employees lit a fire in the grate and set apple-green tea lights and votive candles on the credenza. The candles added a soft shimmer to the room and a scent of spring to the air. The overhead light was lowered to a mellow afterglow, and on the CD player, The Dubliners, a popular Irish folk band, sang a ballad about how lonely life was around Athenry fields.

Danny took Clara's second emerald cocktail out of her hand and set the glass down. "One last dance?"

"Of course." She smiled. "I am having a brilliant time tonight. Everything was planned perfectly."

He led her to the middle of the living room. As he took her in his arms, his gaze kindled with the promise of tantalizing kisses. She felt her own response, yearning for his body to stay pressed to hers, the softness of his caress. As they slow-danced, she listened to the heartbreaking lyrics of "The Fields of Athenry," which told the tale of a man sentenced to forsake Ireland because he'd stolen food for his starving family.

When the poignant ballad came to an end, Danny gathered her nearer and placed his chin on her upswept hair. "Thank you."

She toyed with the reddish hair at the nape of his neck. "For what? I should be thanking you."

He tipped up her chin and held her gaze. "For your smile, your love of life, your appreciation. For being you—breathtaking, valiant and incredibly dazzling in that red dress. And for making my time in Farthing so memorable."

She touched her fingers to his cheek. "It sounds like you're ... you're leaving?"

"Armed with my franchise agreements and a half-dozen lawyers, my franchise expansion begins in Europe."

She had difficulty swallowing the ache in her throat. "When?"

His arms tightened around her. Briefly, he closed his eyes. "Tomorrow I leave for London. And then ..." He gestured wordlessly, indicating more places and miles than he could name.

There it was. The irrevocability in his tone, the finality of their relationship. It was useless to reply with any note of longing in her voice. A while ago, he'd let her know in no uncertain terms that his departure was not open for discussion.

She lowered her head and studied his broad chest, his forest-green cashmere sweater reminding her of a woodland filled with lonely pines. "How long will you be traveling?"

He shifted. "A few months, which may be extended,

depending on any unforeseen red tape along the way. It'll definitely be a long while."

She avoided his probing gaze. Her heart beat sluggish.

She should be happy for him, she told herself, because the business venture he'd worked on for so many years was coming to fruition. Victory was well within his grasp. And she should tell him how happy she was—except that a sharp sadness threatened to carve a hole in her lungs every time she took a breath.

Somehow, she managed a weak smile that she was certain didn't reach her eyes. In an effort to dispel the melancholy mood settling over them, she changed the subject. "Thanks for giving Seamus extra hours at work this week. And his substantial raise has been brilliant. He bought a new car, because it was going to cost too much money for my car to be fixed. Seamus is putting his hard-earned money to good use."

Danny cocked an eyebrow. "I haven't given him a raise, Clara. And your brother called in sick the past seven days, although he reported for work today."

"You must be mistaken." She scanned the near-empty room, realizing that Seamus must have slid out of the party without a word. She considered the time, just before eleven o'clock, then zeroed in on her sister. Anna and Ian were sharing bites of salmon hors d'oeuvres while Ian dangled Anna's leopard stilettos from his beefy fingers.

Clara pulled out of Danny's arms and headed toward her sister.

"Hi Clara! Great party—which is why we're still here." Anna laughed. "You know me, the type of person who comes for the wedding and stays for the christening, just like the old Irish saying. Of course, we were also waiting for the rain to stop because getting soaked while riding a motorcycle is no fun."

Grinning, Clara hugged her sister. "You and Danny managed to pull off a wonderful shocker birthday celebration that I'll reminisce about for the rest of my life."

Anna's own smile was just as wide. "And I got a job at his coffee shop. I start tomorrow."

"Congratulations."

"Yeh, it'll be grand. Now that my disability insurance had ended, I realized it was time to get a real job with a great boss." Still grinning, Anna's honey-colored eyes met Ian's hazel gaze. "We danced every fast dance and my feet are never going to forgive me. Tonight, I'll be riding on your motorcycle barefoot, cupcake."

A moonstruck-looking Ian gawped at Anna. "I love your feet."

"And I love yours." Anna and Ian glued their lips together, the irresistibly offbeat couple clearly in love.

Clara folded her hands together and waited. When their kiss ended, she said, "I was so preoccupied with all the guests, I didn't realize Seamus had snuck out early. He wasn't with a woman, was he? He said he'd met someone."

Anna shook her head. "He hasn't been with any woman since Fiona."

"And he looked half-cut again after drinking all that vodka tonight," Ian put in.

"Seamus doesn't drink vodka. He used to drink whiskey, but not anymore." Clara touched her neck and asked haltingly, "Again? You've seen him out drinking?"

Ian kept his arm firmly around Anna. "Aye. We talked on several occasions at the local pubs this week and got along well."

"Seamus has an addictive personality, especially when he drinks and gambles, and one drink can easily lead to more." Clara chewed her bottom lip. "You must be mistaken about the vodka."

"Vodka is the drink of choice for an alcoholic because it's clear and can go undetected."

"Where would Seamus get the vodka? Did Danny—"

"The boss instructed no alcohol at your party," Ian said. "Your brother must've walked in with his own drink."

"Wait." Clara paused, letting the conversation lag as she rewound Ian's earlier remark. "How could you have seen Seamus in the local pubs? You were in Dublin this past fortnight." She narrowed her eyes. "Weren't you?"

Ian pulled at the collar of his beat-up leather jacket and shot Anna a helpless glance. "I have a terrible memory," he began. Ian yanked a roll of antacids from his pocket and dashed one in his mouth as Clara saw Danny approaching in ground-breaking strides. "Sometimes I lose my motorcycle and ..."

A knot was forming in Clara's stomach. "Surely you'd remember where you were all week." She whirled on Danny, feeling a swell of genuine wrath. "Your bodyguard's been following me, hasn't he?"

"Aye."

"Aye? Aye? You've all lied to me!" She whirled to her sister, but Danny stopped her with his hands on her forearms.

"I couldn't leave you alone in Farthing without my protection, Clara." He held her firmly. "Not until Jack Connor ..." His voice trailed off.

"I told you I could take care of the Jack Connor problem by myself."

Danny quirked a brow. "You haven't done a very good job. However—"

She flung off his hands and cut him off with an abrupt shake of her head. "Neither have you."

"I couldn't bear the thought of you possibly getting hurt.

Do you truly believe that I deserve your animosity for wanting to protect you?"

Slightly mollified, she replied, "I can take care of myself."

"Let's talk this out alone, all right? There's something I need to tell you." He looked around the room. Except for the four of them, the only people left were the waiters. He gave Ian and Anna a meaningful look, dismissed the waiters, and then gathered some empty plates and headed for the kitchen.

"We were about to leave, anyway," Anna said, grabbing her stilettos from Ian. As he went to retrieve her leather biker jacket and their motorcycle helmets, she spoke to Clara in a low voice.

"Don't be angry at Danny. He's an honorable man. And he loves you, and he declared it to all your guests tonight when he gave his toast."

"He quoted Oscar Wilde, whom he admires as much as Francis Bacon," Clara refuted. "I've been Danny's diversion while he's spent his working hours in Farthing opening another profitable business."

Anna scoffed. She took Clara's cold hands in her warm ones and nodded toward the kitchen. "You're wrong. Go to him."

Clara yanked her hands from Anna's grip. "Don't pass that yoke to me. I have little enough self-respect to salvage after what Jack Connor did to me. And I won't sacrifice any progress I've made these past two years to appease a billionaire businessman just because he's given me a surprise party."

Ian reappeared, assisted Anna with her jacket, and handed her a motorcycle helmet. "The rain has let up. We should head off."

Clara turned away from them, intending to tear down all the decorations and straighten Danny's flat. Then she'd extinguish the votive candles and fold the linens into a neat pile. And then she would walk home.

Anna's stern tone checked her in midstep. "You know that progress you refuse to sacrifice? That's what Danny admires most about you—your indomitable spirit. Go into the kitchen, apologize for your uncalled outburst, and thank him for arranging such a lovely party." With that, Anna tucked her hand into the crook of Ian's elbow and exited Danny's flat.

* * *

CLARA WALKED over to the cherry-wood credenza, piled high with an assortment of birthday gifts. So considerate of all the guests, she thought, examining each brightly colored tag. Every person had brought something, except for Seamus. Odd, considering their conversation in front of the coffee shop a few weeks prior.

I'd figured on walking to the city centre and buy you a gift with some of the money I earned. You've ruined my birthday surprise for ya by all your harping.

She fingered the exquisite diamond necklace around her neck.

For you, luv, Danny had said eagerly, a tender, expectant gleam in his eyes when she'd unwrapped his gift. *I hope you like it.*

With her sister's advice overriding her excuses, Clara silently counted to sixty. Tackling difficult discussions and admitting she was wrong didn't mean she'd lost control, she told herself.

She took a deep breath and joined Danny in his small, efficient kitchen. She noted his stiff back as he dried forks and spoons on a dishtowel.

Obviously aware of her presence, he turned and said, "Tea?"

Despite his rigid stance, his voice was gentle. He looked

tired, a weariness softening his handsome features. He'd been awake since dawn.

"Thanks." She smoothed her dress. "Look … When I—I realized that Ian had been following me and everyone had been lying, I overreacted. Jack lied many times and I always felt so hurt and defenseless when I found out the truth." She shook her head. "I was so gullible."

Danny's hand tightened on the dishtowel. "You're doing it again, daring to compare me to that monster."

"I'm not. Let me finish explaining."

"Your brother told me that your ex would beat you when he was drunk." Danny dropped the dishtowel on the counter. "Do I seem that type of man to you? Someone who would drink, and beat you, and manipulate you?"

"Of course not." She dug her nails into her palms and let a slow breath in and out of her lungs. "The reason you asked Ian to stay in Farthing was for my benefit."

Danny swerved to the sink and filled the electric kettle with water. When he curved back around to face her, his jaw was still tense. "I knew you were against the idea. However, your safety was more important to me."

She twisted her hands together. Her voice cracked. "Then afterward, Jack would apologize over and over until I'd relent and forgive him."

His cell phone in his pants pocket buzzed several times. He scowled.

She shifted. "Shouldn't you answer? The call might be important."

He slipped the phone from his pocket and glanced at it. "It's Aiden. He's busy doing whatever accountants do best. He can wait." Danny sent a quick text and shoved the phone back in his pocket. He gazed at her for a long while and his features softened. "My apologies for the interruption, Clara. Please continue."

She swallowed. Tears burned her throat. He always placed her needs above his own.

"I'm not used to a man being so kind to me and sometimes I don't know how to respond. I …" Her voice cracked again.

It was the closest justification she could offer. Danny would understand. He knew how difficult it was for her to apologize after dealing with Jack. She'd been so confused. After a while, she hadn't known what was wrong, what was right.

Danny didn't respond. Perhaps he wanted more. More of an apology, more awkward reasons that might only justify his anger. Or perhaps this entire argument gave him the opportunity to sever a break—from her, from her family, from Farthing.

He leaned against the kitchen counter and closed his eyes.

She waited, watching him, remembering his generosity, his thoughtfulness, and her defenses crumbled. Sadness and despair welled at the realization that he was leaving in a few hours and, if she didn't right her wrong, she might never see him again.

"I apologize," she said. "My reaction to your protection was unwarranted."

She lowered her guard because she trusted him and wanted to be close to him, leaving no emotional barriers between them. And if apologizing to a considerate and kind-hearted man made her vulnerable, so be it, because it was time to break loose from the damaging, traumatic chains that Jack had shackled around her.

Danny opened his eyes. Understanding, affection, and unmistakable desire smoldered in his gaze. "I accept your apology. And I was wrong, too, for being dishonest. I should've risked your anger and told you that Ian would be staying in Farthing to ensure your safety."

She smiled at him. "So you're afraid of my anger?"

"You put the heart crossway in me, especially when your eyes shoot daggers." With a chuckle, he brought her into his arms. His mouth came down ravenously on hers. She parted her lips to receive him and looped her arms around his neck, forming her body to his, softening against his solid form. When the kiss ended, he kept his arms around her.

Clara didn't move, protected in his embrace, feeling safe and secure and cherished.

He pressed his lips to her hair. "Your apology means so much to me."

She brushed a single tear from the corner of her eye. "I was afraid I'd open an emotional floodgate that I'd be power-less to stop, that I'd feel defenseless and out of control."

He cradled her in his arms. "And now?"

"I was wrong about that too."

And with that admission, she felt empowered, not defenseless.

He rested his cheek against her head and sighed. "It's late, and I should start preparing for my departure tomorrow morning. However, I'd like to continue our relationship long-distance." He lifted her chin and stared at her. "I hope you feel the same way."

She nodded.

"While I'll be traveling a great deal, I should have reason-able Internet connection, and we can talk by phone every evening. You know I'm a planner."

"I know."

"Are you willing?" he asked quietly.

Her throat clogged. She couldn't find her voice.

He cupped her chin. His blue eyes gleamed with purpose. "Long-distance relationships require a great deal of commit-ment. Network connections are spotty, plus I'll be circum-navigating language barriers, time changes and jet lag. If your schedule allows, perhaps you can meet me on occasion? I'll arrange and schedule your flights." He brushed his lips across hers. "I'll miss you too much if I don't see you every day."

Through happiness and unabashed tears, she managed, "I can't fly to a different country every day. However, I will try to see you as often as I can."

"What more can a man ask for?" Slowly, he bent his head, his mouth lingering over hers. Their breaths merged. His kiss was longer, primal, claiming her.

When he lifted his head, he said with a grin, "One of my international franchisees is in Rome. You can join me there and show me all the shops you pilfered. That is, *if* they're still in business." He waited for a beat, the teasing grin gone. "I also want to see your orphanage. Do you remember the town you were in?"

She shook her head. "My Irish mom said the town was close to the Egadi Islands. She may have mentioned Palermo. That town may be miles away from your coffee shop."

"No matter. We can fly there or take a train. I'll investigate. Also, we can research your long-lost Italian brother's whereabouts."

"I remember his name was Luciano." She ran her hand along the sleeves of Danny's sweater. "I don't know if my orphanage is there anymore, or if my adoption records are available."

"We'll find them. In addition, the weather will be warmer in Italy, which will help your breathing."

"Yeh." Because in that moment, she knew. She needed to be with him.

"That's it? You're agreeable?"

"I don't strike you as the agreeable type?"

He laughed and kissed her. "Good. Everything's settled." He drew out a copy of his itinerary from a kitchen drawer.

"Take this so that you can keep track of me. And I assume you'll be in Farthing, waiting for my return. The key word is that you'll be waiting for me." Although his tone was light, the heat from his smile warmed her blood.

Briefly, she closed her eyes, then smiled at him and nodded.

His cell phone buzzed, persistent, and Danny uttered a quiet Irish curse. His laughter had faded. "My business leaves me no peace," he muttered.

"Your business is a large part of your life."

"Too large a part, I'm beginning to realize."

An insistent knocking at the door drew a more colorful oath from him.

She pulled out of his arms and tucked his itinerary in her handbag. "Go. I'll follow. It must be important."

Danny stalked to the door and threw it open.

A disheveled Aiden raked a hand through a knot of his carrot-red hair. "I'm sorry to bother you, Mr. Brady."

"Perhaps I wasn't clear enough." Danny placed his hands on his hips. "I texted that I wasn't to be interrupted."

"My apologies, sir. Could you step into your board-room? Your computer files—there's an alarming discrepancy. The numbers don't add up—at least not accurately." Aiden, the bespectacled guy who was never rattled, was wiping his hands against the thighs of his pants as he spoke.

Standing behind Danny, Clara clasped her fingers and glanced outside as an explosion of hard rain hit the glass.

"Can't this wait?" Danny was asking Aiden.

"I was vetting all the payments, and one particular invoice did not go through the proper procedure," Aiden said.

"What's the name of the company?"

"RC Dougal Restaurant Supplies."

Danny scrubbed a hand over his face and hesitated. She

caught the hesitation before he said, "That's the name of the factory Clara works for."

Aiden shook his head. "The factory in town is RJ Dougal Restaurant Supplies."

"I don't understand," Clara murmured, willing her heart to stop racing.

"I suspect that your Farthing business account has been compromised, sir," Aiden continued, "I've summoned the Gardaí because this incident has all the makings of a cybercrime."

*a*iden and Danny hastened to the boardroom with Clara at their heels. Danny quickly took a seat at the computer desk while Clara and Aiden stood behind him.

"There, sir." Aiden leaned over Danny and pointed to the computer screen. "An invoice for the café in the amount of fifty thousand euros was submitted by RC Dougal Restaurant Supplies, and our accounting program paid it."

"Normal," Danny said.

"However, this payment did not go through the proper procedure. The banking information for this supposed company is not valid because the company doesn't exist."

Danny's fingers tightened around the computer mouse.

"At first, I assumed the money transfer was normal—"

Danny lifted his brows. "Transfer? To where?"

"Most likely to an existing hijacked account. All of this was done outside of normal banking hours. My assumption is so that it would go undetected. Did anyone else have access to your boardroom?" Aiden asked.

Danny frowned. "No. This room is always locked with a deadbolt."

"I checked the lock. It doesn't appear to have been broken." Aiden enunciated each word grimly. "What about your computer files, sir? Who has security access and password information?"

"No one except you and me." Danny clicked to another screen and said absently, "This Internet connection seems slow."

"Aye." Aiden's eyes narrowed through his thick glasses. "If someone took control of your computer from a remote location, both computers are connected. However, slipping in and out of the boardroom would have been easier *if* the hacker knew your account password. Then it's simply a matter of logging onto your computer and doing whatever you want. Like uploading a phony invoice from a flash drive and telling the accounting program to pay it."

"Who could have done this?" Danny tapped his fingers on his desk and glanced briefly in Clara's direction. "I changed my password a few weeks ago."

She stiffened. Her mind raced with possibilities. Had she mentioned to anyone that she suspected Danny had used her name in his new password? Anna? Seamus? Colum? Even so, he'd used a combination of characters for his password.

Still, was this entire incident somehow her fault?

She braced her hands on Danny's chair for support. Her knees had started quaking.

"An employee, perhaps, who's down on their luck?" Aiden was asking.

"I trust my employees with my life." Danny leaned back in his chair. "Ian, Kathleen, and several others have been with me since I started my first coffee shop. I only hired one new employee, a dishwasher, within the past couple of weeks." Danny lifted his gaze to Clara. Under his breath, he asked, "Any thoughts on this matter?"

"Thoughts?" she echoed, surprised that she'd managed to

keep her tone composed and reasonable. Very softly, very carefully, she asked. "Perhaps your computer has a virus?"

"A computer virus can't lift fifty thousand euros from a business account," Aiden said sharply.

Of course, she realized that. And through her mounting apprehension came one adamant denial: Seamus, Danny's notable and newest hire, couldn't possibly be at fault, no matter if all the evidence in the world pointed to him.

Her dear brother had lost his beloved wife, and then had turned to alcohol and gambling for consolation. That was understandable. Everyone made missteps and needed a second chance. With the help of his loving family, he was slowly piecing his life together. Hadn't he seemed more upbeat lately? The job at the coffee shop had given him self-respect, as she had hoped. Besides, if Seamus was hiding any illicit, secretive activities, she would know. He lived with her, and, for the most part, she knew his whereabouts. Furthermore, her brother was a chatterbox who couldn't keep anything to himself. A cybercrime took advanced, careful expertise.

Through the boardroom's window, flashing red lights from the street below brought her rioting thoughts under control.

Danny, Clara, and Aiden leaned forward and peered out. Under a sky filled with angry, ragged clouds, two Gardaí stepped from a patrol car. One of the men looked retirement age; the other was stout with a fringe of brown bangs. They both wore peaked hats and formal uniforms and swung their nightsticks in unison. Opening identical black umbrellas to protect themselves from the heavy rain, they marched briskly up the steps to the coffee shop. Clara's heart beat more slowly with each of their quick strides.

* * *

CLARA CHECKED HER WATCH, noting that it was well past midnight. A long, excruciating hour had passed. She stood to the side as the stout garda--his name was Jimmy Doherty--squinted at Danny's computer screen, while the older garda went over a report with Aiden. This was Danny's world, where staggering sums of money were invested.

Garda Doherty leaned forward to get a closer look at the security camera's video feed. "Nothing is showing on the DVR for the night of March eighteenth. The adapter, cable, and power port seem to be working."

"Then how could there be no feed?" Aiden asked.

"It may have been cut off." Doherty unbuttoned the top silver button of his black jacket. "Did the coffee shop experience a power outage?"

"Not that I was made aware of," Danny answered.

Clara glanced at him. He stood to the right of his computer desk, his features drawn. His replies had been thorough and composed as he'd answered unending questions. All the while, he'd seemed to be moodily contemplating the situation and never met her gaze. Exhaustion, she'd decided. He'd been awake for almost twenty-four hours and had to catch an early plane to London.

"It doesn't look as if anyone broke into the boardroom," Aiden commented.

The older garda returned to the door and inspected the lock. "The doorframe hasn't been forced in and the deadbolt doesn't show indications of being visibly tampered. We'll send a locksmith out tomorrow to be certain. Might've been a professional break-in. These types of thieves are savvy and don't usually leave a trace. The chief constable will want to have a look too."

"An extra set of keys to the boardroom went missing recently and haven't been found." Danny rubbed a hand through his hair. "Regardless, someone hacked into my computer files. And my email. And my online identities."

"Happens all the time, sir. We'll report it as a cybercrime," Doherty replied.

Clara concentrated on his shiny black boots, the silver buttons of his somber uniform that seemed ready to burst around his thick waistline, his fringe of thick brown bangs.

A recollection flickered. Wasn't he the garda who had arrested her the night she and Jack had attempted to steal money from Clara's friends, the Murphys?

She shuddered. Garda Doherty had hauled her to the dank, cramped cell and locked her in. The peeling blood-red paint and sharp walls had reminded her of the suffocating closet she'd been locked in all those years ago at the orphanage.

She fingered the cold stones of the diamond necklace around her neck. "Computer hacking is a crime?" she asked.

"Aye, and punishable with a fine and imprisonment from one to twenty years." He tipped his head. With a dawning look of recollection, he asked, "You're Clara Donovan?"

She chewed her bottom lip and nodded.

"It seems as if I've seen a lot of *you* these past couple of years." He spoke loudly, bluntly emphasizing the word *you*. He caught the older garda's gaze, who lifted his brows in amused derision.

Danny turned a questioning look on Doherty. "Where? When her brother was in prison?"

"Ask her. The Murphys are such nice people."

With a curt nod to the men, Danny drew Clara into the hallway and closed the door behind them. "Am I missing something?"

"Is this an interrogation?"

"It's simply a question demanding an answer. Who are the Murphys?"

181

She paused. His abrupt demand fired her indignation. "I told you to check the past copies of the Farthing newspaper."

"I obviously haven't had time to be going through old newspapers."

She threw him a scathing look to match her tone. "Why not? Because you've wasted so much time in Farthing around me and my family? Sorry that we've become such a burden to an important man like you." She whirled, intending to walk away.

He grabbed her by the forearm and angled her to face him. "Clara, what did the garda mean?"

She thrust her hands against his chest, forcing a space between them. "He was in the patrol car the night Jack Connor shoved me."

"Jack did more than shove you, so don't cover up for him."

"I'm not. I—"

"And that incident didn't happen two years ago." Danny released her forearm so suddenly that she reeled. "So tell me what everyone seems to know except me."

She took a deep, pained breath and closed her eyes, torn between indecision and decisiveness. *Help me to be forthright,* she prayed, before realizing that the person she was praying to was Danny. He was compassionate, and kindhearted, and possessed an integrity and empathy rarely found in a person. He of all people would understand.

She could lean on him, be honest with him, trust him, because …

Dear saints in heaven. Because she loved him.

She could scarcely move because of the realization. Her heart filled to bursting. Had her deep feelings been there all the while, tamped down by her shame, her denials, her struggle to be totally self-sufficient?

She'd told herself that she and Danny had grown close

because of the traumatic events they'd shared. Yes, they'd become good friends. She cared a great deal about him.

She fought the impulse to grab his hand and declare her love.

She didn't. Instead, she fastened her gaze on his face, taking reassurance from his calm expression.

Cautiously, she began answering his question. "A couple years ago, I stole money from my friends, the Murphys. They own a furniture store in town. Jack had convinced me that we needed the money for the rent and that we would repay them." She swallowed, the memories pressing so close that her ribs felt squeezed together. "I was so nervous that I stumbled out of the store while the burglar alarm was going off. I lost one of my shoes and dropped my purse when I started running. And what I did was so very, very wrong." She trembled. The sound of Jack's drunken, high-pitched laugh still sounded in her ears.

Danny's blue eyes were inscrutable. "You knew it was wrong and you still went along with Jack's scheme? The Murphys were your friends."

She flinched at the sting in his tone. "Before the robbery, Jack had assured me that the Murphys were rich and would never miss the money. He said they'd never suspect me because I was 'their charming and honest friend.'" She squeezed her eyes shut, humiliated and furious at herself. And the shame, always the shame.

Why had she believed Jack? She'd been in a daze when she'd been with him, constantly responding to his demands as he manipulated and altered her beliefs. As a result, she'd lost sight of her own values. And, in ironic hindsight, he hadn't cared about the rent. He'd wanted the money for his drink and drugs.

The older garda opened the boardroom door. "Do you want to press charges if we pick up any suspects, sir?"

"Absolutely," Danny said. "Whoever did this will pay for their crime."

"Can you both step into the room in case we have any further questions?"

Danny nodded. His expression had changed from alarm, to anger, to carefully neutral. And he hadn't commented on her admission.

As the men formed a conclave in the boardroom, Clara pressed a hand to her forehead. Fifty thousand euros was an astronomical sum. No one in Farthing would ever be able to reimburse that amount of money.

In a swish of ruby-red silk, she sank onto the espresso-colored leather couch. She eyed the doorway, noting that Danny's fern needed watering. Plus, the magazines on the coffee table were in disarray. She'd neatly sort the pile and then water the fern. Surely, there was a sink and watering can somewhere.

However, her nerves were playing havoc. Deciding that she couldn't sort, or water, she laced her shaking fingers on her lap. Listening to the men's muted voices, she closed her eyes.

When she heard Danny say thank you to the Gardaí and *slán* to Aiden, she opened her eyes. He came to the sofa and took a seat beside her.

"How are you faring?" he asked. "You must be exhausted."

"Not as exhausted as you, I'm sure. What time do you leave in the morning?"

"Seven." He pulled his phone from his pocket and texted someone. "I'll sleep on the plane."

"Don't you need to go to Dublin first?"

"Aye." He snapped his phone shut and slipped it into his pocket. "Ian will drive me. He just left your sister's flat and is on his way here. He'll take you home. He can use my car."

"You're … you're not taking me home?"

"I have a lot to wrap up before I leave. Aiden is contacting a few of my accounting and computer employees. They'll be changing and safeguarding all my computer accounts after this hacking."

She tried to swallow and had difficulty. "That's understandable, considering you'll be gone for several months."

He hadn't smiled, hadn't wrapped an arm around her, hadn't so much as met her gaze. His manner was coolly polite, as if he was speaking to an acquaintance, someone he had little interest in conversing with.

His gaze shifted to his watch, and he rose. Without a word, he walked over to the picture window. Despite the hour and steady downpour, the town was aglow with corner streetlamps and bustling pubs, typical for a Saturday night in Ireland.

With his back to her, he stared out at the rain for a long while. He was so still, she wondered for a moment if he were breathing.

His cashmere sweater fit his broad form splendidly. He was athletic, commanding. He was a man who would always succeed, able to carry any burden weighing down on his strong shoulders.

Although the boardroom was warm and brightly lit, an unsettling chill settled over the room. With a determined lift of her chin, she decided to venture into the deafening silence. They only had a few minutes before Ian arrived.

"Are you angry at me for some reason?" Despite her resolve, she heard the tremor in her voice.

He swung around. Anguish and hopefulness, two contradictory emotions, flickered across his face. He rubbed the back of his neck. "Should I be angry? Angry at you?"

"No, unless you've suddenly grown an aversion to celebrations and sur-surprise birthday parties." She hadn't meant to stammer. And she'd spoken louder than she'd intended.

He didn't seem to notice. Instead, he expelled a long sigh. His sharp gaze seemed to pierce through her, and she directed her own gaze at the rain spitting against the window. She kept her head high, her chin determinedly set. And she waited, although she wasn't sure what she was waiting for.

"Clara, where was your brother last evening?"

She heard her own sharp intake of breath. Danny's voice was so implacably calm.

Very deliberately, she shook the wrinkles from her silk dress and stood. "You know where he was. He spent the day working in your hot kitchen and attended my surprise party."

"I meant last evening. March eighteenth."

"I don't know. I'm trying not to nag Seamus about his whereabouts because he gets furious when I do."

Frantically, she sifted through her memory. Seamus had gone out to settle a car deal on March 17, St. Patrick's Day. And tonight, March 19, was accounted for. Her mind was in turmoil as she tried to recollect the day in between. Hadn't Seamus said that he was working on March 18?

A vision of her brother from two years ago, strong-willed and protective, a sprinkle of reddish-brown bristles along his chin, flashed in her memory. He'd safeguarded her from Jack Connor so bravely.

And then another image from a few weeks past. Seamus, his mouth twisted in hopeless despair, that heart-wrenching night atop Farthing Bridge when he'd contemplated suicide.

"It's better if I end my life. I'm on me tod, I'm all alone," Seamus had sobbed.

"You mentioned that Seamus was buying a car," Danny was saying. "Where did he get the money?"

"He said it was a private deal. Why? There's no crime in a man buying an old banger of a car to get around. It's further proof that he's exchanging his bad choices for good ones."

She could see the conflict in the set of Danny's jaw as he stepped forward, his tall form seeming to loom over her. Automatically, she stepped back before changing her mind and standing her ground.

He put one hand on her arm. "I don't believe that Seamus pulled off a cybercrime from a remote computer location. He must have either stolen the key to the deadbolt from Ian when the keys went missing, or broken into the boardroom. Somehow, he managed to avoid the security camera."

"How dare you accuse my brother!" Angrily, she shrugged off Danny's hand. "Seamus would never do such a terrible thing and steal money right out from under you. You're his employer and his new job is the main reason he's finally beginning to respect himself. You saw him tonight at my party. Did he look like a criminal to you?"

"Did you talk with him?"

"No. Although I wanted to, I never had the chance."

"Because he was probably avoiding you. He was buzzed on vodka most of the night."

She didn't speak as a glacial blast of silence encased them.

"Unfortunately," Danny finally said quietly, "I may be forced to press charges against Seamus, now that Aiden and the Gardaí are privy to so much information."

White static went through her brain, a forewarning of impending disaster. She knew that he might suspect Seamus, and had half expected his questions. However, she hadn't expected his unsympathetic confrontation and accusation, and a fierce wave of protectiveness for her brother rose in her.

In quiet defiance, she repeated, "My brother is not a thief."

Danny looked away, seeming to mentally review the

evidence. "Perhaps he's been gambling again. Perhaps he was desperate."

She bristled. "He has no reason to be desperate. He lives with me and we share the cost of his food and I charge no rent. Plus, one of the reasons he's buying a car is so that I won't have to use public transportation to travel to and from work anymore. Please." She reached out and touched Danny's sleeve. "Seamus is kind and considerate and generous. We all go through hard times and he's made a remarkable recovery. He's vowed that he isn't gambling anymore. And, emotionally, he wouldn't be able to survive being hauled into a garda station for questioning."

"And I have a cyber nightmare ahead of me. The need for all these fixes will impede the smooth flow of my businesses as the computer system is being changed and upgraded. Not to mention the money taken—"

"It's all about the money for you. Not about people, nor their lives, nor their hardships. And—"

He interrupted with an ironic laugh. "Despite what you may think, I don't care about the money."

She almost lost her determination to continue. However, Danny had shown her that persistence paid off, and *that* realization gave her resolve.

"You care about being a winner." She stiffened her stance, meeting his cool gaze with as much confidence as she could muster. "You're so driven. And for what? Coffee? Can't you be satisfied with all that you've already accomplished? You *are* successful. You don't need any more money or international franchises to prove that."

In the glare of the overhead florescent lights, she saw the fury, then sadness, emanating from him. They were standing so close, within arm's reach, yet so far away. She dropped her hand.

"You don't understand," he said softly.

"Help me to understand."

A heavy-booted stride had them glancing toward the hallway. Ian had undoubtedly arrived.

Clara started for the door. "I'll get my things from your flat."

"I told Ian to retrieve your gifts and personal belongings and pack everything into my car."

She pressed back the tears threatening to flood her eyes. "You're quite efficient," she managed to say. "Of course, you're an entrepreneur, and all your jobs and appointments must be completed on schedule."

He jerked, then said curtly, "Aye, they must."

She swiped a tear that had managed to trickle down her cheek. Surely, he would take her in his arms and reassure her that this was all a grave misunderstanding.

At first he didn't move. He folded his arms, seemed to think better of it, and stepped forward. Lightly, he placed both hands on her shoulders. Any hint of the sparkling, teasing gaze she'd come to treasure had long disappeared from his eyes.

"Clara."

She stared up at him, at the persistent pulse drumming at his temple. Hesitantly, she laid a hand against his cheek. "Please, don't do this to Seamus, to us." She felt more tears, made no attempt to wipe them. "Please. I love—"

He shook his head, effectively stopping her from continuing.

"I must ask you one more question," he said. "This is difficult for me. Please understand that I have no choice." He blew out a ragged breath. He couldn't quite meet her gaze. "Clara, where were you the evening of March eighteenth?"

CHAPTER 18

*S*he visibly whitened as his words registered. And Danny knew, having asked the question he didn't want to ask, shouldn't have asked, that she'd never forgive him.

He wasn't prepared, however, for the sharp crack of her hand against his jaw.

"You think it was me? You think I was the one who hacked into your computer and stole your precious money?" She reared back and hurled a curse at him. "How dare you? You are nothing but a wastrel, a no-good bowsie who only thinks about himself!"

She lifted her arm, ready to strike him again.

He grabbed her hand. "Of course I don't think it was you. I think it was your conniving brother who coerced you into committing this crime."

"Did I waltz past your fancy security surveillance camera, your always devoted barista, Kathleen, plus shut the power to your entire shop so that I could steal fifty thousand euros?"

He shrugged with an indifference he didn't feel. "If anyone could pull off a crime like that, you could."

Her eyes widened in confusion. "Because I stole from some shops when I was five years old?"

"You're conveniently forgetting your crime from a couple of years ago."

Her lips parted and she blinked rapidly. "My crime? My *crime*, like I'm some sort of hardened criminal? I never ended up stealing any money from the Murphys, and I served my night in jail." She visibly shuddered and rubbed her hands up and down her arms as if to warm herself. "My crime was splashed on the front page of the Farthing newspaper and I felt such shame afterward. Wasn't that punishment enough for my foolish mistake? Or would you prefer that I serve my sentence for a lifetime?"

"Of course not." He released his grip on her wrist. His gaze raked her features, searching for guilt. He saw only her anguished expression and her trembling chin; heard her soft sobs. And in that instant, he knew that no matter how much misguided devotion she felt for her brother, she would never have taken part in Seamus's misdeeds.

Danny swallowed the unaccustomed tightness in his throat. "I'm sorry, luv."

She was sobbing harder now.

"I'm … I'm sorry. I—I didn't mean to sound so harsh. It's late." His excuses were hollow, because there were no excuses.

He watched her exquisite features crumple, and his heart seemed to crumple too. Her shiny hair had fallen from its upsweep, tumbling in waves around her face.

She twisted from him, her shoulders shaking. She was crying, and she didn't want him to see. She was so proud, had fought so hard to break free from her shameful past. And he was driving her away, just as he'd driven away everyone he had ever loved with his harsh judgments.

Instinctively, he placed a hand on her shoulder. "Luv,

please don't cry. I never meant to hurt you. I'm not thinking straight. I'll make it up to you. I'll buy you—"

"Don't touch me." She shrugged him off. "Don't ever touch me again. Don't ever come near me or my family. We don't need you, your posh gifts ..." She whirled, unfastened the diamond necklace around her throat and threw it on his computer desk as if the stones were filthy.

He ached to take her in his arms and absorb the hurt he had caused with his terrible charge. He wanted to thread his fingers through her hair, kiss her nape, inhale the fresh, lemony scent of her. "Please, keep it. I picked it out in London especially for you. It's my birthday gift."

She tightened her fists at her sides. "I don't want anything from you." Her voice was fainter, her tone broken.

"Seamus coerced you," he said quietly, trying to talk reasonably. "He's obviously off the rails."

"No. He lives with me, we have long chats." She drew in a shaky breath. "He wouldn't need fifty thousand euros."

"Gambling debts add up quickly, and unscrupulous men may have pushed Seamus to the brink of desperation. And, if you'd be honest with yourself concerning your brother for longer than ten seconds, you'd realize that Seamus has had a lot of extra time and money unaccounted for."

"People fall ... people fail ... Everyone deserves a second chance. He's doing well, has a job ..."

"Your brother has perfected the art of persuading you to feel sorry for him. It's time he stood on his own two feet without you making excuses for him every inch of the way."

She cut him off. "He said he was working and saving his money. He said—"

"And I'm his employer, and I can say for certain that he's hardly put in one full day of work since he was hired."

"Seamus leaves my flat at the same time every day."

"And where he goes is anyone's guess. My guess is liquor

and gambling." With a heavy sigh, Danny looked up at the ceiling. "Clara, please. At least, entertain the thought that Seamus may have committed this crime."

She shook her head. "No."

A click of boots in the hallway was followed by a knock on the door.

Ian entered the boardroom quietly. Working an antacid around in his mouth, he kept his gaze on Danny while handing Clara her raincoat. "I'm warming the car, boss, and ready to return Clara to her flat."

"Not yet, Ian." Clara lifted her hand and turned to Danny. "You've forgotten about Jack. It could easily have been him. He's stolen plenty of times. He gambles. He drinks."

She waited until Danny met her gaze. Everything grew quiet.

Danny drew in a heavy breath and released it before he spoke. "Clara, that's what I've wanted to tell you all evening and I haven't had the chance. Since the Gardaí haven't been any help, I hired a private detective to follow Jack Connor. He was picked up a few days ago near Dublin."

Her hands went to her face. "What was Jack doing in Dublin?"

"Apparently, he was trying to get to me," Danny said, half to himself. "Aiden said the money lifted from my Farthing account occurred on March eighteenth and Jack wasn't anywhere near Farthing. He's been locked in county Dublin prison the past three days for violating parole."

* * *

DANNY STOOD by the window in his flat. He'd abandoned the task of sorting files, leaving the computer fixes to his experts. For him, the burden was emotional. He felt violated.

Someone had accessed his online information, which he considered private.

Silently, he replayed his last scenes with Clara before he finally shut down his computer. She'd hardly bidden him a civil good-bye, even when he'd assured her that he wouldn't press charges against her brother, although he would be forced to dismiss Seamus from the dishwasher job. He'd also offer Seamus a month-long compensation in wages.

She'd said nothing in return, silently assessing him and then requesting that he never contact her again. He'd insisted she take the diamond necklace because it was a gift, and she'd reluctantly placed the necklace in the pocket of her raincoat. Then he'd watched her walk away. Her spine had been straight, her chin held high.

Her unconquerable spirit had been ever-present, even when he'd charged her with theft. He kept envisioning her in that silky dress, its deep red color enhancing the creamy olive tones of her flawless skin, her silver earrings glinting in the overhead lights. She'd been enraged, her face heated, her hand raised, ready to strike him a second time. She'd resembled a stormy, outraged goddess.

And she'd never looked so irresistibly gorgeous.

He walked down the hall to his flat and fixed a cup of tea. Clara's lemon scone recipe, written in her scholarly scroll, sat on the kitchen counter. He'd shared the recipe with his bakers and kept her hand-written recipe for himself.

He stared at it and sighed. He wasn't certain what made him more furious—his infatuation with her, or his inability to concentrate whenever she was near. He was in his thirties, considered one of the most successful businessmen in all Ireland, and she'd trimmed him down to staring at a lemon scone recipe.

Somewhere along the path of his disillusioned, cynical life, Clara Donovan had taken the eye out of his head. He'd been smitten with her, a part-time dance teacher who lived in a small town that he hadn't even known existed. Despite the turbulence surrounding their relationship, he had enjoyed every minute of their time together. He'd started to dream that their moments together could last forever.

He wet his tea and added a great deal of cream to cool it. He sipped. Still too damn hot. He shook his head.

He'd seen what he'd wanted to see—a life with his precious Clara. He loved her desperately. And now, somehow, he needed to come to grips with the fact that her engaging smile, her eternal optimism, was gone from his life.

He carried his steaming tea to the living room and stood at the window, looking down at the street. Rain bore down endlessly, beating against the cobblestone sidewalks. The roads were rapidly becoming infinite lakes of grey, mud-spattered water.

He took a dull swallow of tea, quelling the urge to ring Clara, closing his eyes to memorize every detail of her exquisite features—as well as her wit and her jaunty smile. For he knew, he'd never see her again.

With a rough sigh, he shoved away from the window and set his cup on the cherry credenza. He'd instructed Ian to return before dawn so that they would reach Dublin by early morn.

He should be packing, Danny's practical side insisted. Six months of travel was a long time. Instead, his gaze canvassed the remnants from Clara's birthday party. The green balloons were sinking. The slices of apples had browned, and the strawberries smelled unpleasantly pungent. Kelly-green confetti littered every inch of the cream carpeting.

If she'd seen it, Clara would have begun straightening the mess immediately. Except that Clara wouldn't ever know, because she wasn't standing beside him.

With a vicious jerk, Danny tore the festive streamers

from the lampshades and threw them on the floor. This was all her brother's fault. He'd been a dark cloud, hovering above every moment of Danny's relationship with Clara. He was the painful trigger, and Danny resented Seamus more and more. Seamus's drinking and gambling, his resultant lies, had set off this devastating chain of events.

Why did people—his parents, Seamus—act the way they did and not overcome their addictions? He didn't know. He just knew that Clara was still crying when she left.

On his way to his bedroom to begin packing, Danny picked up several discarded napkins. *The Ground Café* was proudly stamped on each, along with the recognizable pot of gold logo.

"Always the businessman, yeh?" Clara had said, grinning while she'd sat in his car and dabbed at her eyes, the night Jack Connor shoved her.

Or when she'd sat pertly, engrossed in *Entrepreneur* magazine, a frown of concentration on her beautiful face. She'd mentioned her hope to someday open a dance studio in town, and that she required money for expenses.

Danny crushed the napkins in his hands. His mouth twisted. Perhaps Seamus had convinced her that they would split the fifty thousand euros so that she could open her own business. After all, Jack had convinced her to steal from the friends.

Danny threw the crushed napkins in the wastebasket.

No.

His exquisite Clara would never have stolen from him, certainly not for her own gain. Moreover, he'd offered the money outright to open her business. She'd looked him straight in the eye and refused his offer.

Women couldn't be trusted, a small voice argued in his sleep-deprived brain. Hadn't his ex-wife, Kyla, proven that? Women wanted him for his wealth, the prestige of dating an up-and-coming billionaire. No woman wanted him for himself.

Except for his Clara. She'd been furious at his deception when she'd found out his real identity that first day at the coffee shop. The bittersweet memory made his heart skip a beat. He'd vowed that he wouldn't fall in love, because love had no place in his demanding, stressful life.

But he had. He'd fallen in love with a magnificent, tenacious woman who saw the good in everyone. Once, he'd dreamed about marriage to a woman like her, settling down in a small town, having children.

Restlessly, he paced the soundless room which no longer radiated with her disarming humor and jaunty animation. Hours earlier, she'd chatted and laughed, her splendid silk dress rustling gracefully as she'd engaged with her guests. Now she'd walked out of his life.

And with her departure, he felt empty.

Perhaps the mellowing effect of the rain against the window was why he'd slumped on the couch and eventually closed his eyes. He awoke to the harsh sound of Ian knocking on his flat door. He opened his eyes with a start and gazed out the window. Dawn was streaking across the early morning sky.

"Ready, boss?" Ian stepped in and peered at Danny. "I'll drive. You look terrible."

"Thanks," Danny said wryly. As quickly as he could, he packed his bags and briefcase, and then went to the kitchen and grabbed Clara's hand-written recipe, putting it in the inside pocket of his sport jacket. He'd have just enough time to shower in Dublin before boarding the plane for London.

"Remove the Francis Bacon painting and deliver it to my home in Howth," he instructed Ian as they passed the watercolor in the hallway. "And instruct Kathleen to return to my Dublin shop by the end of the week, then meet me in Italy.

She wants to work there a few months and brush up on her Italian, because she met some Italian guy online. I assume you'll be in Farthing a while longer to look after the coffee shop?"

"Aye. Anna lives here." Ian bent a thoughtful eye toward Danny. "Does that mean you won't be returning to Farthing, boss?"

"Never again will I set foot in Farthing."

The men rode the lift to the main floor of the coffee shop in silence.

He wouldn't look back, Danny told himself. He wouldn't look back.

Mist swirled around him as he stepped outside. He slid into the passenger seat of his silver Mercedes and Ian took the wheel. As the car glided through rain-slicked streets, Danny snapped open his briefcase and leafed through a stack of documents, looking for the paperwork he'd need in London. Only once did he peer out the window to admire the early sun rising against a crimson sky. The way the sun filtered through tawny clouds signaled an end to the rain, at least for a day or so. Clara wouldn't need to worry about a downpour when she walked to the bus stop.

The quaint town of Farthing was Clara's town. It had never been his town, just as she had never been his damsel in distress, because she hadn't been the one in distress. In the end, he'd needed her more than she'd needed him.

Muttering an Irish curse, Danny extracted his gold pen and a pad of white paper featuring The Ground Café logo from his briefcase. He ignored Ian's brutal set-down that he get some sleep before he collapsed from exhaustion.

"I am so exasperated," he said, shaking his head. "So frustrated with Seamus. Doesn't Clara see he's the problem? He's impossible. He's an addict. Why doesn't he change his behavior?"

"Perhaps you can't change him," Ian said softly. "Perhaps you can only change yourself."

"What's that supposed to mean?"

Ian's sigh was polite. He added a small shrug.

With unswerving determination, Danny wrote up a formal deed, including instructions to draft a check to Clara Donovan in the amount of thirty thousand euros. On a separate sheet, he added a note: "Per our agreement, this check is for your lemon scone recipe, and to assist Seamus in repaying his gambling debts. It is my hope that you enjoyed our time together as much as I did."

He hesitated. She would probably be furious when she received the check. However, the thought of her struggling each day to make ends meet was intolerable. If, by God's good grace, her brother actually stayed on the rails, then Clara wouldn't need to keep bailing him out of debt, and she could use the funds to make her life more comfortable. She deserved this check, and so much more.

He folded the papers, instructing Ian to get them to his solicitor in Dublin and tell him to draft the check to Clara immediately.

"The funds may take a wee bit longer to clear because of the cybercrime and resultant investigation," Ian reminded him.

With a clipped acknowledgement, Danny shoved the deed and note in an envelope, sealed it, and placed the envelope on the dashboard. Leaning his head against the leather seat of his Mercedes, he resisted the impulse to rip the envelope open and write the words to Clara that were in his heart:

"Please, luv, can we start again? I'm sorry for my hurtful accusation. It was so wrong. This wasn't the way I wanted your birthday celebration to end. If I can take you in my arms once more, I promise I'll brighten every hour of your life with love and laughter. I'll make it up to you. We can visit Italy together, the Egadi Islands, and you can show me ..."

No.

Danny discovered that he could swear fluently in Gaelic. Disregarding Ian's scowl, he reached for the documents in his briefcase that he'd neglected. He'd plunge himself into the minutest of details involving each franchise in Europe and America, thereby occupying every second of his waking hours with one mission in mind.

Forgetting Clara.

CHAPTER 19

*A*s the following week went by, Clara found that she could sometimes go an hour or two without thinking about Danny. Anna knew better than to mention him, or her new waitressing job at the coffee shop, or Ian, for that matter, although Clara knew that Ian was still in Farthing.

Gradually, Clara was finding a quiet stability in her routine, although her eyes were continuously red from crying and her heart was broken. Danny had called every day, his caller ID flashing across the screen of her cell phone. She'd refused to pick up the phone. She'd told him not to contact her, but he made his own rules. Besides, she didn't want to risk speaking with him, fearing that she'd burst into tears before she was able to utter a word.

In her flat one damp, grey evening, she lit a fire in the hearth. On impulse, because she missed hearing Danny's voice, she played his CD, the one he'd given her from the coffee shop.

His soft Irish ballad brought her to her knees, and she wept so hard that she feared she might never stop. When there were no more sobs left inside her, she stared at the cheery fire in the hearth and forced herself to stand. Her throat ached as she vowed she would never cry for him again. She was self-reliant, dependent solely on herself. Stiffly, she placed the CD in its case and tucked it in the bottom of her bedroom bureau.

To make matters worse, Seamus had grown more diffi-cult. Since losing his job at the coffee shop, his temperament had been surprisingly mellow. That is, until he erupted in anger and aggression because of something she'd uninten-tionally said. He'd blame her, and she'd apologize. Somehow, his mood changes were always her fault.

He slept in most mornings, often waking famished, and constantly sipped from a coffee thermos. Despite his overeating, he seemed to be rapidly losing weight and spent a great deal of time in the bathroom.

Her workweek ended with the same routine she'd estab-lished before she'd met Danny: walking to her preschool dance class. The days were getting longer, and for a change, the twilight sky was devoid of clouds. The warmer weather had soothed her cough, and her disposition lifted with each step. Teaching dance gave her such delight and took her mind from her melancholy. If only she could do it full-time. She so enjoyed her young students' energy and imagination, their bright-eyed sparkles of giggle.

When she arrived at the dance studio, Colum O'Brien stood in the middle of the rehearsal room amidst seven active preschoolers.

"Who can jump on one foot all the way to the barre?" he was asking.

A freckle-faced little boy hop-scotched to the ballet mirror and made a funny face, while another ran in rapid circles around Colum.

Giving Clara a wave, Colum wiped his sweaty brow and

declared, "I am so relieved you are here, Miss Donovan. Things were getting a wee bit chaotic."

"My pleasure, Mr. O'Brien," she returned with a laugh. "Children, let's join hands and sing our good-bye song. Show me how *slowly* you can move."

When the parents entered several minutes later, Clara hugged each departing child. Afterward, Colum perched his slim hip on the reception desk and silently applauded. "One would think that a grown man with over twenty years of professional dance training and experience could handle a group of four-year-olds," he said.

Clara grinned. "The key is structure. Children like routine, including a clear beginning, middle and end."

"I prefer teaching adults. At least they listen to my instructions." Colum grabbed his parka. "After that energetic class, I need a smoke."

"I thought you were quitting?"

"Next week." He dug around in his pocket and drew out a cigarette and lighter. "Can we chat?"

"Sure. My class doesn't begin for another hour."

They made their way to the front stoop.

While cars whizzed by, Colum assessed her with an astute, green-eyed gaze. "So, I enjoyed your birthday party," he said, a bit too pacifyingly.

The slight wind burned her puffy eyes and sent the hood of her jacket fluttering behind her. She jammed her hands in her pockets. "Thanks. Everyone seemed to have a good time."

"Your Brady fellow worked hard to pull off the surprise. He wanted each detail to be perfect and rang nearly everyone himself, making them promise to keep your party a secret."

She stared fixedly at a rut in the road and pinched her lips together.

Colum paused, seeming at a loss for words, and blew a ring of smoke in the air. "I caught one of his interviews on television the other night. He was leaving London and flying to ..."

"Spain," she provided. She'd memorized Danny's itinerary. "And before you ask, he won't be returning to Farthing."

"So I've heard." Colum scowled, then patted her shoulder. "If you ever want to talk about what happened, I'll be happy to listen. I like Danny Brady. He's a good chap."

She bent her head, attempting to dull the longing she felt whenever she heard Danny's name.

Colum was so understanding. Their friendship made her want to babble, to tell him that her heart had been shattered, but the words lodged in her throat.

"Danny's doing what he does best," she replied tonelessly. "He's making a fortune and—"

Colum checked her words. "He rang me this week. He wants to talk to you. He said he's called you numerous times and you haven't picked up."

"He never left a message."

"A hollow excuse and you know it." Colum waved one hand in the air. "You can't resolve a disagreement by not speaking to one another. Mr. Brady and I enjoyed a lengthy chat the night of your party, and he couldn't take his eyes off you the whole while. It was obvious that he's in love with you. In my opinion, his love is so strong that even *he* doesn't recognize it." Bleakly, Colum smiled. "Judging by the shuttered look in your eyes every time his name is mentioned, you feel the same way about him."

"He's undoubtedly regretting the day he ever met me." Ruefully, Clara dragged her thoughts away from her first meeting with Danny at the bottom of Farthing Bridge. "He came to our town for one reason, the successful opening of his fiftieth coffee shop."

Colum's forehead knit into a frown. "Don't fault him for

his ambition. Recently, I read a magazine article featuring an account of his early years and his very difficult upbringing. He's accomplished everything on his own."

She rolled her eyes. She wasn't in the mood to extoll Danny's virtues. "As a result, his priorities are expensive homes and cars and his precious money. Not people. Not—"

Before she could finish, a yellow taxi pulled to the curb. Madame Sophie stepped out, scowled at the cigarette dangling from Colum's fingers, and marched to the stoop. Neatly installing her matronly form between Clara and Colum, Madame Sophie adjusted her hip-length kimono wrap and greeted them.

"Good. I need to speak with both of you." She peered over yellow reading glasses at Clara. "Ms. Donovan, your teaching this year has been—"

"I'll pack my things," Clara broke in, blindly grabbing Colum's arm for support. Her feelings were raw, and two letdowns within a few days would undo her. Wildly, she rehearsed how she was going to accept the fact that Madame Sophie was firing her in front of Colum without running down the street like a blubbering fool.

"Ms. Donovan, your teaching this year has been exemplary," Madame Sophie finished. "So, I loathe being the person to break bad news on such short notice. However, I'm closing the dance studio at the end of March. We can't afford to make ends meet and I'm retiring gracefully."

"Which means that both Clara and I will be losing our jobs in less than a week." Colum's ruddy complexion turned so ashen, Clara feared he might get sick. Already, he was reaching for another cigarette.

Madame Sophie's index finger pointed reprovingly to a rundown building across the street, another building with its paint peeling, the potholes in the street. "This little town doesn't have the resources to support the arts."

Tears brimmed in Clara's eyes. "What about our end-of-the year dance recitals? The students will be so disappointed. They've been practicing all year long."

Madame Sophie cast the dance building a swift, fault-finding perusal. "I've exhausted all our resources—fund-raising, begging for corporate donations, raising our tuition. Maintenance costs are rising. The studio requires a major updating."

Colum leveled Madame Sophie a furious gaze. "I've taught dance my entire life, plus, my nephew relies on me. His graphic design business is in the beginning stages. If you had shared the studio's dire financial problems, I would have been looking for another job."

He inhaled a final puff and threw his cigarette to the ground. Head down, his shadow lengthened as he stalked away.

* * *

THERE WERE two reasons why Clara scrubbed her flat the following day.

The first was because she was upset about the dance studio closing, and her restless fingers needed something to do.

The second was because the diamond necklace that Danny had gifted her the night of her birthday party had gone missing. Panicking, she'd retraced her steps and scoured every inch of her bedroom. After she'd returned to her flat the night of her argument with Danny, she'd been certain that she'd placed the necklace in her jewelry box.

She took a few deep breaths, trying to focus and keep her mind clear. She'd chased away Seamus's clutter and checked under every piece of furniture.

Perhaps Seamus had seen the necklace. She made a

mental note to ask him when he slipped in for the evening. *If he slipped in for the evening.* Offhandedly, he had mentioned that he and Liam had gambled all week because Seamus was on a winning streak. He'd assured that the pastime took away his thoughts of suicide and depression, and that gambling was harmless. After all, he wasn't bringing illegal drugs into her flat.

Clara had lectured him about the dangers of addiction before he'd stormed out and slammed the door behind him.

She'd brushed off his terseness. He was still having a hard time coping with Fiona's death. Plus, he was under stress because he'd lost his dishwasher job and was having difficulty finding employment.

In the meantime, he'd purchased an orange sports car to "cheer him up," and had parked the car ostentatiously outside her flat. And the car wasn't an old banger, as he'd initially claimed. When she'd questioned the expense—a new convertible, no less, in a country that experienced rain over two hundred days a year—he'd snapped that he'd received a generous compensation from Mr. Brady and needed transportation because he was looking for a job.

All of her cleaning hadn't turned up the necklace, so she went to the kitchen to bake. She started to dice lemons for a batch of scones, and then switched on the television in the living room. The low hum was company in her quiet, lonely kitchen while she measured flour, baking powder, and sugar for the dough. She set the dough to settle and reached beneath her kitchen cupboard for cleanser to scour the sink, surprised to find a half-empty bottle of clear liquid that she hadn't noticed before.

Detergent? She opened the bottle and sniffed.

No. She wrinkled her brow. Her stomach clenched. Vodka.

A deep, familiar Irish brogue coming from the television

brought her into the living room with the half-empty bottle of vodka in her hand. Danny Brady appeared on the screen. Sounding like a Dubliner, he spoke at length into a microphone, explaining— to a well-known, gorgeous female newscaster—his newest coffee franchise in the south of Spain.

Her gaze riveted to the television, Clara assured herself that she wouldn't be affected by watching him, and that she'd view the interview only for a second and then return to the kitchen to finish the scones.

The harsh studio lights brought out the reddish tinge in Danny's brown hair. He was so handsome, looking into the camera with his china-blue eyes, suited in a navy sport coat and white button-down shirt. The newscaster gushed throughout the interview, and Clara didn't miss how she lightly touched Danny's sleeve. When the interview ended, Clara felt her insides die a little beneath an anguished pang of jealousy. Her hands were cold, her legs were trembling.

Women had always made themselves readily available to him.

Fifteen minutes later, with tears streaming down her cheeks, Clara clicked off the television and crossed to her bedroom. She placed the bottle on her bureau and cried out her sorrow in her pillow—for the half-empty bottle of vodka, for the dance studio's closing, for her lonesome life without Danny.

An hour later, she was still huddled in a cocoon on her bed when an insistent rap on her flat's door forced her to answer. The postman stood at the entry and handed her a thickly padded sealed envelope. She brought the envelope into the kitchen, unsealed it and pulled out official-looking papers. A check for thirty thousand euros was clipped to the top of the documents.

Thirty thousand euros.

Clara dropped the check on the table. She'd never seen such a large sum. Her hands shook as she read the documents, punctuated by legal terms she scarcely understood. "In consideration of the Buyer," and "Bill of Sale," and "The Seller." At first, she assumed the packet pertained to Seamus's sports car and that she'd mistakenly opened a post intended for him.

And then she realized that the check was signed by Danny Brady.

Her fingers shook as she spread out the neatly folded note, stamped at the top with The Ground Café's logo. In Danny's bold scroll, he'd written: "Per our agreement, this check is for your lemon scone recipe, and to assist Seamus in repaying his gambling debts. It is my hope that you enjoyed our time together as much as I did."

She squeezed her eyes closed.

"I'd consider buying your recipe. How does a flat fee of ten thousand euros sound?" Danny had asked.

"Twenty thousand is fairer."

Her eyes snapped open.

Her pride insisted that she tear up his check and toss it into the fireplace to burn. He had shattered her to the core, taken away her self-esteem and proven that he didn't trust her.

Her heart, however, whispered otherwise.

An image of Danny's tormented face when he'd apologized for his accusation rushed into her thoughts: *Luv, please don't cry. I never meant to hurt you. I'm not thinking straight. I'll make it up to you.*

He was good-hearted, so generous to her and her family. And Colum said Danny loved her, and that nothing could be resolved if she and Danny never spoke.

Colum was right. She'd never been so unhappy. She was living in a suspended state, flanked by memories of her joyous past days with Danny and a desolate future without him.

Anxious and indecisive, she rubbed her neck, took a deep breath and slowly exhaled. Perhaps they could begin where they'd left off, before the terrible accusations and bitter argument.

She envisioned Danny's face, and a deep longing swelled in her heart. He was so splendid, and she missed him so much. Perhaps she should call him, thank him for his generosity. She'd begin by telling she forgave him. Everyone made mistakes and he had apologized.

She reached for her cell phone. Smiling, she envisioned the broad grin spreading across his face when he answered and heard her voice.

But what would she say?

She took a quick breath, a fluttery feeling in her stomach. She stared at the phone, her mind groping frantically for reasons why she shouldn't call him. He would be busy, he wouldn't have time to listen to her. He probably was angry because she hadn't picked up his calls. Or worse, he'd act cool and indifferent. Furthermore, there was a time difference and it was an hour later in Spain. He might have retired early for the night.

She set the phone down.

The next time he rang her, she would answer his call, thank him, and thus, salvage her self-esteem.

She stared at the check. With these funds, she could keep the studio open. And she would be able to do what she loved best—teach dance, while creating a lively and diverse cultural centre in Farthing. She could connect with other arts groups and civic leaders, as well as philanthropists like Danny. Together, they could entice families to stay in her hometown rather than relocate to bigger cities.

She could advertise, design a fresh, new look for the

studio. To help prevent injuries, she'd install a floating floor for the dancers. She'd paint the studio walls in gentle, inspiring hues—light beige, muted blues and gold. The lobby could incorporate fun, bright colors—teals and shocking pinks. Most important, Colum could continue to teach dance. He wouldn't need to scramble for another job.

She flew to the sink, filled a kettle with water for tea and set it on the stove to boil. Her mind busied with plans because there was so much to tell Danny. And he could offer insight regarding Seamus's behavior. Her pride might suffer considering her refusals of his advice, yet she wanted to discuss the matter with him.

Her spirits lifted. She could lean on Danny's broad shoulders. After all, relationships were a give and take partnership.

She beamed, picturing their joyful reunion. In person, she would finally tell him what was in her heart. Her handsome, bold, sophisticated man.

Her Danny Boy.

CHAPTER 20

*D*anny attempted to tune out the talkative businessman sitting next to him in first class by staring down at the international permits on his lap, all the while pondering why he hadn't chartered a private plane. They were headed for Rome, Italy, although the plane had been delayed several hours in the Spanish airport. Consequently, he was several hours behind schedule.

In three days, he'd be in America. His coffee franchises were scheduled to open on the east coast in New York City, Atlanta, Miami, Charlotte, and Boston.

He scrubbed a hand over his face. The Spanish coffee shop, located near Malaga in southern Spain, had experienced unexpected complications. Furthermore, although his expert staff had reinstated his computer accounts, the continual phone calls and meetings had been a cyber nightmare.

He tipped his head against the seat and tried to rest. He couldn't seem to keep his mind on his work. Every time he closed his eyes, the image of Clara's stricken face when he'd accused her of stealing tore at him. When would he be able to arrange his thoughts back into a semblance of working order?

When she finally decided to answer her damn phone, that's when. He needed to talk to her.

"Beautiful scenery."

Danny opened his eyes.

The businessman's gaze was roving appreciatively over Kathleen's voluptuous curves. She sat across the aisle, attractively dressed in a clingy jersey knit top and short skirt. She met the man's gaze with a teasing grin before crossing her legs and returning to the magazine on her lap.

With a lingering, leering chuckle, the businessman looked back to the window. "We're flying over the three Egadi Islands."

"Aye, I've heard of them," Danny said.

Do you remember the name of the town?

No, although my Irish Mom said the town was close to the Egadi Islands.

He stared out the window, watching the loops of clouds swirling in the sky, evolving from white to grey. He yearned to have the swirls block out the ever-present sting of memories and resultant pain in his gut.

To distract himself he turned to chat with Kathleen, asking if she'd heard anything recently from her Italian boyfriend.

She shook her heard. "Not since yesterday. I hope his villa is actually as nice as the internet photos he texted."

She'd flown from Dublin to Spain to meet with him to help with the opening of the Spanish coffee shop. She'd help with the launch of the Rome coffee shop as well, and then stay to oversee it after Danny departed. The Italian coffee market was highly competitive, and Kathleen was ever competent in dealing with distributors. Besides, her new Italian boyfriend lived there. Or at least, she assumed he did.

"Hopefully, you're not in for a surprise—with either the boyfriend or his villa," Danny said. "Internet relationships can be tricky, and people are sometimes not who they portray themselves to be through texts and photos."

"How close is your hotel to the coffee shop, just in case?" Her low laugh had a slight catch.

She was too accessible, Danny thought, too willing to please men—any man. And her eyes weren't a deep, warm brown.

He glanced at his watch. The plane was scheduled to land in forty-five minutes. As soon as he reached his hotel, he'd ring Clara. If she didn't answer, he'd leave a message this time, then continue ringing until she picked up. Persistence. It had worked well in business, it would work well with—

He didn't complete the thought.

Hoping it would soothe him during his whirlwind journey, he'd brought his acoustic guitar with him. So far, he hadn't had the opportunity to strum a note, neither in France nor Spain. Perhaps in Italy, on a warm, balmy night, he'd sit on his hotel balcony and finish his song for Clara.

"I'm American," the businessman said. "And I own a home in Italy and speak fluent Italian."

Danny nodded absently. "Bravo."

"You?"

"Irish. I own a home in Ireland and speak fluent English and a wee bit of Gaelic."

"Gaelic is a difficult language."

"Aye."

The businessman pressed closer to the window. "Looks like a storm brewing."

Danny resumed his appraisal of the permits.

A bump. An unexpected jostle. No warning.

The businessman lifted the plane's shade higher. "Turbulence from the winds," he observed knowingly. "I'm a seasoned world traveler."

"Good to know," Danny replied, thinking he would have been better off saying nothing, because the businessman would probably start talking again.

The plane shuddered and dropped altitude. The pilot came on the loudspeaker and advised passengers to fasten their seat belts because they were making an unexpected, forced landing at a small airfield near Cosenza, Italy.

"Not an emergency." The flight attendants reassured passengers, scurrying down the aisle as the plane continued to dip. "Only a precaution. Brace, brace, brace."

Danny felt woozy, his brain drifting.

The plane tilted and oxygen masks were deployed.

The last thing he remembered was smelling smoke, followed by a loud bang.

CHAPTER 21

*C*lara stood on the stoop of the dance studio with
Colum. The two of them had just spent the day
painting the interior of the studio.

She pulled in a deep breath and pointed to her new sign,
large pink letters against a white backdrop. "Hang the sign a
little more to the left," she instructed Colum's nephew.

"Miss Clara's School of Dance." Colum gazed at the sign
and smiled broadly. "Congratulations. You've saved the arts
in our little town. Not to mention my job."

"And my thanks to your nephew for designing the sign so
quickly. He's very artistic. We should consider offering art
classes in the future." She couldn't help an entrepreneurial
smile. "Remember, this is all because of a lemon scone recipe."

"A fair exchange. I'm sure Mr. Brady was delighted when
you told him about your business venture."

Clara shoved her hands into the pockets of her new,
caramel-colored jacket and released a ragged sigh. "I haven't
heard from him since his check arrived. Maybe he sent me
the money to assuage his guilt for his accusations. Now his

conscience is clear because he's paid for his recipe and is well rid of me."

"I like him," Colum replied, giving her a hard, quick embrace. "However, I like you more. And I don't like the idea that he's hurting you, whether intentional or not."

As she brushed away a tear, her cell phone buzzed. She'd become an expert in the art of weeping, she thought sheepishly. Ever hopeful, she glanced at the caller ID before answering the call. She sighed again and then said, "Hi, Anna."

"Don't sound so thrilled to hear from me."

"Sorry. I'm at the dance studio with Colum."

"You've been very mysterious the past few days."

"I'm working on a surprise." Clara glanced at the sign. "You'll see it tomorrow."

"I have a surprise too. Can you stop by the coffee shop? I'm finishing my shift and I want to show off … the baked goods display. Your lemon scones are selling well."

The thought of entering the coffee shop, especially since her last encounter with Danny, caused Clara to falter. "I've seen my lemon scones before and they're not a surprise," she evaded.

"This is important to me."

Apparently eavesdropping, Colum mouthed, "Go ahead. We're done here."

"I'll head over now, Anna." Clara nodded and bid Colum a silent farewell. With her cell phone pressed firmly to her ear, she headed toward the coffee shop.

"The lobby is near empty." Anna continued their conversation while Clara walked. "Ian is in Dublin and Kathleen flew to Italy."

"Kathleen flew to Italy?" Clara parroted. She stopped, swaying in place as the realization hit her. Danny was in Italy with Kathleen, which was why he no longer bothered to ring. He'd lost interest, pure and simple.

She shook her head. She should've called him but she'd gotten cold feet. And she'd wanted to salvage her wounded pride, plus give them both a cooling-off period before they spoke. In the meantime, he'd moved on, resuming his affair with the sultry and dazzling Kathleen.

Clara frowned at the wetness burning the back of her eyes. Now she knew exactly what being in Danny's arms meant—and Kathleen might be enjoying his breathtaking kisses and warm, teasing smile.

Her shoulders shook with soundless sobs as Anna clicked off.

The coffee shop hadn't changed, Clara mused, when she pushed open the door ten minutes later. The aroma of dark, rich coffee beans surrounded her. An Irish fiddle and harmonica were the featured instruments on the Irish music piped in the background.

She rode the escalator to the second floor and spotted Anna behind the display counter. As usual, Anna oozed attractiveness. Her name was pinned to her starched white blouse, the dazzling white in sharp contrast to her tanned skin. Her black slacks hugged her appealing curves.

"What's the craic?" Anna asked.

Clara gave a noncommittal shrug. "I don't have much of a life at the moment."

Anna's response was a half smile. "You look wrecked, as if you haven't slept."

"I've had a difficult week."

Anna added a look of frustrated annoyance. "You're not answering Danny's calls."

Clara didn't respond. Anna had obviously been talking with Ian. Or Colum. It seemed like the entire town knew about the argument.

"The coffee of the day is hazelnut. Wanna try some?" Anna busied herself behind the counter.

"Coffee's too bitter. I'll have a glass of mint green tea."

"Our hazelnut coffee is sweet. We add cinnamon and a touch of sugar."

Clara shoved her hair off her forehead. "No, thanks. I'd like iced tea."

Anna poured the tea and set the cup on the display case between them. She huffed an overstated sigh. "You're so bull-headed, you know that? Once you get something in your mind, you don't listen to reason."

Clara grabbed the cup, squeezing it with a death grip. "I'm unreasonable because I don't drink coffee?"

"You're just … unreasonable."

"In case you're confused, Danny was the person with the unreasonable accusations," Clara reminded with a broken laugh.

"Then you're merely bullheaded. You've been seeing a man who owns a chain of coffee shops and you refuse to try his coffee."

"Don't patronize me."

Anna grinned. "You realize that we're quarreling about coffee?"

"Coffee, tea. All roads seem to lead to Danny Brady." Clara attempted to keep the sadness from her voice. "I wish …" That torrent of tears threatened to emerge.

When she couldn't continue, Anna softly said, "I invited you here to see your lemon scones. Aren't they brilliantly displayed?" Anna's fingers, their nails sporting a deep purple polish, fluttered in the air around the display case. A shining diamond ring glittered on the fourth finger of her left hand.

Clara grabbed Anna's hand. "You're engaged?"

Anna hooted elatedly. "Ian taped my engagement ring inside my motorcycle helmet. I went to put it on last night

219

and nearly had a cow when I saw the ring. Then he got down on one knee and proposed, right in the middle of a rainy street. My fiancé is a romantic."

"So you accepted his marriage proposal?"

"Of course! He's a romantic cupcake." She sighed. "Today he had to drive to Dublin for business but he should be back later this evening. I haven't seen him all day and I miss him."

Clara's lips trembled with elation for her sister while she blinked back hopeless tears for herself. "Have you told Seamus about your engagement?" she asked.

"I haven't seen much of Seamus these days."

"Neither have I." Clara chewed her bottom lip, undecided if she should tell Anna about the half-empty bottle of vodka she'd found, and that the diamond necklace had gone missing.

Anna's cell phone buzzed. She fumbled in her pocket for it and read the text. "Ian can't remember where he left the keys to his flat, and he wants me to check in the boardroom," she reported, and then tsked. "Danny will personally wring Ian's neck if Ian lost another set of keys. Come upstairs and help me look for them."

Clara lowered her eyes. "I'll wait in the lobby."

Anna's exasperated frown swung in Clara's direction. "I was in the boardroom earlier because I brought Aiden a cup of tea while he labored over the coffee shop's yearly audits. I left it unlocked, so you won't be blamed for breaking in. No worries."

Anna's bluntness jerked Clara out of her tortured reverie. "No, I'll—"

Too late. Anna was already pushing her in the direction of the door marked Private, then onto the lift to the third floor.

"Francis Bacon is gone," Clara noted as they crossed the hallway.

"Ian returned the painting to Danny's home in Howth,"

Anna explained as the women stepped into the boardroom. She tossed her hands to her hips. "Now where could my forgetful cupcake have misplaced the keys to his flat?"

While Anna went through computer desk drawers, Clara examined the drooping fern by the doorway. She knelt and began pulling dried leaves off the bottom stem. Out of the corner of her eye she spotted a familiar looking men's cap, half hidden and wedged between the fern and doorway. Doing a double take, she slowly and deliberately fingered the stiff brim and plaid tweed. Then she gasped.

Anna hurried over. "Nice cap." Her statement held a question.

Clara moved back slightly, staring at the cap as if it were about to begin speaking. "This cap belongs to Seamus. He bought it in Donegal."

And when had she last seen Seamus wearing the cap? Surely it must've been before her birthday.

Anna lifted her eyebrows and grabbed the cap from Clara. "What's it doing here? He worked in the kitchen."

Absently, Clara rubbed her forearms. All the pieces of Seamus's never-ending mysteries registered in mere seconds. His excuses, his denials, slipping in and out of her flat at all hours. The missing diamond necklace. The half-empty vodka bottle.

Her mouth opened, closed. Her chest tingled. "Seamus was in the boardroom on March eighteenth." She tried to rein in her disbelief, heard her voice choke up. "I can't believe this. Seamus lied to me. He's lied all these months."

Anna's face had gone pale. She openly gaped. "Seamus stole the fifty thousand euros?"

Clara's thoughts scrambled. No, it couldn't be true. No one could spend that amount of money, although Danny had said that gambling debts added up quickly.

Feeling lightheaded, she rushed to the leather sofa and sank into the cushions.

Anna followed.

"This explains …" Clara covered her face with her hands. "This explains Seamus's new sports car … and all the other unanswered questions that have baffled me." Repeatedly, she shook her head. "I chose to ignore what I didn't want to see."

Dear saints in heaven. Seamus, her dear brother, was an addict. A gambler, an alcoholic and a liar. And his suicide attempt had been a cry for help.

She dropped her hands. Her job title as loving sister hadn't been sufficient. She hadn't helped him. She'd only enabled him.

Anna was gaping at her. "Now what?"

Clara leapt from the couch, grabbed her sister's hand and dashed for the door. "Now we can only hope it's not too late."

CHAPTER 22

"*B*oss, where have you been?"

Danny leaned forward in the ripped bus seat, straining to hear Ian's voice crackling through his cell phone's static interference. He rubbed his bleary eyes. He'd had little sleep, and weariness had taken a firm hold in his veins.

The small airport where the plane had landed three days earlier had boasted no showers, rigid benches that ensured impossible sleeping, and a near-empty vending machine selling stale candy and bottled water. The bus was the opposite of luxury, smelling of chewed tobacco and diluted diesel. With any luck it wouldn't break down, Danny thought, although the brakes squeaked at every twisted turn in the road.

"I've been holed up at an Italian airfield in a remote town with no cell phone connection," he explained.

"I thought you and Kathleen were flying directly to Rome."

"We hit a bad storm as we approached Italy. One of the plane engines stalled and we had to make an emergency landing. They found significant damage to one of the blades. No worries," Danny hastened to assure Ian. "Our pilot was very competent and got us safely on the ground. I was able to shower at a youth hostel in Cosenza this morning. However, I've lost three days of valuable time, plus have been virtually unplugged from the rest of the world."

He'd found a quiet seat in the rear of the bus, setting his briefcase and carry-on luggage beside him to dissuade anyone from joining him. Intent on working the entire six-hour bus ride, he'd extracted the Spanish permits from his briefcase. Sleep would have to wait.

The talkative businessman and Kathleen had … well, never stopped talking since they'd landed at the small airfield. Danny flashed a look at them a few seats ahead of him and grinned slightly. Heads together, they sat deeply engrossed in conversation. Again.

"I'm in Farthing," Ian was saying through the static. "Anna and I are engaged."

Squelching his unexplainable annoyance at that announcement, Danny asked a bit too abruptly, "Should I be surprised?"

"Not at all. You are aware of how close Anna and I had gotten."

He seemed to be waiting for a reply.

Danny tried not to sound irritated. He tapped his gold pen on his knee. "Ian, I am genuinely happy for you both. However, to ring me with this news when I have so many important matters facing me seems—"

"Have you … spoken to Clara?"

"Not since the night of our argument." Danny softened his curt tone. "I've tried, although she hasn't responded."

"She's staging an intervention for Seamus."

Danny sat straighter. "What? When?"

"Seven o'clock this evening. I'll be there with Anna and

Colum. We're meeting at the dance studio in Farthing." Ian hesitated. "You should be there too, boss."

Slowly, Danny set down the permits and pen on the empty seat beside him and stared out the graffiti-stained window. He shifted in his seat, and one shoe seemed stuck to the floor. He lifted his foot. A thick wad of bubblegum was stuck to the sole of his shoe. He picked at the gum with his fingernail. It had to be at least ten years old. "I'm in Italy, remember? Once I arrive in Rome, I'll only have three hours to open my new franchise."

An uncomfortably long silence ensued.

"You should be in Farthing," Ian said again.

Danny's jaw tightened. "I leave for America in the morning."

"We all have a copy of your itinerary, boss."

Was there really a note of sarcasm in Ian's voice, or was it the terrible static on the line?

"So then you know what you're asking is physically impossible. My franchise agreements are all legally signed and sealed, and my biggest profits await across the pond."

"She found Seamus's tweed cap in your boardroom."

Danny was silent as he envisioned Clara's pain at that discovery.

"You charged Seamus with stealing, and you were right," Ian continued.

Of course he was right. Seamus needed professional help. Clara had attempted to solve Seamus's problems, deflecting his troubles by taking on his burdens.

Danny forced a laugh. "I saw through Seamus's lies all along. If she'd only listened instead of—"

More static.

"What's that, boss? I can hardly hear you."

"I said that she should have listened to me."

The phone went silent. Ian hadn't hung up, had he?

He resisted the urge to fling it out the bus's grimy window.

He shook his head, steepled his hands. He should be feeling satisfaction.

Instead, he felt shallow.

Why?

Seamus was the reason he and Clara were separated, and, if Danny was honest, he resented Seamus. Although resentment didn't feel very good.

Didn't matter. How could he let Seamus off the hook after the havoc he had caused? Danny could never forgive him. Just as he couldn't forgive his parents. They'd caused Glenna's untimely death. How could he ever forget their mistakes?

He reached for his permits, intending to drown himself in his work.

A picture came to mind, frozen in his memory.

Clara, at Glasnevin cemetery: *You're not forgetting. You're finding your own happiness. Otherwise, these resentments will gnaw at you and you'll never be at peace.*

This anger. These resentments. He blew out an exhausted sigh and set the permits aside. He had to let it all go.

He didn't understand people's mistakes. And he didn't need to understand. Or judge. He couldn't change Seamus nor his parents. He *could* change his reactions. Perhaps he'd been angry at them because of his own addictions and inability to forgive himself.

He drew in a long breath. Seamus had held Clara as an emotional hostage, manipulating her so that she felt guilty whenever she confronted him. However, enabling Seamus had come from a good place in her heart, and she'd freely forgiven him for his mistakes. Sure, she'd been sidetracked and in denial. But she was also the closest Danny had ever come to meeting an angel.

His sweet, non-Irish damsel.

She had tried to tell him that she loved him and what had he done? He'd held up his hand to interrupt her. All he'd offered in return was his distrust and crippling accusations.

And still she'd rallied, dauntless and spirited.

He grinned. She could be a real spitfire.

He placed the pen and permits in his briefcase and retrieved her lemon scone recipe from his jacket pocket. Aye, he'd carried it with him, Clara's recipe written in her scholarly hand.

He ran his thumb along the recipe and pressed it to his lips. He detected a subtle fragrance of lemon, cheerful and uplifting. Clara's fragrance.

His heart thumped in slow, aching beats.

He missed her desperately. He missed their connection. They'd been separated far too long.

CHAPTER 23

*C*lara pushed open the doors of the dance studio with her spine straight and her shoulders set. Today was the day.

She had told Seamus to come by after her class ended at seven o'clock. She hadn't told him why, giving only a brief excuse about seeing her new studio.

Two days earlier, she had contacted the Flyaway Treatment Center to stage his intervention. She had presented the center with a large donation, thanks to Danny's generous check. Bryan, the interventionist, had arranged everything, beginning with choosing Ian to act as the point of contact. The plan was for Ian to meet Seamus at Clara's flat, then the two men would ride Ian's motorcycle to the dance studio.

Liam hadn't been informed, as Clara had feared he might sabotage the intervention. And, she suspected that Liam was also involved in the cybercrime. Perhaps he had guided Seamus on the phone through the entire process when Seamus had been in the boardroom.

She took a calming breath, arranged bottles of water on a round table, and glanced at her watch. Time ticked slowly, although only a few minutes remained until the men were scheduled to arrive.

For the umpteenth time, she straightened the five chairs she'd set in a circle. One for herself, Ian, Anna, Seamus, and Bryan, who would orchestrate the intervention. Colum would wait outside the building, standing by to lend moral support. These were the team members. Together, they'd rehearsed a consistent message and well-thought-out plan. They'd gathered their information and shared it with one another. The entire picture of Seamus's destructive behaviors was now clearly mapped out. Besides his gambling and alcohol addiction, he'd been stealing. The diamond necklace and hacking into Danny's accounting system still hadn't given him enough funds. He'd obviously risked his money gambling beyond his ability to pay, because Seamus owed a large amount of money to numerous bookies reaching as far as Donegal.

The previous day, the team members had staged a rehearsal, deciding who should speak and in what order, and the general thrust of what each person would say. It had been a long and intense training session. There would be no room for indecisiveness once the intervention began.

An addiction specialist had counseled the team, and Clara had gained a better understanding of Seamus's compulsive actions. His suicide attempts had been an effort to alert those around him that something was seriously wrong. He was obviously depressed. Despite the negative consequences, he had been struggling to find an escape from his grief and hopelessness after Fiona's death. He'd denied and hid and refused to acknowledge that he had a problem.

Clara had arranged for Seamus to travel directly to the treatment center following the intervention. His admission was set, his suitcase packed. A specialist stood ready to escort Seamus quickly out of the studio through a side door.

Bryan drew Clara and Anna aside. "No half measures. No caving in," he reminded the women. "Your brother has fallen off his tightrope for the last time. He's holding on by the proverbial thread. Don't waste this opportunity, and keep in mind that it's not your job to help him back up. I'll guide you through the confrontations."

Clara nodded. She wanted her brother to be able to walk with his feet firmly planted on the ground. This intervention was his opportunity.

The outer door slammed. All heads jerked up.

"Here they come." Anna gestured to the lobby and grabbed a bottle of water. "Remember, I'll go first."

Clara glanced at the note to Seamus that she had drafted, and then nodded to Bryan that she was ready.

Seamus and Ian walked in, their shoes echoing on the new floating dance floor.

"What's the craic?" Seamus's bewildered gaze shot around the studio.

Clara wiped her sweaty palms on her slacks, pushed her hair from her forehead, and rose swiftly to her feet. She looked at Seamus. Her gaze never flinched.

* * *

DANNY TOLD himself that if the Gardaí wanted to stop him for speeding, first they'd have to catch him. He pressed his foot on the Mercedes's gas pedal, grateful for the long stretch of open road. He was not grateful, however, for the rain that had decided to beat against his windshield, nearly blinding him as he took the last curve into Farthing too fast.

He found a spot a half block away from the dance studio, and parked behind a familiar candy-blue and yellow motor-cycle. The rain had stopped as quickly as it had started.

Ireland. Who said it always rained?

He checked his watch. Seven thirty. He was late for the intervention, although considering he'd flown from Italy to Dublin, then raced to a Dublin florist shop to pick up two dozen red roses, he'd completed the journey quickly. The one-hour time difference between Italy and Ireland had worked in his favor.

He observed an unfamiliar sign hanging above the entrance as he approached.

Miss Clara's School of Dance.

He grinned, mesmerized for a moment.

Colum O'Brien, wearing a camouflage-colored parka, was perched on the stoop. He held a cigarette in his hand and seemed to be having a love/hate relationship with it.

Danny nodded a greeting. "How are ya?"

"Grand."

"Is Clara inside?" He attempted to step past Colum, who was doing a brilliant job of blocking the doorway.

"Of course she's here. She owns it." Colum eyed Danny with a suspicious frown and then glanced at the roses. "And where has the likes of you been lately?"

"Traveling."

Danny was preoccupied in trying to find the best way around Colum without shoving the man out of the way.

Colum scraped back his thick salt and pepper hair. "Now you're in a hurry? After breaking her heart?"

Silence for a beat.

"Let me pass." Hadn't he said that once already?

Colum rose, staying right in front of Danny. "You left her in Farthing to deal with Seamus, to pick up the pieces of her life after your accusations. I hope she tells you how much she's accomplished since you decided to disappear."

Danny glanced at the sign, then meaningfully toward the door. "That answer is perfectly obvious."

"You'd better be planning to make it up to her."

Danny had immediately liked Colum when he first met him. And, although it was absurd, he was coming to like Colum even more. The man was proving to be Clara's devoted friend, a man of honor who expected the same integrity from those around him.

"That's why I'm here," Danny replied evenly. "I'm going to try very, very hard, as soon as you let me in."

Colum's expression softened. With a sigh, he threw his half-smoked cigarette to the ground. "It'll take more than roses."

"I can't change what I've done, but I can learn from her how it's supposed to be done. I'll do whatever's necessary. I love her."

"I know." Colum appeared to smile, although he crossed his arms. "Sorry. I still can't let you inside. There's an intervention going on, and only family is allowed."

"Ian's back there. He's not family."

"Ian and Anna are engaged. He's considered family."

"Clara and I are engaged too."

Or at least they would be, if he ever was able to actually talk with her.

Colum's eyebrows flew up. "You and Clara are engaged? Since when?"

Danny paused. "We'll be engaged in less than two hours."

The last of the hostility in Colum's face faded. Mischief flickered in his green eyes.

"I'll hold onto your flowers and walk you inside. You may need a friend with the crowd you're about to face."

CHAPTER 24

*T*he entire intervention had taken less than thirty minutes.

"Thank you for all you've done for me. I love you." Clara fiercely hugged her dear brother before he turned and started for the door.

The love and support from his sisters, and the fear of looming consequences, had prompted Seamus to go willingly to the Flyaway Treatment Center. Bryan had told Clara that quick action was necessary, before Seamus's defense mechanisms and excuses kicked in. The window of opportunity was a small one.

Seamus had been quiet and reflective when the intervention was over. He'd seemed to appreciate the objective competence of the specialists, and had paid especially close attention to Ian.

"I will be there, every step of the way," Ian had assured Seamus. "I'm a recovering addict too, you know."

As Seamus left with the two professionals and Ian, Clara lifted a prayer of thanks. The first step to Seamus's recovery had begun. And it had all happened in thirty minutes.

Anna gulped her water and sank into a chair. Her hands trembled. "You know what it's like to have the wind knocked out of your lungs? That's how I'm feeling—physically and mentally exhausted."

Clara drew a deep breath and nodded. She felt the same—emotionally drained.

"I'm meeting Ian outside as soon as Seamus is safely on his way. Wanna join us?"

Anna's tone was genuine and imploring.

Clara shook her head. "You need time alone with your new fiancé. You don't want a sister tagging along. I'll head back to my flat." Her cold, empty flat. "Besides, Colum and I need to straighten the studio before we leave."

"You can always change your mind. I told Ian that this intervention either called for a swear word or food."

"And you picked?"

"Food. Join us if you want." Anna stood and finger-combed her canary-yellow hair strands into place. "What do you think of my new hair color?"

"Still matches Ian's motorcycle."

"Ian likes it. He's thinking of dying his hair to match mine."

"Now there's a visual."

Laughing, Anna slung her purse over her shoulder. Then she paused, studying her sister's face. "Have you heard from him?"

Anna didn't need to say Danny's name. Clara knew who she meant.

"He hasn't made the slightest effort." Somehow, she kept her voice from breaking. She looked away for a moment and focused on the ballet mirror. "And it doesn't matter anymore."

She knew that she wasn't fooling Anna for a second.

Tears sprang into Anna's amber eyes. "You managed a

wonderful intervention, Clara. You did the best thing for Seamus."

"Thanks. It was a concerted effort. We're a great team."

"Ring me if you change your mind and would like to join us." After a nod of assent from Clara, Anna headed for the lobby.

Clara turned to face the mirror again, allowing her relief at the successful intervention to flow through her. She still held the note she'd read to Seamus, and she looked down at it, reading the last line aloud. "So you see, Seamus, the Flyaway Treatment Center is your best option."

She looked up to see a tall, handsome man with reddish brown hair and china-blue eyes step into the room.

Their gazes met.

"Missus, are you trained for this?" he asked.

CHAPTER 25

$\mathcal{D}$anny kept walking toward her and without hesitation took Clara in his arms.

Desperately, she tried to understand what was happening. Danny was here. He was here. This good-looking, grave man who was staring down into her eyes.

Slowly, tears slid down her cheeks. She stood motionless, unable to move, scarcely breathing.

He hadn't uttered another word.

"Danny," she whispered. "How? When?"

His strong arms held her closer, as if he could absorb the sadness he had caused her.

"If you ever think again of not answering the phone when I ring, I'll put you on redial and never give you a moment's peace."

She tipped her head back and saw the anguish on his face, raw and exposed.

"And if I answer on the first ring?"

Tenderly, he kissed her cheeks, her temple, her hair. "Then I'll finally be able to talk to you."

She reached her arms around his broad shoulders. "And what will you say?"

"I only know a few words." He framed her face, brushed his lips against her temple. "Clara Donovan, I'm sorry. And I love you so very, very much."

His mouth captured hers. She kissed him back with an eager desperation equaling his. When the kiss ended, she stayed in his arms. Her fingers stroked the silky hair at his nape.

"I can't believe you're actually here, in Farthing. This past week, everything's felt so—"

"Desolate? Empty?" She loved his persuasive baritone voice, the voice that had haunted her dreams.

"Lonely." Her voice broke. "Danny Brady, I've missed you more than you will ever know."

His response was his lips parting hers.

* * *

CLARA LOOKED SO beautiful and Danny concentrated on memorizing each detail of her exquisite face and perfect figure. For several minutes, he hadn't been aware that anyone else was in the dance studio. That is, until he heard two people clearing their throats.

"You're kidding," he said, glancing over his shoulder to a beaming Ian and Anna.

"What's the craic?" Anna's face was wreathed in mischievous laughter.

"How long have you two been standing there?"

"Only a minute," Ian replied. "I didn't know anyone could travel that many miles so quickly."

"Now you know."

"Glad you could make it, boss. Are you flying to America in the morning?"

Danny shook his head and held Clara tighter. "Kathleen is handling the American franchises."

"I thought she was staying in Italy with a new guy she met on the Internet."

"That guy turned out to be a thirteen-year-old kid playing a hoax. However, she met a hotshot American businessman on the plane, so they'll fly to Boston together. And there are competent employees to handle the Rome coffee shop." Danny kissed Clara's shiny hair. "I need to spend my time on more important things."

"Well, I'm glad you two are all settled, because I'm starved." In the true nature of a matchmaker whose mind turned to food once the match was settled, Anna added, "Danny, Ian and I are headed to your shop for free Guinness cake. Then we're taking a week's vacation because Seamus's intervention wore us out."

Ian sheepishly looked at Danny. "Hope you'll agree, boss. Anna wants to visit Portugal."

"My birth country," Anna declared. "I can hardly remember any details from when I was a child and I want to visit with my favorite cupcake." She blew a kiss in Ian's direction although he was only standing a foot away from her.

"Perfectly fine. Enjoy your time off," Danny said.

"There goes a week's profit," Clara murmured.

Danny laughed and shrugged. "We'll walk out with you and Ian, Anna."

Clara perused the chairs, the empty water bottles. "Not yet. I need to clean—"

Danny shook his head and firmly took hold of her hand. "Tomorrow."

Colum sat on the stoop as the foursome stepped outside. He held two dozen roses. "Forgetting something?" he asked Danny.

"A wee bit wilted," Danny apologized as he handed the roses to Clara.

"They're beautiful. They just need a little water. Thank you."

They all wished Colum a good evening and started to leave. Colum called after them, "Congratulations on your engagement."

Anna glanced back. "You already congratulated me and my cupcake."

Colum shook his head. "Not you. Clara and Danny."

Clara stopped in midstep. She turned to Danny. "We're engaged?"

"Aye," Danny said. "I wanted Colum to be the first to know."

The rain had started as Anna and Ian hopped on his motorcycle. "Does it ever stop raining in this country?" she asked him.

"How would I know? I'm only in my thirties." Ian laughed at his own joke.

With a grin and a farewell, Clara slipped into Danny's silver Mercedes.

He turned on the engine and let it idle. Then he reached for her and held her in his arms for a long while. "For our honeymoon we'll travel to Italy," he said. "I've seen the Egadi Islands, from the air, at least. They look beautiful. Then after our honeymoon, we'll find your orphanage. If it's still there, I'll set up a fund for the children. And together, we will confront your bad memories."

"Always the planner. Don't forget my brother, Luciano."

"Aye."

"Where are we going?" she asked.

"Your flat."

She stared up at him. "Can I tell you something?"

He nodded.

"I'm sorry that I didn't listen to you about Seamus."

"The main thing is that Seamus is going to get the treatment he needs." Danny pulled her closer. "You'll see, he'll be better soon."

"And I'm sorry about the diamond necklace. During the intervention, Seamus confessed that he stole the necklace you gave me, but Ian and I will check the pawn shops and try to find it."

"No worries. You're more important than a thousand diamonds." He gazed into her glorious eyes. His precious Clara.

She snuggled nearer and he kissed her tenderly.

When the kiss ended, she asked, "Now can I ask you a question?"

"Always."

"Why did you return to Farthing?"

He grinned. "I like your smile. I like your lemon scones. And I love you."

He waited a beat for her reply. When one wasn't forthcoming, he continued, "And I want to sing the last two lines of my favorite song to you. I hope you will finish it for me."

"Is it the song you've been working on?"

He shook his head. "It's better than anything I ever attempted to write. May I?"

Tears welled in her eyes. She nodded.

To the tune of "Oh Danny Boy," he sang, "'Oh Clara Donovan, if you'll not fail to say you love me—'"

Clara's smile was radiant as she finished the chorus:

"'Oh Danny Brady, Oh Danny Brady, I love you so.'"

The End

A NOTE FROM JOSIE

Dear Friend,

Thank you for reading *Oh Danny Boy*. I hope you enjoyed it. I have had the opportunity to visit Ireland many times and wanted to capture the essence of one of my favorite countries in the world.

If you loved this sweet romance as much as I loved writing it, please help other people find *Oh Danny Boy* by posting your amazing review, as well as for the bundle: Irish Hearts

Oh Danny Boy is available in ebook, paperback, Large Print paperback, Hardcover, and audiobook.

I'd love to meet you in person someday, but in the meantime, all I can offer is a sincere and grateful thank you. Without your support, my books would not be possible.

As I write my next sweet or inspirational romance, remember this: Have you ever tried something you were afraid to try because it mattered so much to you? I did, when I started writing. Take the chance, and just do something you love.

My Spotify Play List for Oh Danny Boy is here.

With sincere appreciation,
Josie Riviera

Want more sweet Irish romances?
A Chocolate-Box Irish Wedding
1-800-IRELAND
Maeve
Irish Hearts:

IRISH SCONE RECIPE

Enjoy this Irish Scones recipe, brought to you by a granny in County Derry, Ireland.

Irish Scones:

2 cups flour
1/2 tsp. salt
1/4-1/2 stick margarine
2 tsp. baking powder
4 oz. buttermilk
Set oven to 450F. Grease cooking tray and sift dry ingredients. Cut and rub in margarine.

Mix quickly and lightly to a soft dough.

Turn onto a floured table and knead.

Roll and cut out small scones.

Brush with egg or milk.

Bake 10-15 minutes in preheated oven.

I have converted grams and milliliters and rounded off. Hopefully errors have not occurred! I also learned that sweet milk is buttermilk, and cooking butter is margarine.

Enjoy!

ACKNOWLEDGMENTS

An appreciative thank you to my patient husband, Dave, and our three wonderful children.

ABOUT THE AUTHOR

Josie Riviera is a *USA TODAY* bestselling author of contemporary, inspirational, and historical sweet romances that read like Hallmark movies. She lives in the Charlotte, NC, area with her wonderfully supportive husband. They share their home with an adorable shih tzu, who constantly needs grooming, and live in an old house forever needing renovations.

To receive my Newsletter and your free sweet romance novella ebook as a thank you gift, sign up HERE.

Become a member of my Read and Review VIP Facebook group for exclusive giveaways and ARCs.

josieriviera.com/
josieriviera@aol.com

ALSO BY JOSIE RIVIERA

Seeking Patience

Seeking Catherine (always Free!)

Seeking Fortune

Seeking Charity

Seeking Rachel

The Seeking Series

Oh Danny Boy

I Love You More

A Snowy White Christmas

A Portuguese Christmas

Holiday Hearts Book Bundle Volume One

Holiday Hearts Book Bundle Volume Two

Holiday Hearts Book Bundle Volume Three

Holiday Hearts Book Bundle Volume Four

Candleglow and Mistletoe

Maeve (Perfect Match)

A Love Song To Cherish

A Christmas To Cherish

A Valentine To Cherish

A Christmas Puppy To Cherish

A Homecoming To Cherish

A Summer To Cherish

Romance Stories To Cherish

Romance Stories To Cherish Volume Two

Cherished Hearts Six Book Volume

Aloha To Love

Sweet Peppermint Kisses

Valentine Hearts Boxed Set

1-800-CUPID

1-800-CHRISTMAS

1-800-IRELAND

1-800-SUMMER

1-800-NEW YEAR

The 1-800-Series Sweet Contemporary Romance Bundle

Irish Hearts Sweet Romance Bundle

Holly's Gift

A Chocolate-Box Christmas

A Chocolate-Box New Years

A Chocolate-Box Valentine

A Chocolate-Box Summer Breeze

A Chocolate-Box Christmas Wish

A Chocolate-Box Irish Wedding

Chocolate-Box Hearts

Chocolate-Box Hearts Volume Two

Chocolate-Box Double Hearts

Recipes From The Heart

Leading Hearts

New Year Hearts

SENIOR HEARTS

Summer Hearts

Christmas in the Air (1-800-Book)

A Very Christian Christmas

Most books are available in ebook, audiobook, paperback, Large Print paperback and Hardcover.

Many are FREE on Kindle Unlimited!

MAEVE (A SWEET CONTEMPORARY ROMANCE) PREVIEW

"It'll do you good to get away from Ireland. We've had a rainy summer."

"Rainy summer?" Maeve Doherty grinned at her best friend, Colleen O'Keefe, who was busily swiping Maeve's phone. "When can you recall a non-wet summer in Ireland?"

"A year ago. It was on a Thursday."

Maeve laughed out loud. As always, her flaming-haired friend's sunny disposition lifted her spirits.

Colleen chuckled in return. Her tailored canary-yellow pantsuit, with matching pumps, fit her full-figured body impeccably. Maeve glanced at her own worn linen skirt and smoothed her wrinkled polyester blouse. When had she last taken time for herself? She'd forgotten, it had been so long ago, with all the worry and sleepless nights.

Colleen plunked into an oversized chair in the lobby of the building that housed the Merrimac Company. The women were purchasing agents for a small Irish hotel chain. Their duties included placing orders for everything from hotel furniture to cleaning supplies, and comparing various prices and the quality of the merchandise.

Colleen pointed with one of her French manicured fingernails at Maeve's phone screen. "If I'm reading this email correctly, you've been offered a free week at the paradise island of your choice, compliments of the Perfect Match dating agency."

Maeve pulled up a chair across from her friend. "Aye."

Keeping her fingertip on the blinking cursor, Colleen paused. "You plan to accept, don't you?"

"Whatever the catch is, it's not worth a week anywhere on the globe."

"This offer is from Amy Yates, your friend from America, and her husband, Dawson. And it's a personalized invitation." Colleen scanned Maeve's phone screen. "A free vacation, a romantic getaway, a chance—"

Maeve held up a hand. "Aye."

"So it's legit," Colleen declared gaily. "I remember you said they owned the agency."

"Aye."

"Which island are you choosing?"

"I'm not choosing any island because I'm not going."

"How about Corsica, France?" Colleen obviously pretended she hadn't heard Maeve. "You've always wanted to learn French. And isn't there a famous museum there you've always wanted to visit?"

"Maison Bonaparte, the ancestral home of the Bonaparte family." Maeve nodded. "The museum is located in Ajaccio, Corsica."

"Then go."

"Yes, someday, on my own, using my own money—not obligated to a matchmaking agency."

Colleen pushed her glasses up her nose and peered at the phone. "All expenses are paid and the terms and conditions are clearly spelled out. All you have to do is agree to spend the week with your match or risk being charged for the vacation."

Maeve lifted a skeptical eyebrow. "That's all?"

"It's a massive marketing campaign to introduce their new business," Colleen reminded her. "You're helping them as much as they're helping you."

"I love history, but I'm not that desperate to see Napoléon Bonaparte's death mask. I'd prefer spending a cozy week in my flat reading a pile of European history books." Maeve tapped her fingers together and drew in a breath. "Figure in a hot cuppa Irish tea and lemon scones from The Ground Café and I'll be merry as a leprechaun."

"You're emotionally spent," her friend said quietly. "And you gave Amy Yates permission to plug your name into the Perfect Match database."

Maeve turned a despairing look on Colleen. "Aye, in a

flash of desperation when I feared any opportunity for love was passing me by. I'm over that."

Was she?

Once she'd recovered from the sadness and shock of learning her twenty-year-old brother Owen had been diagnosed with cancer, she'd settled into the daily task of tending to him when he opted to move in with her rather than live with their mother. She'd given up every pastime she enjoyed to care for him, including auditioning for minor acting roles, something she loved.

Now that Owen's radiation treatments were over and his caregiving routine had become stable, perhaps she could ease up a bit, take a breather. Perhaps ...

"Maeve?" Colleen prodded. "Owen is in remission and he can go live with your mother for a week. She's able-bodied and can tend to him. You're only twenty-six. Live your life."

"Most days my mother isn't capable of washing a dish, let alone attending to a sick adult. She had a hard-enough time being a parent when Owen was well."

"Your mother lands in the middle of drama because of the type of men she sees, and her ongoing dilemmas can't always be your problem." Colleen leaned back in her chair. Her normally keen bright-blue gaze softened. "Enough about your mother. What's the craic with you? Are you sleeping okay?"

Maeve shrugged. "I'm always tired, although everyone is exhausted nowadays because of our hectic lifestyles."

"Grab this chance. Go. Believe me, if it weren't for my boyfriend, Colin, I'd take your place."

Colleen and Colin had an on-again, off-again relationship that had lasted for over a year. Currently, it was on again.

A reassuring grin crossed Colleen's freckled face. "Along with Owen's healthcare providers, your mother will mind him brilliantly. I want to see an optimistic smile on your face again. I'm sure you'll have a lorry-load of stories to share when you get back."

Maeve shook her head. "Because of all the days I missed when Owen became ill, I'm on the verge of losing my job. I certainly can't afford to take off any more time. Besides, his medical bills are mounting, and our private insurance only covers part of them."

"You're physically and mentally exhausted. *Your* health is important too. You need the time away to maintain your sense of balance."

"Aye, perhaps," Maeve admitted. Her brother's cancer journey had been a lengthy road crowded with difficult decisions and the challenges of radiation treatment.

"The Merrimac Company wants to branch out of Ireland and explore resort areas for other hotels. Pitch the idea to our manager. Tell Mrs. McShea it's a working holiday. Just think you'll get paid for sitting on a beach in a bikini."

"I don't swim, and I've never worn a bikini."

"Live a wee bit, Maeve. Spend your days lying in a lounge chair and looking out at the Mediterranean. You once told me there are over two hundred beaches in Corsica. Imagine the sun, the surf—"

"Colleen—"

"The sand." Colleen laughed. "It's a win-win. Besides, who can pass up the chance to meet Mr. Right?"

"I'm too busy to fritter away my valuable time on a man. And there's no such man as Mr. Right, at least not for me."

"How do you know? Make the time."

"Suppose he's not interesting?"

"Suppose he is?"

"What about Crinkles?"

"Your dog is accustomed to your ma's flat." Colleen tapped the phone screen again. Amy says her agency's matchmaking algorithms are the best and they're launching this campaign to prove it."

"And if you keep scrolling, you'll see they want people who've been unlucky in love."

Like her.

Maeve studied Merrimac's lobby—a gleaming brown floor, mahogany table, anything but her friend's sympathetic stare. She'd spilled out more than she'd intended.

A year ago while visiting a cousin in America, she'd met Amy while shopping in an exclusive boutique, not realizing at first that she was chatting with the owner of the boutique. They'd become instant friends, and they shared coffee and heartfelt conversation after the store closed. That evening, Maeve had poured out her sadness to her new-found confidante.

Finbar, Maeve's boyfriend of two years, had broken up with her—not even in person—but through a dismissive text.

"No more," she'd declared to Amy. "Men and their hollow promises are not to be believed."

Wasn't Maeve's father, who'd left her mother without an explanation, further proof of her statement? He'd said he'd return. He never had.

"Maeve? Maeve?" Colleen yanked Maeve from her upsetting remembrances. "I'm partial to the final line of your dating profile." She read aloud: "'Love comes in many forms, and I believe in a commitment to one person.' Colleen looked up at Maeve. "Aww, that's very sweet. You expressed yourself perfectly."

Heat rose in Maeve's face. "I'm starry-eyed and foolish for writing something so reckless. No one stays with one person forever."

"Some do. Some people have a love that lasts. Where are those rose-colored glasses you used to wear?"

"I've put them away and become realistic."

"Dust them off. What if Mr. Right is waiting for you in Corsica?"

"He won't be, although just to be sure ..." Maeve grabbed her phone from Colleen and included another line at the bottom of her dating profile.

Be warned ... I'm a workaholic.

Colleen squinted at the screen. "Being a workaholic is supposed to deter him?"

"I'll plead nine-to-five obligations."

Plus, any other excuses necessary to safeguard her heart.

"So, it's settled." Colleen flashed a quick smile. "You'll accept Amy's offer and choose Corsica."

"Aye." Maeve feigned enthusiasm, then blew out a breath.

She'd go, she'd rest, she'd work. But she wouldn't risk falling in love.

Once was enough. Besides, if there was a perfect match for her on God's emerald-green planet, she'd have found him by now in Ireland.

"That's grand," Colleen said. "Finally, you're doing something for yourself." With a flourish, Colleen stood and walked over to Maeve, throwing her arms around her. "Get ready, my dear friend, for an amazing adventure!"

*** End of excerpt *Maeve* by Josie Riviera
Copyright © 2018 Josie Riviera
***

Want more? Keep reading Maeve on Amazon.